W9-BDB-134

A Cousin's
CHALLENGE

WANDA & BRUNSTETTER

A Cousin's
CHALLENGE

INDIANA COUSINS | BOOK 3

**Doubleday Large Print
Home Library Edition**

BARBOUR
PUBLISHING

This Large Print Edition, prepared especially for Doubleday Large Print Home Library, contains the complete, unabridged text of the original Publisher's Edition.

© 2010 by Wanda E. Brunstetter

ISBN 978-1-61664-375-1

All scripture is taken from the King James Version of the Bible.

All German-Dutch words are taken from the *Revised Pennsylvania Dutch Dictionary* found in Lancaster County, Pennsylvania.

For more information about Wanda E. Brunstetter,
please access the author's Web site at the following
Internet address: www.wandabrunstetter.com

Cover design by Müllerhaus Publishing Arts, Inc.,
www. Mullerhaus.net

Published by Barbour Publishing, Inc., P.O. Box 719,
Uhrichsville, OH 44683.

Printed in the United States of America.

**This Large Print Book carries the
Seal of Approval of N.A.V.H.**

Dedication/Acknowledgments

To Ada Nancy Smoker, who has taught many deaf children over the years and provided me with much information about the hearing impaired. To Sandy Rose for the information on hearing loss she shared with me. To Deborah Trevett for sharing with me some things about her own loss of hearing. To the following Indiana friends who answered many of my questions during the making of this series: Irene and Melvin Miller and family; Betty and Richard Miller and family; Orley Lambright and family; Karen and Dave Lehman, Katie and Mary Yoder; Marilyn Hostetler; Mary Alice and Harley Yoder and family; Doretta and Mark Yoder; Orley and Dianna Yoder and family; Harley Miller; Bob Kurth; and Arlene and Wayne Randolph. I also wish to thank my editors, Rebecca Germany and Becky Durost Fish, for their help with the editing process. Thanks also to the following people who shared some of their humorous stories with me: Jake Smucker, Betty Miller, and Lorine VanCorbach.

**I will instruct thee and teach thee in
the way which thou shalt go:
I will guide thee with mine eye.**

PSALM 32:8

CHAPTER 1

Quiet darkness met Jolene Yoder as she stepped into Aunt Dorcas's kitchen. After losing her hearing two years ago in a van accident, she'd become used to the quiet. There were even times when she saw it as a blessing rather than a hindrance. Oh, she missed some things—twittering birds, rain splattering on the roof, the soft *mew* of a kitten, and her mother's gentle voice. What she didn't miss were blaring car horns, squeaking doors, roaring thunder, and the shrill voices of people shouting.

She flipped on the light switch and glanced around. Aunt Dorcas was obviously not at home. If she were, she'd be in the kitchen, starting supper. Maybe she was still at the sewing circle, where she and several women from her Mennonite church were making quilts and other items for the Mennonite Relief Sale that would take place later this fall.

Someone touched Jolene's shoulder, and she whirled around.

"Sorry if I startled you," Uncle Charlie signed.

"It's okay," Jolene spoke as she signed. She understood that tapping her shoulder was sometimes the best way to get her attention. "I thought Aunt Dorcas would be home by now. Do you know why she's so late?"

"When she left this morning, she said she planned to make a few stops on her way home from church this afternoon." Uncle Charlie spoke rather than signed, and Jolene interpreted by reading his lips.

"Guess I'd better start supper so we can eat as soon as she gets home."

"Would you consider making chicken potpie?"

She nodded and grinned. Uncle Charlie might not have a Pennsylvania Dutch background, but he sure liked Pennsylvania Dutch food.

"If you don't need me for anything, I think I'll go back to the living room and finish reading the newspaper," Uncle Charlie said.

"I can manage, so go right ahead."

"We've sure enjoyed having you here." He patted her arm and ambled from the room.

She quirked an eyebrow. What had Uncle Charlie meant when he'd said "enjoyed"? It sounded as if he thought she had plans to leave.

Jolene shrugged and turned toward the stove. He probably hadn't meant anything.

She had just started the broth for the potpie when Aunt Dorcas got home. "Sorry I'm late," she both said and signed. "It took me much longer to do my errands than I expected, and traffic was terrible between here and Lancaster."

"No problem. I've already started supper." Jolene motioned to the bubbling broth on the stove, filling the room with a savory fragrance. "It shouldn't take too long."

Aunt Dorcas pulled out two chairs at the

table. "Would you sit a minute? I'd like to talk to you about something." Her expression was solemn.

"Is something wrong?"

"While you were at the dentist's this morning, I talked to your mother on the phone."

"How is she? Are things going well at home?"

Aunt Dorcas nodded. "She had a message for you."

"What was it?"

"The school board met yesterday, and they asked if you'd come home."

Jolene's eyebrows rose. "How come? They know I can't teach anymore."

"Two deaf children have moved with their family from Millersburg, Ohio, to your hometown of Topeka, Indiana. Their parents have the Rh factor, and the children haven't been able to hear since they were born. They've each had a year of schooling, but they need someone who can sign and read lips to continue their education."

Jolene shook her head. "Huh-uh; I'm not ready for that."

"You've been with us two years now and have become proficient at signing and reading lips," Aunt Dorcas said. "I think you're more than ready to go home and teach those special children."

"Why don't their parents send them somewhere else to learn? There are lots of good schools for the deaf, like the one here in Pennsylvania where you've taught."

"They did take the children somewhere to learn how to sign, but they want the family to be together at home now." Aunt Dorcas placed her hand gently on Jolene's arm. "They want you to provide their basic schooling and teach them how to read lips."

A gentle breeze floated through the open window and fluttered the curtains. Jolene shivered. She felt comfortable and confident here in Pennsylvania. She'd made friends with some of the deaf students Aunt Dorcas taught. The thought of going home sent a ripple of apprehension up her spine.

"You've missed teaching school; you've mentioned it so many times," Aunt Dorcas said.

"I know, but this would be different. I'd be teaching children who can't hear."

"That's right. And since *you* can't hear, who better to teach them?"

Aunt Dorcas's innocent question pried through Jolene's numbness, and she turned to stare out the window. She tried to envision what each person in her family was doing right now, for she truly did miss them. She tried to picture herself back home again, teaching two deaf children how to read and write. She thought about her cousins and how nice it would be to spend time with them again. She even thought about her buggy horse, Belle, and wondered if the easygoing mare missed her.

After several minutes of contemplation, Jolene turned to Aunt Dorcas and said, "Call Mom, and tell her to let the school board know that I'll be home by the end of the week."

CHAPTER 2

The clean scent of freshly laundered sheets on Jolene's bed brought a smile to her lips. She'd arrived home last night and had been greeted enthusiastically by her family. Her brother Andrew had even given Jolene one of his balloon creations made to look like a flower. She was grateful that she knew how to read lips, since no one in her immediate family knew how to sign. She wanted to begin working on that right away and hoped that once Mom, Dad, and Andrew learned, one of them might be willing to sign during their church services.

Jolene slipped out of bed and stretched

her arms over her head. She padded across the cold hardwood floor in her bare feet and stared out the window. The morning sun cast a golden haze over their corn-field. Her nose twitched as the smell of burning leaves, a sure sign of fall, drifted through the open window. *Dad must be working in the yard already.* He'd always gotten up early to do his chores so he could be in his buggy shop by eight o'clock.

Jolene turned away from the window, and her gaze came to rest on the hope chest sitting at the foot of her bed. She'd received it as a birthday present when she'd turned sixteen and had started filling it right away with a variety of things she might need when she got married. *I guess that may never happen, since I don't have a boyfriend,* she thought. *Even if I did have one, would any man want to marry a woman who can't hear?*

Knowing she couldn't give in to self-pity and needed to get downstairs to help with breakfast, Jolene moved over to her dresser. She picked up her hairbrush and began brushing her long hair, which hung below her waist.

Sometime this morning, she wanted to

see her cousins Loraine, Ella, and Katie. Then this evening, she planned to meet with the school board and talk about teaching the two deaf children who'd moved to the area.

Uneasiness tightened her chest. Was she really ready to begin teaching again? What if the children were difficult to teach? What if she didn't have all the skills she needed? Maybe she'd made a mistake in agreeing to take this position.

A vibration she felt told Jolene someone must be knocking on her door, so she turned from the window and yelled, "Come in!" At least she thought she'd yelled the words. Since Jolene could no longer hear her own voice, she couldn't be sure how loud she'd spoken.

When the door opened, her brother Andrew stepped into the room. "Mom said to tell you that breakfast is almost ready."

Jolene was glad Andrew had spoken slowly while looking directly at her. Otherwise, she couldn't have read his lips. She smiled and said, "Tell her I'll be down as soon as I get dressed and have my hair put up in place."

Andrew hesitated a minute as though

he might want to say something more, but then he gave a quick nod and hurried out the door.

Jolene sighed. Did Andrew feel uncomfortable talking to her? Would he be willing to learn sign language so they could communicate better? She certainly hoped so.

～❧ ❧～

"Is Jolene up?" Mom asked when Andrew entered the kitchen.

"*Jah.* Said she'd be right down." Andrew poured himself a cup of coffee and took a seat at the table. "It's hard to think of her being *daab*. I mean, she seemed to understand every word I said to her. It made me feel like she's not really deaf."

"Remember what she told us last night? She was reading your lips, the way your *daed*'s sister taught her to do while she was living in Pennsylvania." Mom set a plate of toast on the table.

"It just seems strange to me, that's all." Andrew blew on his coffee and took a tentative sip. "Do you think she'll be able to teach those daab *kinner*?"

Mom's forehead wrinkled. "Of course she can teach the deaf children. Jolene was a good teacher before she lost her hearing, and I'm sure she'll be a good teacher to the daab kinner, too."

He drummed his fingers along the edge of the table. "You think she'll expect us to learn how to talk with our hands?"

"Uh-huh. Before Jolene went to bed last night, she told me and your daed that she hoped we would all be willing to learn signing." Mom took a jug of Dad's homemade apple cider from their propane-operated refrigerator. "Jolene's right, Andrew. If we're going to communicate with her and tell her what others are saying, we need to learn sign language."

"But if she can read our lips, why do we have to learn how to sign?"

Mom set the cider on the table and took a seat across from him. "We need to understand the signs Jolene uses when she talks, and we need to learn to sign. It will help us all if we can communicate that way. And when others are speaking, like the ministers during church, hopefully one of us will be able to sign so Jolene will know what they're saying."

"Maybe those two daab kinner, too?"

"Jah. It would help them as well."

"Sorry I'm late," Jolene said when she

entered the room. "It felt so good to sleep in my own bed that I slept longer than I thought I would."

Mom smiled. "That's okay. Your daed's still outside, so we won't be ready to eat until he comes in."

"Dad went back to bed?" Jolene asked with a look of surprise.

Mom's eyebrows shot up. "I think you *missverschtch* what I said."

"Didn't you say that Dad's in bed?"

Mom shook her head and then glanced over at Andrew with a strange expression. He was beginning to realize that just because Jolene could read lips it didn't mean she understood every word they said.

Jolene moved closer to Mom. "Would you please repeat yourself? It would help, too, if you spoke a little slower this time."

"Your daed is still outside doing his chores," Mom said slowly. "We'll eat when he comes in."

Holding her right hand in front of her body, Jolene then brought it up and rested her thumb on her chest. "I. . ." She flicked her index finger off her thumb in front of her forehead. "Understand. I understand."

Mom looked over at Andrew. "We should both try that."

He grunted. "It looks too hard."

"Would you show us again?" Mom asked Jolene.

Jolene repeated the sentence, as well as the action with her hand, while Mom and Andrew tried to follow along.

"Don't think I'll ever catch on," Andrew mumbled as he tried to flick his thumb the way Jolene had done.

"Sure you will. It just takes practice," Jolene said. "There's a lot I can teach you if you're willing to learn."

"We'll all learn." Mom smiled. "You can start by giving us a lesson this evening after supper."

≈ ≈

As Lonnie Hershberger stepped into the barn, he was greeted by the unmistakable sound of grunting pigs awaiting their breakfast.

He groaned. Slopping hogs was not his favorite thing to do. But as much as he disliked it, he'd follow through on the promise he'd made to Pop to help out whenever he could.

Lonnie and his family had moved from Arthur, Illinois, to Middlebury, Indiana, a few months ago. Soon after their arrival, Lonnie had begun working for Rueben Yoder, tuning wind chimes. Lonnie had been playing the harmonica since he was a boy, and he had a good ear for music. Learning to tune the chimes had come easily to him, and he enjoyed his new job more than any other he'd held. Certainly more than working with pigs.

When Lonnie and his folks had first moved to Indiana, he'd thought he would miss Illinois. But the only thing he missed was his girlfriend, Carolyn, whom he'd been writing to at least once a week. In Lonnie's last letter, he'd invited Carolyn to visit Indiana. He hoped he'd receive a letter from her soon and that she'd be willing to come.

He dumped the food into the trough and watched as the mother hogs rustled their snouts into the slop, while their babies nudged the sows' udders for milk. The greedy little piglets bit each other and carried on as though they were starving to death.

"Knock it off!" Lonnie reached over the stall and nudged one of the piglets with a stick, hoping to break up the fight. The mother pig let out a high-pitched squeal, jerked her head around, and bit Lonnie's hand.

"Ow!" Fiery pain shot up his arm. "Let go, you stupid *sau!*"

The sow hung on, tearing into Lonnie's flesh. He ground his teeth together as sweat beaded up on his forehead and trickled onto his cheeks. "Let go!"

He swatted the sow's rump with the stick. When she finally let go, he breathed a sigh of relief but winced when he saw blood oozing from the wound in his hand.

A wave of anger swept over him. "Oh, great! Now I'll probably need stitches!" He kicked the stall door as another burst of pain shot up his arm.

CHAPTER 3

When breakfast was over and the dishes were done, Jolene slipped on a sweater. "I'm going over to see Ella," she said to Mom, who sat in front of her quilting frame on the sunporch. "Then I plan to stop and see Loraine and Katie."

"That's a good idea. I'm sure they'll be real glad to see you again." Mom had turned her head toward Jolene, and when she spoke, her lips moved slowly, making it easier for Jolene to know what she'd said.

"I'll be back in time to help with supper," Jolene signed as she spoke. Even though Mom didn't know how to talk with her hands yet, Jolene thought it was good for her to see the hand positions. This evening when the family gathered for their first lesson, she would show them some specific words and letters.

Mom smiled as her fingers moved deftly, creating an intricate pattern on the quilt that was taking shape on her quilting frame. "Could you hand me those *schpelle*?" she asked, pointing to the container of pins on the sewing machine.

Jolene picked up the pins and gave them to Mom. "Guess I'd better get going."

"*Danki,* and have a *gut* day."

Jolene nodded and scooted out the door. Her nose twitched as the distinctive odor of wood smoke drifted across the pasture from their neighbor's chimney. There had been a day when she probably wouldn't have noticed the smoke, but her sense of smell had gotten keener since she'd lost her hearing.

As Jolene walked toward the barn to get her horse, a blustery breeze hit her full in the face. She looked up and saw the branches in the trees way up high hitting each other. Then she glanced at the dead leaves on the ground and noticed the wet, earthy smell they gave off. They were well into fall, and soon winter would be ushered in by cold snow and harsh winds. Maybe by then, her family would be able to communicate through signing, and she'd feel more at ease. She'd been gone so long that she almost felt as if she didn't belong here anymore. She'd been comfortable living with Aunt Dorcas and Uncle Charlie. Even though she'd missed her family in Indiana, Pennsylvania had begun to feel like her home. Maybe after a few more days, she'd feel like she was part of the family again.

Something soft and fuzzy brushing Jolene's leg brought her thoughts to a halt. She looked down and smiled at the silver-gray kitten staring up at her. It couldn't have been more than a few weeks old.

She bent over and picked up the kitten. Its nose felt soft, like a swatch of velvet, and Jolene felt the vibration of the kitten's purrs against her chest. "Where's your *mamm*, little one? Should we see if she's in the barn?"

The kitten opened its tiny mouth in a silent *meow*. Jolene patted its soft, furry head. "We'll find your mother, don't worry."

When Jolene opened the barn door and stepped inside, she was greeted by the aroma of sweaty horse flesh mixed with sweet-smelling hay. She smiled. Some things never changed.

She spotted Fluffy, the mother cat, sleeping in a pile of straw, and placed the kitten beside her. As Jolene was getting ready to open the gate to her horse's stall, Andrew showed up.

Jolene saw his lips move as he turned his head toward the stall, but she had no idea what he'd said. She tapped his shoulder. "I didn't understand you. Please, look at me when you speak."

He turned toward her with a sheepish expression. "Sorry. I was just saying that I heard you were going over to see Ella, so I thought I'd get your horse hitched to the buggy for you."

Even though it had been some time since Jolene had hitched a horse or driven a buggy, she was sure she could do it. But she didn't want to appear ungrateful, so she smiled and said, "Danki, I appreciate that."

Andrew touched Jolene's arm. "I'm sorry for the way I acted this morning. I'm just not sure I can learn to talk with my hands."

She thumped his arm. "I learned how to do it. I'm sure you can, too."

"Guess we'll have to see how it goes." Andrew took Jolene's horse, Belle, from her stall. As he led Belle out of the barn, Jolene followed.

She marveled at the agility of Andrew's sun-bronzed hands as he worked easily to hitch Belle to the buggy. He'd done it much faster than she ever could.

When Andrew finished the job, he held the horse while Jolene climbed into the buggy. "Guess I'd better get my own horse and buggy ready to go now," he said, poking his head into the buggy and looking directly at Jolene. "I need to get to the harness shop or I'll be late for work."

"All right then. Have a good day." Jolene picked up the reins and got the horse moving. When she reached the end of the lane, she was relieved to see that no cars were coming in either direction. Getting the feel for driving the buggy again would be easier with less traffic on the road.

As Jolene traveled along, she felt the rhythmic vibrations of the horse's hooves pounding against the pavement. This was another sense that had increased since she'd become deaf. Even though she couldn't hear any cars that came up behind her, she could sense their presence by the vibration of the wheels on the road and see them by looking in her buggy's side mirrors.

Jolene relaxed against the seat, enjoying the fall foliage and gazing at the many Amish farms scattered along this stretch of road. Despite the comfort she'd come to know in Pennsylvania, she had missed Indiana and its wide-open spaces. Even though this area was often visited by tourists, it wasn't nearly as congested or commercialized as what she'd seen in Lancaster County, Pennsylvania.

After a short drive, Jolene guided Belle up the driveway to Uncle Rueben and Aunt Verna's place and pulled up to the hitching rail near the barn. Just as she was climbing down from the buggy, Ella came out the front door and sprinted across the lawn.

"*Ach,* it's so good to see you!" Ella said, rushing up to Jolene. Her pale blue eyes filled with tears, and she gave Jolene a welcoming hug. "Are you able to read my lips?" she asked after she'd pulled away.

"Jah, but it would be easier for me to

know what you're saying if you could talk with your hands."

"I'm not sure I could learn to do that. I think it would be too hard."

"It's not that difficult. I'm going to teach my family, and I'd be happy to teach you if you'd like to learn."

"I'm willing to try." Ella motioned to the house and then turned her head in that direction.

Even though Jolene could see Ella's lips move, she had no idea what she'd said. She stepped in front of Ella. "In order for me to read your lips, I need to see your face."

A blotch of red erupted on Ella's cheeks. "Sorry about that. What I said was, 'Let's get your horse put in the corral; then we can go inside for a cup of tea while we get caught up on one another's lives.'"

"That sounds good, but I can't stay too long. I want to stop and see how Loraine and Katie are doing."

"If you stay awhile, you won't have to stop and see them, because they're both coming over here soon."

"They are?"

"Jah. We knew you were supposed to

get home last night, so we made plans to meet here and then go by your place and take you out for lunch."

"That sounds nice, but it'll be harder for us to visit at a restaurant with so many people around."

"What if we stay here and have lunch?"

Jolene smiled. "That's fine with me. I'd be more comfortable eating here than at a restaurant, anyway."

They'd just gotten Belle put in the corral when a horse and buggy came up the drive. Thinking it must be Katie or Loraine, Jolene turned and waved. After the buggy had pulled up to the hitching rail and the driver got out, she was surprised to see that it wasn't either one of her cousins. It was a young Amish man with wavy blond hair. She was sure she'd never seen him before.

Ella must have known him, though, for she rushed right over. They talked a few minutes, but with their backs to Jolene, she had no idea what they were saying.

Finally, they turned, and the young man followed Ella as she headed back toward Jolene. His chiseled cheeks and promi-nent jaw dwarfed his narrow nose, and his eyes were the rich brown color of spring soil. Jolene couldn't help but feel his curious gaze, and her face heated.

"I'd like you to meet Lonnie Hershberger," Ella said, looking at Jolene. "He and his family moved here a few months ago, and Lonnie's been working for my daed, tuning and cutting the pieces of pipe that make up our wind chimes." She looked over at Lonnie and smiled, and then she motioned to Jolene and looked back at her. "This is my cousin Jolene. She's the one I told you had been living in Pennsylvania, where she learned to sign and read lips."

"It's nice to meet you." Lonnie shook Jolene's hand. That's when she noticed a large bandage wrapped around his other hand.

"One of my daed's ornery pigs bit me this morning," Lonnie explained. "The wound was so bad that I had to get stitches and a tetanus shot."

Jolene grimaced. "Does it hurt much?"

"Not so much at the moment, but it sure did when the *dumm* sau bit me." Lonnie's thick eyebrows almost met his nose when he frowned.

"Will you be able to work today?" Ella

asked. Her question was directed at Lonnie, but she was turned toward Jolene enough so that she could read her lips.

Lonnie's frown deepened. "Afraid not. With only one good hand, I won't be able to cut any pipes."

"That's too bad. I'm sure Papa will be sorry to hear about your hand," Ella said.

"Guess I'd better go tell him right now. Is he up at the shop?" Lonnie asked.

"Jah."

Lonnie gave Jolene a brief nod. "Nice meeting you."

"It was nice meeting you, too."

As Lonnie headed up the driveway toward the shop, Ella turned to Jolene and smiled. "He's nice, and he's sure got an ear for music. Before Lonnie came along, Papa couldn't find anyone besides himself to tune the chimes. We're fortunate to have Lonnie working for us."

Jolene didn't voice her thoughts, but seeing the way Ella's face lit up when she talked about Lonnie made her wonder if there might be something going on between them. As they reached the porch steps, Jolene said, "Lonnie's nice looking, don't you think?"

Ella's eyebrows shot up. "After only one meeting, are you interested in him?"

Jolene shook her head vigorously. "Ach, no! I just meant. . ."

Ella touched Jolene's arm. "I hope you don't have any ideas about Lonnie, because he's got a girlfriend back in Illinois, and I believe she might be coming here for a visit soon. I suspect from what Lonnie's said that he hopes to marry her."

Jolene's mouth dropped open. Before she could explain her question, a cloud of dust swirled across the yard as another horse and buggy rolled in. The lathered-up horse, flipping its head from side to side, headed straight for the barn.

CHAPTER 4

I'm sorry to hear that," Rueben said after Lonnie told him about the sow biting his hand. "Guess you won't be able to work today."

"Probably not for a few days. Hopefully by Monday I'll be able to use my injured hand." Lonnie grimaced as frustration boiled in his soul. He wished he didn't have to miss any work. He'd been trying to save up enough money so he could ask Carolyn to marry him, but the more work he missed, the longer it would be before he felt free to ask. Of course, Pop thought

Lonnie ought to work for him full-time, slopping and butchering pigs. What was the fun in that? Making wind chimes was a lot more enjoyable.

Besides, Rueben appreciated Lonnie's work; he'd said so many times. And he didn't criticize everything Lonnie did the way Pop often did. Nothing seemed to be good enough for Pop: not the way Lonnie groomed the horses, not the way he butchered hogs, not even the way he fed the stupid swine. In Pop's mind, there was always a better way of doing things. His way; that's what he thought was best.

"You're lookin' mighty glum," Rueben said, nudging Lonnie's arm. "Are you that upset about missing a day's work?"

"Guess maybe I am. Can't afford to miss too many days, that's for sure." Lonnie glanced around Rueben's shop. Pieces of pipe that he'd cut yesterday lay on a table where Charlene, Rueben's seventeen-year-old daughter, was busy stringing the chimes. On another table lay several more pieces of pipe still needing to be cut and tuned. Lonnie figured Rueben would probably take over his job until he returned to work, which meant he wouldn't be free to make deliveries and pick up supplies, like he normally did.

"I know what you mean about not wanting to miss too many days of work," Rueben said. "In this day and age, we all need some kind of steady employment." His deeply set blue eyes darkened as he pulled his fingers through the ends of his full, red beard. "So many businesses are going under. I'll admit that I'm a little worried about whether folks will keep buying wind chimes with the economic distress we're facing right now."

"I'm sure everything will be okay," Lonnie said. "Many businesses outside of our area buy your chimes. If you were only relying on local businesses, it might be a concern, but jobs aren't as scarce in some other places as they are right here."

Rueben's face relaxed a bit. "You've got a good point. Guess I need to let go of my worries and leave my business in God's hands."

"That's the best way, all right. Think I'd better head for home and put some ice on my hand. Since there's no church in our district this Sunday, I probably won't see you until Monday."

"See you then," Rueben said with a nod.

Lonnie went out the door, but he'd only taken a few steps when he spotted a horse and buggy coming up the driveway at a very fast pace. The horse was lathered up, and no one was driving the buggy. He raced down the driveway, waving his hands, hoping to detour the horse. Ella, who'd been standing near the corral next to her cousin, started after the horse at the same time.

The horse was almost to the barn when it screeched to a stop and stood pawing the ground.

Ella grabbed the horse's bridle. "Whew. . . that's a relief! I thought for sure that crazy animal was going to run into the side of our barn."

"I wonder whose rig this is and how come there's no driver," Lonnie said.

"I have no idea where the driver is, but this is the horse Papa sold my cousin Katie's daed a week ago. He's always been a bit of a challenge."

"Your cousin's daed or the horse?" Lonnie asked with a chuckle.

Ella grinned. "There might be times when Aunt JoAnn thinks Uncle Jeremy's a bit of a challenge, but I was referring to the horse."

Lonnie studied Ella for a minute. Her reddish blond hair and pale blue eyes stood in sharp contrast to Jolene's dark brown hair and vivid blue eyes. It was hard to believe they were cousins. In the few minutes he'd visited with them before going to Rueben's shop, Lonnie had determined that the young women's personalities were very different, too. Ella could be quite outspoken and was a take-charge kind of person. Jolene, on the other hand, seemed a bit more reserved. Maybe that was because she couldn't hear.

Lonnie was grateful for his two good ears. He didn't know what he'd do if he couldn't hear the beautiful melody of the wind chimes he helped create. The melodious sounds made him think about David in the Bible and the harp he used to play.

Ella's eyebrows drew together as she frowned. "Since this is the horse my daed sold Uncle Jeremy, I'm wondering if Katie should have been driving the buggy."

"What do you mean, 'should have been'?" Lonnie questioned.

"Katie's supposed to come over here this morning, and so is my cousin Loraine. Maybe the horse got away from Katie before she could get into the buggy." Ella stroked the horse's mane. "Is that what happened, big fellow? Did you get in a hurry to go and then decide to head over here because it's the place you know best?"

The horse nuzzled Ella's hand in response.

"Would you like me to look for Katie on my way home?" Lonnie asked. "If she's out searching for the horse, I might see her walking alongside the road."

Before Ella could respond, another horse and buggy rolled into the yard. When it pulled up to the hitching rail, Ella's cousins Loraine and Katie stepped down. Katie looked relieved when she saw her horse, but Loraine didn't seem to notice. She was too busy greeting Jolene.

"I was trying to get in my buggy to come over here when the horse took off without me. I'm glad to see he came here and isn't out on the road running for who knows where," Katie said.

"That's what I thought might have happened," Ella said. "Guess it'll take some time for the horse to get used to its new home and owners."

"I would have used my horse, Dixie, but I thought I'd give Dad's new horse a try." Katie smiled. "There was a day when something like this would have put my nerves on edge, but I'm dealing better with everything now." She turned to Jolene and gave her a hug. When she pulled back, she smiled and said, "It's so good to see you again. Welcome home."

Jolene smiled. "It's good to see you, too."

Lonnie turned to Ella. "Would you like me to help you put the horses in the corral?"

"I appreciate the offer," Ella said, "but it might be hard for you to do with only one good hand."

"Ach, my! What happened to your hand?" Loraine asked.

Lonnie explained his accident and then grimaced. "My hand's starting to throb again, so I think I ought to head for home."

"That's probably a good idea," Ella said. "It might help if you put some ice on it."

"That's just what I was planning to do." Lonnie gave Ella a nod and sprinted to his buggy.

~❧ ❧~

After the horses had been put away, Ella led the way to the house, where Jolene and her cousins took seats around the kitchen table. Ella's mother, Aunt Verna, set a pot of tea and five cups on the table and then joined them.

"Jolene and I decided we'd like to have lunch here today instead of at a restaurant," Ella said. "It will be easier for us to visit without so many interruptions."

"That's fine with me," Loraine said. "Sometimes it can be awfully noisy at a restaurant."

"And since we won't have to travel anywhere, it'll give us more time to visit. Oh, and it'll be easier for me to read your lips if you all look at me when you talk," Jolene quickly added.

"There's some leftover chicken noodle soup in the refrigerator," Aunt Verna said. "I'll heat that up and make sandwiches to go with it." She got up from the table. "I'll get it started right now while you young women visit."

The sunlight streaming through the kitchen window spread a warm glow across the table. When Jolene took a sip of tea, she felt its warming comfort flow through her. It was nice to be with her cousins again. This was the first time they'd all been together since the horrible accident that had changed each of their lives in some way.

"How does it feel to be home?" Loraine asked, touching Jolene's arm.

"It feels good, but I'm a little *naerfich* about teaching again."

"I don't think there's any reason for you to feel nervous. You were a good teacher before, so I'm sure you'll do fine," Katie said.

"This will be different, though. The children I've come home to teach are deaf like me, which could be a challenge."

"What kind of challenge?" Loraine asked.

"What if I can't communicate well enough with the children? What if they don't understand what I'm saying?"

"You'll do fine," Ella said. "Just believe in yourself and ask God to help you."

Jolene sighed. "Since I lost my hearing from the accident, I've lost some of the confidence. I—I'm not sure I'll fit in."

Aunt Verna turned from the stove and stood in front of Jolene. "You're still the same person, so you'll fit in just fine." She patted Jolene's shoulder and then hurried back to the stove.

Feeling the need to change the subject, Jolene turned to Loraine and asked, "How are Wayne and Crist doing with their taxidermy business?"

"Pretty well, but with jobs being scarce and money so tight, they're concerned that folks might stop bringing things in to be stuffed. If that should happen, they'll need to find some other way to make a living." Loraine smiled. "I do have some good news to share with you."

"What's that?" Katie asked.

"Wayne and I are expecting a *boppli*. We're hoping and praying that this baby will be healthy and I'll be able to carry it to full term."

"That is good news," Ella said. "I'll be praying with you about the baby."

Jolene nodded, and so did Katie, although Jolene couldn't help but feel a bit envious. She longed to be a wife and mother.

"I'm so pleased that you'll be here when Freeman and I get married in the spring," Katie said to Jolene.

Jolene smiled. "At least I won't miss this wedding." She turned to Loraine. "Sorry I had to miss yours, but Aunt Dorcas needed my help after her carpal tunnel surgery."

"I know, and I understand. We're just glad you're home now."

Aunt Verna peered out the kitchen window. Frowning, she turned to face them again.

"What's wrong?" Ella asked.

"Not what, but who. Eunice Byler's buggy is in the yard, and she's heading for the house. She probably came by to deliver the soap I ordered from her awhile back."

"Don't you want the soap, Mama?" Ella asked.

"Of course I do."

"Then why are you frowning?"

A rosy color flooded Aunt Verna's cheeks. "Eunice tends to be quite the gossip. Once she gets going, it's hard to make her stop." She glanced at the stove then back again. "I hope she doesn't expect an invitation to join us for lunch."

"Who's Eunice?" Jolene asked.

"She and her family moved here after you went to Pennsylvania," Ella said.

Katie grimaced. "Eunice used to have her *kapp* set for Freeman. I think she was very disappointed when he chose me instead of her."

When the back door opened, Jolene leaned forward, anxious to meet Eunice. All this talk made her curious about just what kind of person Eunice was.

CHAPTER 5

When Eunice stepped into the Yoders' cozy kitchen, a tantalizing aroma wafted up to her nose. Her stomach rumbled, and she licked her lips. Maybe she would be invited to stay for lunch.

"*Guder mariye*," Eunice said, smiling at Ella, who sat at the table with Loraine, Katie, and a young woman Eunice had never met.

"Our morning's almost over, so I guess I'll say good afternoon." Ella glanced at the dark-haired woman who sat beside her. "This is my cousin Jolene. She's been living in Pennsylvania for the last two years and has returned to Indiana to teach the two daab kinner who moved here a few weeks ago."

"Oh, you're Andrew's sister, aren't you?" Eunice asked without looking at Jolene.

Jolene gave no response.

Eunice frowned and repeated her question.

Still no reply.

"Humph! Well, don't answer me then," Eunice muttered.

"Jolene's deaf. You have to look directly at her when you speak so she's able to read your lips."

Eunice's face heated. How could she have been so stupid? She remembered now that Andrew had told her about his sister losing her hearing in the accident they'd been in two years ago.

Eunice knew that if she was going to get Andrew to be interested in her, she needed to get to know his sister.

"Your *bruder* Andrew did mention that you've been living in Pennsylvania." Eunice spoke slowly, emphasizing each word as she looked at Jolene. "I should have remembered that you'd lost your hearing."

"Did he tell you that I've come home to teach Sylvia and Irvin Troyer?"

"I didn't know that until Ella mentioned it just now." Eunice shifted uneasily. It felt strange to speak to someone who couldn't hear. It was hard to believe that Jolene could know what she was saying by reading her lips. "I hope that the Troyer children are well mannered and easy to teach. Fern and I are good friends, and she's told me some stories about some of the more stubborn scholars she teaches." She wrinkled her nose. "Makes me glad I'm not a teacher."

"I'm sure there are a lot of rewards in being a teacher." Ella looked at Jolene. "Isn't that right?"

"Were you speaking to me?" Jolene asked.

"Jah. I said that I'm sure there are lots of rewards in being a teacher."

Jolene smiled and nodded. "I've always enjoyed teaching."

Eunice looked over at Katie. She hadn't said a word since she'd entered the room. She knew Katie didn't like her, but did she have to be so rude? After all, Katie was the one who'd ended up with Freeman, even though he'd been Eunice's boyfriend first. If anyone had a reason to hold a grudge, it was Eunice. Everything had been going just fine between her and Freeman until Katie came between them. She guessed it didn't matter anymore, because Katie and Freeman would be getting married in the spring. Besides, Eunice had her eye on Andrew now.

Eunice's gaze went to Verna, who stood in front of the stove, stirring what smelled like delicious soup. The fragrant aroma beckoned her to sit awhile and enjoy the warmth of Verna's kitchen. "What are you cooking?" she asked, moving closer to the stove. "It sure smells good."

"It's chicken noodle soup," Verna replied rather stiffly. "We'll be having it for lunch."

Eunice hesitated, still hoping she might be invited to join them. When Verna said nothing, Eunice handed her the paper sack she held. "I brought the soap you ordered."

"Just put it on the table," Verna said over her shoulder. "I'll get my purse and pay you in a minute."

"Would you like me to get your purse, Mama?" Ella offered.

Verna shook her head. "That's okay; I'll get it. Just stay where you are and visit with your cousins."

Ella took a sip of tea and blotted her lips with a napkin.

Loraine leaned closer to Katie. "Have you gotten any new stamps in the stamp shop lately?"

Katie smiled. "As a matter of fact, we have. Last week's shipment had. . ."

Eunice rested her hip against the cupboard as she tuned out the conversation going on at the table. She felt like an intruder and wished Ella or one of the cousins would at least invite her to sit and visit.

Eunice turned and glanced out the kitchen window, allowing her thoughts to wander. *Sure wish I knew if Andrew was interested in me. I wonder if he'll ever ask me to go out with him. If he doesn't, I'll need to look for someone else, because I sure don't want to end up an old maid like Freeman's sister, Fern.*

Tired of feeling left out, Eunice moved over to the table, pulled out the empty chair next to Jolene, and plunked down. When Jolene turned to look at her, Eunice smiled and said, "I don't know if anyone's told you or not, but I sell soaps and scented candles. Maybe you'd like to host a party sometime."

Jolene's eyebrows drew together. "Could you repeat that, please?"

"I sell candles and scented soaps. Would you like to host a party sometime?"

"I—I don't know. Starting Monday I'll be busy teaching, so—"

"You won't be teaching all the time. You could host the party some evening or on a Saturday."

"I'll have to see how it goes."

Eunice was about to say something more when Verna handed her the money she owed. "Here you go. Danki for bringing my order by."

"You're welcome." Eunice waited to see if anyone would say anything else to her. When they didn't, she looked at Loraine and said, "Before I came here, I delivered some candles to Lydia Beechy. She said she'd gotten a letter from her son, Jake, who lives in Montana."

Loraine smiled. "That's nice. I'm sure she was glad to hear from him."

"Didn't you used to go out with Jake?"

"Jah, but that was a long time ago."

"From what I've heard, Jake's always been kind of wild."

Loraine shook her head. "He's not wild, just free spirited."

"Maybe so, but I heard—"

Ella cleared her throat loudly. "How many more deliveries do you have to make today, Eunice?"

"Four, and then I need to go to Shipshe to pick up a prescription for my mamm."

"Is your mother sick?" Verna asked, turning away from the stove.

"Not really, but she needs medicine for her high blood pressure."

Verna's forehead wrinkled. "I didn't realize she had high blood pressure."

"She just found out a few days ago, but the doctor said she should be fine as long as she eats right and takes her medicine." Eunice drummed her fingers along the edge of the table. "Speaking of eating right, have any of you noticed how much weight our bishop has put on lately? Why, I'll bet he weighs nearly—"

"Oh my, look at the time." Ella motioned to the clock. "It's almost noon, so maybe we should get lunch on the table and see if Papa and Charlene are planning to join us today."

"I'm sure they will," Verna said. "Neither one asked me to pack a lunch for them this morning, so I don't think they're planning to eat at the shop."

"What can we do to help?" Katie asked, pushing away from the table.

"Why don't you and Jolene set the table? Then Loraine can fill the glasses with apple cider, while Ella and I make the sandwiches."

Eunice clamped her teeth together. It was obvious that she wasn't going to be asked to stay for lunch. They were clearly hoping she'd leave.

With an audible sigh, Eunice pushed her chair aside and stood. "Guess I'd better get going." She cast a quick glance in Jolene's direction. "It was nice meeting you. I hope we'll get the chance to get to know each other better."

Jolene gave a quick nod. Eunice figured she might not have understood what she'd said. Either that, or she was just plain rude.

"Well, then, I'll be on my way." Eunice hurried out the door. It didn't take a genius to know that her presence wasn't wanted.

~⚜~

Jolene shifted uneasily in her chair. Even though she hadn't liked some of the things Eunice had said, she wasn't comfortable with the way the others had treated her. It was as though they were anxious for Eunice to leave and weren't interested in anything she had to say. Of course, much of what Eunice had said did seem like gossip.

Ella looked over at Jolene and quirked an eyebrow. "What'd you think of Eunice?"

"She seems nice enough, but she's quite the talker," Jolene replied.

"Oh, she's a talker, all right—either yammering away about nothing at all or spreading rumors and gossip." Ella stuck her finger in her mouth, as though she were gagging.

Katie nudged Jolene's arm. "You'd better forewarn your bruder, because I have a hunch that Eunice has her kapp set for him."

"What makes you think that?" Jolene asked.

"Didn't you see the sappy look on her face when she mentioned his name?"

"No, not really. I was concentrating more on trying to read her lips."

Loraine poked Katie's arm and said something to her, but Jolene didn't get what she'd said because she wasn't looking directly at her.

"Was Loraine saying something to me?" she asked, turning to Katie.

Katie shook her head. "She was reminding me of how Andrew rescued Eunice when her buggy flipped over in a ditch several weeks ago. Ever since then, she's been hanging around Andrew every chance she gets."

Ella touched Jolene's arm. "I'd warn him if I were you. . .just in case he has any ideas about going out with Eunice."

"Would that really be so bad?" Jolene asked.

All three heads bobbed.

"I don't think Eunice would make a good sister-in-law—or a good wife, for that matter." Ella's serious expression caused Jolene to worry. If Eunice was as bad as her cousins seemed to think, then maybe she should say something to Andrew. Or would it be better to let him find out for himself what kind of person Eunice was?

～≈～

Lonnie whistled as he headed up the driveway with the mail in his hands. He'd received a letter from Carolyn and could hardly wait to read it. If she agreed to marry him, they'd be living in Indiana, since this was where Lonnie's job was now. Carolyn made friends easily; he was sure she'd fit in and make new friends here.

The tune Lonnie whistled became louder. It was amazing how finding the letter had improved his mood. It was enough to make him forget about the pain in his hand.

The trees lining their driveway creaked as the wind picked up. Lonnie clung to the mail. *Sure wouldn't want Carolyn's letter to blow away.*

He was almost to the house when his twelve-year-old sister Sharon rushed out the door with a panicked expression. "I'm in big trouble, Lonnie. Really big trouble!" She grabbed the sleeve of his jacket.

"What'd you do now?" Sharon was the youngest in his family, and she always seemed to be in some kind of a fix. It had been that way ever since she was old enough to walk and talk.

Her hazel-colored eyes filled with tears. "I—I spilled beet juice on my bed quilt."

"How'd you do that? Your quilt's supposed to be on your bed, not in the kitchen."

"I wasn't in the kitchen. I was cleaning my room and got hungry for a snack." She blinked a couple of times. "I came down to the kitchen and fixed myself a bowl of pickled beets."

Lonnie's forehead wrinkled. "Please don't tell me you took the beets upstairs to your room."

"I know it was a dumm thing to do, but I set the bowl on my nightstand, and then I took a seat on my bed. When I reached for the bowl, I bumped the lamp beside my bed. It jostled the bowl, and the next thing I knew there was a trail of beet juice on the edge of my quilt." Sharon's chin trembled. "Mom's gonna pitch a fit when she and Pop come home from town and find out what I did. I'll probably get a *bletsching* and be given extra chores to do."

Lonnie chuckled in response to her fears about getting a spanking. Although Sharon

was a bit accident-prone, she rarely dis-
obeyed. He couldn't remember the last
time she'd been disciplined harshly by
either one of their parents. "I doubt you'll
get a bletsching, but you might be right
about having to do extra chores." Lonnie
reached for the handle on the screen door.
"Why don't you try washing the part of the
quilt that has beet juice on it?"

"I tried that already, but the red's still
there." Sharon's nose began to run, mixing
with her tears. She sniffed a couple of
times. "You got any ideas what I should
do, Lonnie?"

He shrugged. "If it were me, I'd try putting some bleach or peroxide on the stain,
and then I'd wash it really good."

She swiped at her tears with the back
of her hand. "You think that might work?"

"It's worth a try. Maybe by the time the
folks get home, you'll have the beet juice
out and your quilt will be good as new."

"But how am I supposed to get it dry in
time? There's not much sun today, and
Mom and Dad will probably be here in a
couple of hours. That might not give the
wet spot on the quilt enough time to dry."

"Why don't you drape it over the clothes rack and set it in front of the stove?"

"I guess that might work." Her lips turned up. "Danki, Lonnie; I appreciate your suggestion."

"No problem. That's what big brothers are for." Lonnie slipped Carolyn's letter in his jacket pocket and handed Sharon the rest of the mail. "Put this on the table, would you? I'm going out to the barn to read my letter."

"Sure." Sharon gave him another smile and scurried into the house.

Whistling all the way, Lonnie hurried to the barn.

As soon as he stepped inside, he lit a kerosene lantern and found a seat on a bale of straw. Tearing Carolyn's letter open, he read it silently to himself:

Dear Lonnie,

I received your letter yesterday, inviting me to come to Topeka for a visit. I'd love to see where you live and spend time with you and your family. Mom said I can have some time off from our general store, so my plan is to get a bus ticket and arrive in Elkhart

**two weeks from today. If you could
hire a driver to pick me up, it would be
appreciated.**

Lonnie smiled as he folded the letter
and returned it to his pocket. Then he
leaned his head against the wooden beam
behind him, feeling fully relaxed. Carolyn
was coming for a visit. In just a couple of
weeks, he could ask her to marry him. Except for the throbbing in his hand and the
fact that he'd lost out on some pay, this
day wasn't going so bad after all.

Lonnie closed his eyes and let his mind
wander as he pictured himself and Carolyn on their wedding day. He saw the two
of them standing before the bishop, answering his questions and agreeing to stay
married until they were separated by death.

He continued to daydream, thinking
about how his life would be once they were
married and raising a family of their own.
How many children would they have? If
they had girls, would they have hair the
color of golden wheat and sparkling blue
eyes like Carolyn? Would the girls enjoy
quilting and working with flowers the way
she did? Would their boys take after him,

with wavy blond hair and closely set brown eyes? Would they have an ear for music, like their father had?

Bam! The barn door opened and shut with a bang, and Lonnie's eyes snapped open. Sharon, wide-eyed and red-faced, rushed into the barn. "Lonnie, come, *schnell!*"

Lonnie groaned, feeling irritated by the interruption. "Where is it you want me to go quickly, Sharon?"

Tears coursed down her cheeks. "My quilt's on fire!"

CHAPTER 6

Lonnie's heart pounded as he raced for the house. When he stepped inside, he saw smoke and flames coming from the kitchen.

He grabbed a towel from a wall peg, wet it at the utility sink, and draped it over his head. Then he grabbed a bucket, filled it with water, and dashed into the kitchen. The quilt, which had been hung over a wooden rack near the stove, was in flames. Lonnie threw the bucket of water over it, filled the bucket once more, and doused it again. When the fire was out, he grabbed the soggy quilt and hauled it outside.

"It's ruined!" Sharon sobbed as she dropped to the ground beside the remains of her quilt. "I—I didn't put the rack too close to the stove, so I don't know how it caught on fire."

"What'd you clean it with—bleach or peroxide?" Lonnie asked.

"Peroxide. I found a big bottle of it in the utility room and poured some on the spot where the beet juice was."

"Did you mix it with water or use it full strength?" Lonnie questioned.

"I poured some into a smaller container, and then I put it on the quilt full strength." She hiccupped on a sob. "That stuff smelled horrible; it made me cough and gag."

Lonnie groaned. The peroxide that had been sitting in the utility room had been the 30 percent industrial kind and should have been diluted with water before use. He'd read several articles in *The Budget* about fires that had been started because people had used 30 percent peroxide full strength and exposed whatever they'd been cleaning to the sun or some other heat source. Of course, Lonnie wasn't sure if it was the peroxide that had caused Sharon's quilt to catch on fire or if it had been placed too close to the stove. He'd been in such a hurry to get the fire out he hadn't noticed how close the drying rack had been set. Either way, the quilt was ruined, and his sister would be in trouble with their mother.

"Guess it's my fault this happened," he mumbled. "I should have never suggested that you put peroxide on the quilt." He rapped the side of his head. "Just never dreamed you'd use Dad's 30 percent peroxide at full strength."

"What am I gonna do, Lonnie?" Sharon wailed. "When Mom and Pop get back from town, I'll get a bletsching for sure."

"You won't get a bletsching. I'll explain what happened, and everything will be fine." Lonnie turned toward the house. "I need to get back inside and clear out the smoke and ashes. While I'm doing that, you can get the wheelbarrow."

"What for?"

"So we can haul the quilt out to the garbage."

"Oh, okay." Sharon hurried off toward the barn to get the wheelbarrow, and Lonnie went into the house.

He'd just gotten some windows open

and had begun to clean up the mess when he heard the sound of buggy wheels rumbling into the yard. *Oh, great, the folks must be home.*

By the time Lonnie stepped outside, Mom was already out of the buggy and standing beside Sharon, staring at the ruined quilt while shaking her head. The wheelbarrow was parked nearby.

Tearfully, Sharon explained what had happened.

Mom moaned. "How could you have been so foolish, Sharon?"

"It's not entirely her fault," Lonnie said, stepping between them. "I'm the one who suggested she use peroxide to get out the beet juice. I just didn't think she'd use the bottle of peroxide on the utility porch or that she'd put it on full strength."

"What in the world were you thinking, boy?" Pop asked when he joined them. "You oughta know better than to tell your sister to use that stuff." He grunted, and his pale, bushy eyebrows pulled tightly together. "What a *dummkopp.*"

"I'm not a dunce, and I didn't think she'd—"

Pop glared at Lonnie. "Your mamm worked real hard making that quilt, and I think you oughta pay her what it'll cost to buy material to make a new one."

Mom shook her head. "He doesn't have to do that, Ezra. I've got plenty of material on hand. Enough so that Sharon can make a new quilt for her bed."

Sharon puckered her lips. "But Mom, I don't know how to sew a quilt."

"Then it's time you learned." Mom nudged Sharon's arm. "And for taking those beets up to your room, you'll have extra chores to do for the next two weeks." She grimaced. "The fire never would have happened if you'd eaten the beets in the kitchen like you know you're supposed to do."

Lonnie bent down, scooped up the quilt, and dropped it into the wheelbarrow. He was on his way to the garbage can when Pop, walking briskly beside him, grabbed hold of his arm. "What are you doing home? Didn't Rueben have any work for you today?"

Lonnie held up his bandaged hand. "Couldn't do much with this hurting the way it does."

"You managed to put out a fire and haul Sharon's quilt outside. How do you account for that?"

Lonnie gritted his teeth. Was Pop trying to provoke him into an argument? "Seemed like putting out the fire was an emergency, so I ignored the pain in my hand." Lonnie hurried off before Pop could say anything more.

⚜

As Jolene headed down the road toward the Troyers' place, her stomach twisted with nervousness. What if Sylvia and Irvin didn't like her? Worse yet, what if the children's parents didn't like her? She remembered Aunt Dorcas telling her that it was very important for a teacher of deaf students to get acquainted with the students' parents. This, she'd said, would help the teacher understand the things the children might tell her that had happened at home. Getting to know the parents also helped the teacher see how the parents were dealing with the children and their loss of hearing.

Jolene tightened her grip on the reins. It wasn't in her nature to worry so much or get worked up over things. She knew she needed to relax and commit this to God.

She whispered a prayer, took a few deep breaths, and relaxed her grip on the reins. By the time she'd pulled off the road and was heading up the Troyers' driveway, she felt calmer and a bit more confident.

Jolene pulled up to the hitching rail and stepped down from the buggy. She'd just finished securing the horse when a tall, freckle-faced man with red hair stepped out of the barn. Figuring he must be the children's father and having been told that he could sign, Jolene used signing as she spoke the words.

"I'm Jolene Yoder. I've been hired by the school board to teach your children."

He gave an enthusiastic nod and signed as he spoke. "I'm Harvey Troyer, Sylvia and Irvin's daed. It's good you have come. We know that the teacher at the Amish schoolhouse can't teach them, and we don't relish the idea of sending them away to school."

"I understand."

Jolene spent the next several minutes talking with Harvey about how she'd lost her own hearing and had received training from her aunt in Pennsylvania, who'd been teaching deaf students a good many years. Then they talked about Jolene's previous years as a teacher and how she wanted to be a good teacher to his children as well.

"I hope to not only teach the children their lessons, but also how to formulate words and read lips," she said.

"That would be a good thing." He smiled. "Now let's go in the house so you can meet my wife, Mary, and the children. Sylvia and Irvin both know how to sign and have had one year of schooling, so I don't think teaching them will be a problem."

"I'm looking forward to meeting them," Jolene said.

Harvey led the way, and when they entered the house, Jolene was met by the enticing sweet smell of gingerbread. She followed Harvey into the kitchen, where a woman with light brown hair and pale blue eyes stood near the stove. A little boy who looked to be about three years old played with some pots and pans on the floor near her feet. A wooden cradle sat nearby with a baby inside.

"Mary, this is Jolene Yoder." Harvey motioned to Jolene. "She's the one who'll be teaching Irvin and Sylvia."

Mary smiled as she spoke to Jolene and signed, "I'm happy to meet you." She turned to her husband then and said something. He nodded and left the room. When he returned, two young children were with him.

"This is Sylvia." Harvey patted the brown-haired, blue-eyed girl on the head, and then he did the same to the boy with red hair and freckles. "This is our oldest child, Irvin."

Jolene signed to the children that she was happy to meet them and was anxious to begin teaching on Monday.

The seconds ticked by as the children stared at her, making no effort to sign anything in return.

"I think my kinner are kind of shy right now. I'm sure they'll warm up to you once you begin teaching them," Mary said.

Jolene decided to try again. She got down on her knees, so she was eye-level with Sylvia. *"How old are you?"* she signed.

Sylvia dropped her gaze and scuffed the toe of her sneaker on the floor. After a few seconds, she looked up and signed, *"I'm seven."*

Jolene looked over at Irvin. *"How old are you?"*

The boy shrugged.

Harvey nudged Irvin's arm. *"Your teacher asked you a question."*

The boy gave no response.

"Don't be stubborn now," Harvey signed. *"Tell Jolene how old you are."*

Irvin shook his head.

Jolene had a hunch that the boy might be the defiant type. She'd seen it in a few of the older scholars when she'd taught school before the accident. If that was the case, he'd probably be difficult to teach.

Oh, Lord, she silently prayed. *What have I gotten myself into?*

CHAPTER 7

Jolene glanced around the small classroom she'd been given to teach her two
students. It was upstairs in the small schoolhouse, set apart from the rest of the scholars, but it had been equipped with the
supplies she would need—a blackboard,
chalk, paper, pencils, and plenty of books.
Being in the schoolhouse brought back a
flood of memories from the days when
she'd been downstairs sitting at the desk
Fern Bontrager now occupied. It made
Jolene realize how much she'd missed
teaching.

   She took a seat at the desk that had

been provided for her as she waited for Irvin and Sylvia to arrive. *If the scholars in Fern's class knew how to sign, I'd be able to teach them, not just the deaf children.* She sighed. *Guess I should be grateful for this opportunity to teach and stop wishing for the impossible.*

Jolene felt the floor vibrate, and she turned toward the door. Sylvia entered the room, wearing an eager expression. Irvin trailed behind her, head down and shoulders slumped.

"Good morning," Jolene signed. She pointed to the low-hung shelf across the room. *"You can put your lunch pails over there."*

Sylvia smiled and placed her lunch pail on the shelf, but Irvin scuffed the toe of his boot on the floor and stared up at Jolene like he had no idea what she'd signed.

Twice more Jolene told the boy to put his lunch pail on the shelf, but he didn't budge. It made no sense, because Irvin's father had assured her that both of his children understood signing. She was sure the boy was just being stubborn and testing her patience.

Finally, in exasperation, Jolene signed

to Irvin, *"If you don't put your lunch pail on the shelf right now, you'll have to stand in the corner."*

No response.

Jolene took hold of Irvin's arm and led him to the corner. He stood like that while she showed Sylvia to her desk.

It gave Jolene no pleasure to begin the day like this, but after having taught hearing students, she knew she must be firm without being mean. After ten minutes went by, she turned Irvin toward her and signed, *"Please put your lunch pail on the shelf."*

She was relieved when he shuffled across the room and did as she'd asked. *"Now, please take a seat,"* she signed, and then she pointed to the desk next to Sylvia's.

Irvin glanced over at his sister, back at Jolene, and then ambled over to his desk and sat down.

Jolene sent up a silent prayer. *Thank You, Lord.*

Before starting their lessons, Jolene had the children stand and sign the Lord's Prayer. Then she opened her Bible and signed as she read Proverbs 16:24 out loud: " 'Pleasant words are as an honeycomb,

sweet to the soul, and health to the bones.'"
She decided that the verse was a timely
reminder for her as well as the children.

As they began their arithmetic lesson,
Sylvia gave Jolene her full attention, but
Irvin appeared disinterested, looking away
whenever Jolene signed anything to him,
and drawing silly pictures on his tablet instead of the numbers she'd written on the
blackboard. Jolene knew she'd need to
come up with some way to get through to
the boy. She wished she could talk to Aunt
Dorcas about this. With all the experience her aunt had teaching deaf children,
she was sure to have some idea what
Jolene could do. When she got home from
school today she would ask Mom to call
Aunt Dorcas and relay her concerns.

⚬❧ ❧⚬

Ella and her brother Larry had just taken
a seat in the waiting room at the dentist's
office when Loraine entered the room.

"*Wie geht's?*" Loraine asked, taking a
seat on the other side of Ella.

"I'm doing fine." Ella motioned to Larry.
"He's had a toothache for the last few days,
so he's missing a few hours of school this
morning to get it taken care of."

Larry grunted. "Rather be in school any old day than here right now."

Loraine offered him a sympathetic smile. "You'll do fine. Dr. Hopkins is a good dentist."

"What are you here for?" Larry asked.

"I'm just here for a cleaning and checkup." Loraine turned to Ella. "I'm surprised your mamm didn't bring Larry to the dentist. I figured you'd be working in your daed's shop this morning. We heard about Lonnie's injured hand."

Ella grimaced. "Mama's not feeling well, so she asked me to bring Larry in. Besides, Papa can get along without me for a few hours. I'm just doing the books and helping string some of the chimes. He assured me that he and Charlene could manage fine while I'm gone."

"I'm sorry to hear your mamm's not feeling well," Loraine said. "She seems to be sick a lot, doesn't she?"

Ella nodded and glanced over at Larry. She didn't want to express her concerns in front of the boy, but she was worried about her mother—had been ever since the van accident two years ago, when her brother Raymond had been killed. Ella figured it would be hard for any parent to lose a child, but she thought it was taking Mama much longer to come to grips with Raymond's death than it should have. Unless Mama's fatigue and shakiness were caused by something else. Maybe it wasn't just grief over losing Raymond. Maybe there was something physically wrong with Mama. If she'd only agree to see the doctor and let him run a few tests. But no, Mama thought everything could be cured by taking a dose of castor oil or some concoction made with apple cider vinegar and honey. Not that those things would do her any harm, but they hadn't kept Mama from feeling so tired, and they weren't a substitute for seeing the doctor.

"We're ready for you now," the dental assistant said when she stepped up to Larry.

He looked over at Ella, as if seeking her approval. When she nodded, he rose from his chair and followed the young woman into the other room, walking slowly with his head down.

"He wasn't happy about coming here," Ella said to Loraine. "In fact, he griped about it all the way from our house into town."

"I'm sure he'll be fine once he's numbed up and his tooth stops hurting."

"Jah."

Loraine reached over and touched Ella's arm. "You look like something's bothering you. Are you worried about your mamm?"

"Uh-huh. You know, she hasn't been the same since Raymond died, and I don't think it's just emotional." Ella's forehead wrinkled. "I don't want Larry or my sisters to know that I'm worried about Mama, though. No point in upsetting them, too."

"Have you talked to your daed about this?"

"I've tried, but he's either too busy to listen or makes light of it." Ella groaned. "I wonder just how sick Mama will have to get before she's willing to see the *dokder*."

"Would you like me to see if my mamm will speak to your mamm about seeing the doctor?" Loraine asked.

Ella shrugged. "I doubt she'll make any headway, but if she's willing, then I guess it's worth a try."

"When I'm done here I'll swing by my folks' place and ask her."

"Danki." Ella reached for a magazine

and thumbed through a couple of pages. Aunt Priscilla and Mama had always been close. If anyone could get through to Mama, it might be Aunt Priscilla.

"I have a few worries of my own this morning," Loraine said with a lingering sigh.

Ella, feeling immediate concern, snapped the magazine closed. "What kind of worries? It's nothing about the boppli, I hope."

"No, everything's going fine with my pregnancy. Wayne told me this morning that he's worried because the taxidermy business has slowed down all of a sudden. He's afraid if things get any worse he won't be able to support us." Deep wrinkles formed in Loraine's forehead. "With a boppli on the way, it's even more frightening to think of Wayne being without a job."

Ella's fingernails dug into the armrests on her chair. "So many of our people are out of work and struggling financially. I'm beginning to wonder if things will ever turn around for us."

"It's very frightening," Loraine said, "but we've got to keep the faith and do whatever we can to make extra money. Wayne's good at woodworking, and he's made a few nice pieces of furniture for our house.

He's also made some things for his folks' new home. I suggested to him this morning that he start making more things. Maybe he can sell them to one of the local furniture stores." She smiled, despite her obvious concerns.

"In the meantime, we just need to keep praying and trusting that God will provide for our needs."

～✞～

"Guder mariye," Andrew said when he entered Tiffany's Restaurant in Topeka and found Wayne waiting for him at a table near the back. They'd decided to meet for breakfast before they began work for the day. Freeman would also be joining them.

Wayne looked up at Andrew and smiled. "Mornin'. Is this table okay with you?"

"Suits me just fine." Andrew pulled out a chair and took a seat. "No sign of Freeman yet, huh?"

"Nope. I'm sure he'll be along soon, though. He'd never pass up the opportunity to be in such good company as ours."

Andrew chuckled. "I doubt he's coming here for our company. More than likely it's to fill his belly with ham and eggs."

"You're probably right about that." Wayne

thumped his stomach a couple of times. "I hope he gets here soon, 'cause my belly's startin' to rumble."

A young English waitress came to their table. "Would you like to place your orders?" she asked, smiling at Andrew.

"Just some coffee for now," he replied. "We're waiting on a friend."

The waitress left the table and returned a few minutes later with two cups and a pot of coffee.

Andrew had just poured some coffee into the cups when Freeman walked in. "Sorry for making you wait, but I had a bike that needed fixing right away this morning and it took me longer than I expected." Freeman took a seat. "Have you two ordered your meals yet?"

Wayne shook his head. "Figured we'd wait for you."

Freeman thumped Wayne's back a couple of times. "It's sure nice to have such good friends."

The waitress showed up again and took their orders. While they waited for their food, they visited about the weather and caught up on each other's lives.

It wasn't long until the waitress returned

with their orders: scrambled eggs and ham for Wayne; pancakes with maple syrup for Andrew; and a ham-and-cheese omelet for Freeman.

About halfway through their meal, Eunice showed up at their table. "This is a nice surprise," she said, smiling down at Andrew.

He nodded and reached for his cup of coffee to wash down the hunk of pancake he'd just put in his mouth. "I'm surprised to see you out so early this morning."

"I needed a few things at the Shoe and Boot store and decided to stop here for some breakfast first."

"Oh, I see."

Eunice leaned on the edge of the table. "I met your sister on Saturday, over at Ella's. She seems like a nice person."

Andrew nodded. "Jolene's one of the nicest people I know—even if she is my *schweschder*."

Wayne needled Andrew in the ribs. "You probably wouldn't say that if Jolene was sitting here, would you?"

Andrew shrugged. "I'll bet I would. I say nice things about everyone in my family."

"My sister's pretty nice, too," Freeman put in. "And I'm not ashamed to say it."

Eunice bobbed her head. "Fern and I have become good friends. She's one of the nicest people I know." She gave Andrew another heart-melting smile. "I hope Jolene and I can become friends, too."

"If you want to be her friend, then it might be a good idea for you to learn how to sign so you can communicate with her better," Andrew said. "Sometimes it's hard for her to read lips, so signing's the better way to go." He grunted. "Of course, I've only had one lesson in signing, and I've got a long way to go. I do plan to learn, though, and so do my folks. Jolene's going to have regular signing sessions at our house once or twice a week, so you're welcome to join us."

Eunice moved closer to Andrew. "That sounds interesting, but I'm not sure I'd have time for signing lessons right now. I'm keeping very busy selling soaps and scented candles."

"Well, if you ever find the time, I'm sure Jolene would be willing to teach you."

"I'll keep that in mind, but I'd better get going now." Eunice gave Andrew one last smile then hurried across the room, glancing over her shoulder before she went out the door.

Wayne poked Andrew's arm. "I think it's safe to say that Eunice is definitely interested in you."

Andrew shrugged. "Maybe so; I don't know."

"*Kumme* now," Wayne said. "Are you blind?"

"What do you mean?"

"Couldn't you see the look of longing on her face when she was talking to you?" Wayne bumped Andrew's elbow. "What about you? Are you interested in Eunice?"

Andrew reached for his coffee and took a sip. "She's a friend, nothing more."

"Better make sure you keep it that way," Freeman spoke up. "Eunice might look good in the face, but she's a gossip and has been known to cause trouble with that unruly tongue of hers." He grunted. "I've had firsthand experience with her, so I know what I'm talking about."

"You've got nothing to worry about, because I'm not getting involved with Eunice." Andrew set his cup down and leaned his elbows on the table. "Besides, some people change, and there are some good things about Eunice."

"Name me one thing, besides the fact that she has a pretty face."

"Let's see now. . . ." Andrew drummed his fingers along the edge of the table. "She's *schmaert* enough to have started her own business, and from what I've heard, she's doing pretty well with it, too."

"That's fine as feathers," Freeman said, "but it doesn't make her a nice person."

"She wants to become Jolene's friend," Andrew said. "That seems nice to me. Besides, she's interesting to talk to."

"Oh, jah, she always has a lot to say." Freeman reached for a piece of toast and slathered it with apple butter. "Unfortunately, much of what Eunice says is nothing but gossip."

"You can think whatever you like," Andrew said, "but the Bible says we aren't to judge others, so I'm giving Eunice the benefit of the doubt."

CHAPTER 8

As Jolene pedaled her bike toward the schoolhouse, she reflected on some of the things that had been going on with her two students. It had been a busy week since she'd started teaching the children, and she'd made some headway with Sylvia, but as far as she could tell, she'd made none at all with Irvin. He just didn't seem to want to learn.

Last night after Mom had spoken with Aunt Dorcas on the phone, Jolene and Mom had discussed the situation. Mom said that Aunt Dorcas had talked about her days of teaching and said that she'd had a few students who'd been stubborn and didn't want to learn. It took patience, perseverance, and a willingness to keep trying new things. Aunt Dorcas felt certain that eventually Jolene would find something that would spark an interest in Irvin.

I hope Aunt Dorcas is right, Jolene thought as she turned her bike up the lane leading to the school. *I'll feel like a failure if I can't get through to Irvin.*

Jolene parked her bike beside several others and had just stepped into the schoolyard, when she saw some of the boys from Fern's class pointing at a smaller figure huddled on the ground near a clump of bushes. As she drew closer, she realized it was Irvin.

"What's going on?" she asked Kyle Beechy.

He pointed at Irvin. "I asked him a question, and he wouldn't answer, so I poked him a couple of times. What's the matter with that fellow? Is he dumm?"

"No, he's not dumb. He can't hear what you're saying because he's deaf." Jolene was glad Irvin hadn't learned to read lips yet. The quiver of his jaw and the tears glistening in his eyes let her know that he was quite upset. He didn't need to know that he'd been called dumb.

She reached for Irvin's hand, but he just sat there, shaking his head. *"Come with me into the schoolhouse,"* she signed.

"I don't want to go to school. I want to go home."

"What'd he say?" Kyle asked.

"He said he doesn't want to go to school."

Kyle wrinkled his freckled nose. "He'll be even dumber if he don't go to school." He nudged his younger brother, Elmer. "Ain't that right?"

Elmer bobbed his head. "Jah, that's right. He'll be dumber than dirt."

The boys who stood nearby laughed. Jolene couldn't hear their laughter, of course, but seeing their open mouths and the way they were holding their sides let her know that they were laughing. It made her angry to see Irvin being treated this way.

"It's not right to make fun of anyone— especially someone with a disability." She pointed to herself. "I can't hear, either. Does that make me dumm?"

Kyle blinked a couple of times. "You don't have to yell. I'm standin' right here."

"Sorry." Jolene hoped her words came out a little quieter this time.

"How come you can talk, but that boy don't say a word?" Kyle asked, pointing at Irvin.

"As you know, I lost my hearing two years ago, but Irvin and his sister were born deaf. If a person is born deaf, it's difficult for them to learn how to speak clearly because they can't hear what they're saying." Jolene glanced across the schoolyard and spotted Sylvia playing with Arie Smucker by the swings. It appeared that she'd been accepted—at least by one of the scholars. "I'll be teaching Irvin and his sister phonetics, as well as how to read lips," Jolene said. "Hopefully, they'll be able to talk some, too."

"He won't learn." Kyle shook his head. "He's too dumm to learn."

Jolene clapped her hands in front of Kyle's face. "Stop saying that! Irvin is not dumb!"

Just then Fern rushed up to Jolene, wearing a look of concern. "What's going on here? I could hear you shouting from inside the schoolhouse."

Hoping her voice didn't sound as shaky as she felt, Jolene explained what had happened. She motioned to Kyle and Elmer. "I'll never get through to Irvin if these boys keep making fun of him. Nobody likes to be teased, and I'm afraid if it continues, Irvin will refuse to come to school."

Fern shook her finger at the boys. "You ought to know better than to tease. I want you both to apologize to Irvin."

Kyle turned his hands upward. "What for? He won't hear a word I say."

Jolene compressed her lips to keep from shouting at the insolent boy.

"Jolene can let Irvin know what you say by signing to him," Fern said.

"What's signing?" Kyle asked.

"It's a way of talking with your hands," Fern replied.

"Oh, that." Kyle raised his chin a notch and shook his head. "I still ain't sorry for sayin' he's dumm, and I won't apologize."

Jolene was stunned. She'd never seen a student so defiant before. Irvin had definitely met his match. "He was teasing Irvin by laughing and poking him, too," she told Fern.

Fern tapped Kyle's shoulder and squinted her eyes. "You need to apologize to Irvin, and you'd better do it now."

The seconds ticked by as the boy stared at the ground, making no move to apologize for his behavior.

Jolene ground her teeth together. It was disrespectful for any student to speak to his teacher that way. Seeing the way Irvin had been treated by Kyle made Jolene even more determined to get through to him and see that he received a good education.

Fern took hold of Kyle's arm. "If you won't apologize to Irvin, then you can stay after school for the rest of the week."

He kicked at a clump of grass with the toe of his boot. "I can't stay after school. I've got chores to do at home."

"Then apologize to Irvin."

"Tell him I'm sorry," Kyle said to Jolene.

Fern nudged Elmer.

"Me, too," the younger boy said.

Jolene gave a nod then squatted down beside Irvin and signed, *"Kyle and Elmer said to tell you that they're sorry for teasing you."*

"They'll do it again; you'll see!" Irvin

scrambled to his feet and raced into the schoolhouse.

Kyle and Elmer ran across the lawn and joined some of the other boys who sat on the fence.

Fern turned to Jolene. "I'll make sure every one of my scholars knows that they'll be in trouble with me if they tease your students."

"If they could only communicate with Irvin and Sylvia, things might be better," Jolene said.

"I think I have an idea."

"What's that?"

"How would you like to come into my class a few times a week and teach the scholars to sign?" Fern smiled. "I think it would be good if I learned how to sign, too."

"I'd like that." As Jolene headed for the schoolhouse, she felt a little better about things.

～❧ ❧～

There was a spring in Lonnie's step as he headed for the pigpen with a bucket of slop. He was in good spirits, and it had nothing to do with feeding and watering smelly pigs.

His injured hand felt much better, and

as soon as he was done with his chores, he'd head over to the Yoders' to work for Rueben.

In just one week, Carolyn would be coming. It would be great to see her again, and he had figured out exactly how and when he'd propose. He didn't know what he'd do if she turned him down. He loved her so much, and while she'd never actually said the words, he felt sure that she loved him, too.

By the time Lonnie reached the pigpen, the wind had picked up, scattering fallen leaves all over the yard. If the wind kept blowing, maybe the leaves would blow out of the yard and no one would have to rake them.

Lonnie poured the slop into the trough and watched with disgust as the gluttonous hogs raced for it, grunting noisily while pushing and shoving each other with their snouts.

"Dirty, greedy pigs," he mumbled. "I'm glad I don't have to smell you all day."

Lonnie turned on the water and filled the watering trough before he headed back toward the house. As he approached the place where their propane tank sat, he halted and sniffed the air. The pungent rotten-egg aroma of propane gas drifted up to his nose. Could there be a leak in the line, or had the nozzle on the tank not been closed tight enough?

He was tempted to move closer to investigate but decided that it would be best to call the company that delivered their propane and ask them to come and check things out.

Lonnie hurried down the driveway toward their phone shed, but he'd only made it halfway there when an earth-shattering explosion shook the ground beneath his feet. When he turned his head, he saw flames shooting into the air and a fence post coming straight at him!

CHAPTER 9

Jolene handed Sylvia and Irvin their pieces of paper and asked them to copy the words she'd written on the blackboard. She'd tried talking to Irvin about what had happened outside before school started, but he wouldn't respond to her at all.

Maybe I should have a talk with Irvin's parents. Jolene tapped her pencil on the edge of her desk. *But if they find out that Irvin was teased by those boys, they might take him out of this school and send him elsewhere for his education. I'd really like the chance to prove that I can teach these children, so maybe I should speak with*

Kyle and Elmer's parents instead, and let them know that their boys were antagonizing Irvin. She continued to tap her pencil. *No, that might make things worse. If Lydia or Joe Beechy punishes Kyle and Elmer for teasing, then the boys might try to get even with Irvin and torment him even more.*

She leaned back in her chair and tried to relax, deciding that it was best not to say anything to either set of parents right now. She'd wait and see if the boys could work things out on their own. In the meantime, she needed to concentrate on teaching.

While the children did their assignment, Jolene made a list of projects she planned for them to do—making posters to hang in their class and cutting out pictures to color during recess when the weather turned cold and they couldn't play outside. She hoped that doing some fun projects might draw Irvin out of his shell. She knew it must be hard for the children to have moved from their home in Ohio and come here where nearly everyone was a stranger.

If only Irvin could make some friends, she thought. *Everyone needs a good friend.*

Jolene didn't know what she'd do without the friendship she'd established with her cousins. Even when she'd been living several hundred miles away, she'd kept in touch with Loraine, Ella, and Katie through letters. And even when they'd each gone through trials of their own, she'd felt their love and support.

Pulling her thoughts aside, Jolene glanced at the battery-operated clock on the far wall. It was time to collect the children's papers.

She rose from her chair and stepped up to Sylvia's desk. *"Are you finished?"* she signed.

Sylvia nodded and handed Jolene her paper.

"Thank you." Jolene moved over to Irvin's desk. When she looked down at his paper she was stunned. He hadn't written one single word!

She groaned inwardly and made a decision. As much as it pained her to do it, she would stop by his house after school and speak to his parents about this.

⸺✀⸻

"I thought Lonnie would be returning to work today," Ella said when she entered her father's shop and didn't see Lonnie in front of his workbench.

"I don't know what's up. Last time I saw him he said he'd be comin' in this morning." Papa shrugged. "He's not usually late, so I guess it's fair to say that his hand must still be hurting." He frowned. "But then, he should've at least come by and told me if he didn't feel up to workin' today."

Ella couldn't argue with that, but it wasn't like Lonnie to be so inconsiderate. He'd always come to work early and sometimes stayed late to finish a job. He often whistled while he worked and usually wore a smile, so she knew he must enjoy working here. His hand was either still hurting, or else something had come up at home to keep him from being here today. She hoped it was nothing serious.

For the next hour, Ella worked quietly, inserting some recent purchases and customer invoices into the ledger. While she did that, Papa cut some pipe for new chimes, and Charlene kept busy stringing the pieces of pipe together.

At ten o'clock, the shop door opened and Jolene's father, Uncle Alvin, stepped in.

"Guder mariye," Ella said, smiling up at him. "Did you come to buy a new set of wind chimes or just to visit with Papa awhile?"

Uncle Alvin removed his hat and fanned his face with it, although Ella didn't know why, because it was a chilly fall day. "Came to see if you'd heard about the explosion that took place over at the Hershbergers' early this morning," he said.

"Which Hershberger?" Papa asked. "The bishop or his nephew Ezra?"

"It happened over at Ezra Hershberger's place," Uncle Alvin replied.

A sense of alarm shot through Ella as she slowly shook her head. "We haven't heard anything."

Papa hurried over to his brother. "What kind of explosion?"

"From what I was told, the Hershbergers' propane tank blew up."

"Ach, that's *baremlich*! Was anyone hurt?" Charlene asked, joining the group.

Uncle Alvin nodded soberly. "You're right. It is quite terrible. Lonnie got hit in the head by a flying fence post and was knocked out cold. Heard he was taken to the hospital, but that's all I know for sure."

Ella felt like her heart had leaped into her throat. She hoped Lonnie wasn't seriously hurt. They'd had enough tragedies in their community over the last few years.

☙ ❧

A sharp pain shot through Lonnie's head as he slowly opened his eyes. He blinked at the blurred image of a middle-aged woman looking down at him. She wore some kind of a uniform, like that of a nurse.

He tried to sit up, but his head hurt too much. It was all he could do to keep his eyes open.

The woman shook her head and her lips moved, but Lonnie couldn't make out what she'd said. It must be because his head felt like it had been stuffed with cotton.

"Wh–where am I?" He winced. That was strange. He couldn't hear his own voice, either.

The woman picked up a notepad by his bed and wrote something on it. Then she held it in front of his face. The words were blurred, but he could make a few of them out. *Parents. Waiting room. I'll get them.*

Lonnie grimaced as the truth set in. He was in the hospital, and his folks were waiting to see him. He must have been given some pills that had made his brain feel fuzzy and clogged his ears. But why was he in the hospital?

When the nurse set the tablet down and hurried from the room, Lonnie closed his eyes, struggling for some memory that would let him know how he'd gotten here.

He remembered getting up, eating breakfast, doing a few chores in the barn, and going to feed the smelly hogs. Then, as he'd headed back to the house, he'd smelled something funny.

Another jolt of pain shot through Lonnie's head as the memory of everything that had happened flashed into his mind. He'd been heading to the phone shed to report a propane leak. Then he'd heard a terrible explosion, turned, and saw a fence post coming straight at him. It had hit him in the head with such force that he'd been knocked to the ground. That was the last thing he remembered.

Lonnie felt the pressure of someone's hand on his arm, and his eyes popped open. Mom stared down at him with tears in her eyes. Pop stood beside her, wearing a grim expression.

"Wh—what happened to me? H—how bad am I hurt?" Again, Lonnie couldn't hear his own voice, and that scared him a lot.

Mom picked up the notepad from the table by his bed and wrote something on it. Her lips were pinched, like she was holding back tears, as she held the notepad in front of Lonnie's face.

Our propane tank exploded. Apparently you were hit in the head by one of our fence posts. Your daed found you lying near the phone shed.

Pop's lips moved as he leaned over Lonnie, shaking his head.

Lonnie put both hands against his ears. "I—I can't hear you! Why can't I hear what you're saying?" His throat hurt, and he knew he must be shouting.

Pop stepped away from the bed, and Mom wrote something else on the tablet and showed it to Lonnie.

When the post hit your head, it caused a concussion, and the doctor just told us that there was severe damage to the auditory nerves in both your ears.

"Is—is that why I can't hear?"

She nodded.

"How long until I can hear again?"

Mom slowly shook her head as tears pooled in her eyes and dripped onto her cheeks. *The doctor isn't sure, but you may never get your hearing back,* she wrote on the tablet. *We'll have to wait and see how it goes.*

Lonnie swallowed around the lump in his throat. If he couldn't hear, he couldn't tune chimes. If he couldn't tune chimes, he didn't have a job. If he didn't have a job, he couldn't get married.

CHAPTER 10

Jolene's heart pounded as she stood on the Troyers' back porch, prepared to knock on their door. As soon as school was over for the day, she'd pedaled her bike over here, hoping to arrive before Irvin and Sylvia, who had walked to school. She wanted to speak to the children's parents without the children knowing she'd been here.

Mary, the children's mother, opened the door before Jolene was able to knock.

"I was looking out the kitchen window and saw you coming up the driveway," Mary signed as she spoke. "If you came to see Irvin and Sylvia, they aren't home from school yet."

"I'm glad they're not here, because I wanted to speak to you alone. Is your husband here? I think he should know what I have to say, too."

Mary shook her head. "He's out in the fields, gathering hay. Come inside and tell me what's on your mind." She held the door open for Jolene.

Jolene stepped inside and breathed deeply as the sweet smell of apples and cinnamon wafted up to her nose. "Are you making applesauce?" she asked, hoping to stall for time. She really didn't want to say what was on her mind.

"Jah, I've been working on it a good portion of the day. Just put the last batch in the pressure cooker a few minutes ago." She motioned to the kitchen table. "Have a seat, and I'll pour us some coffee."

Jolene pulled out a chair and sat down. She really didn't have time for coffee but didn't want to be rude.

"Would you like to try some of my applesauce bread?" Mary set a cup of coffee in front of Jolene, along with a plate that held several slices of deliciously moist-looking bread.

"No, thank you. I can't stay that long, but I wanted to talk to you about your children."

"Are they doing well in school?"

Jolene took a sip of coffee as she thought about the best way to say what was on her mind. "Sylvia's doing well and seems eager to learn." She paused and clasped her hands together. The expectant look on Mary's face made this even more difficult. She drew in a quick breath. "I wish I could say the same for Irvin."

Mary's forehead wrinkled. "What do you mean?"

"He's not responsive in class and won't do his lessons. I asked the children to copy some words I'd written on the blackboard, but Irvin left his paper blank."

"He didn't write down any of the words?"

Jolene shook her head.

"Maybe they were too difficult for him."

"They were simple words, and Sylvia was able to write them all."

The corners of Mary's mouth turned down. "I don't understand it. Irvin's not dumb."

"I don't think Irvin's dumb, either, but I do think either he's not happy with me as his teacher, or he's upset because he's new here and hasn't made any friends."

"But there are lots of other boys his age at school."

"That's true, but Irvin keeps to himself, and. . ." Jolene stopped speaking and let her hands fall into her lap. She'd almost told Mary about the teasing that had gone on this morning.

Just then a blast of cool air floated into the kitchen, and Irvin and Sylvia raced into the room.

Sylvia went to the sink for a drink of water, but Irvin halted as soon as he saw Jolene. *"It wasn't my fault,"* he signed to his mother. *"Kyle Beechy's the one who started it."*

Her eyebrows furrowed. *"Started what?"*

Irvin looked at Jolene, as though expecting her to say something.

"I didn't tell your mother anything about what happened this morning," she signed to him.

"Tell me what?" Mary asked her son.

He squinted his eyes and stared at her.

Jolene could almost see the gears shifting in his head. *"It was nothin', Mama."*

Mary, obviously not willing to give up on the subject, signed in return, *"Tell me what happened, Irvin."*

He dropped his gaze to the floor.

Mary looked at Jolene. "Do you know anything about this?"

As much as Jolene didn't want to tell Mary about Kyle and his brother teasing Irvin, she knew it was time to explain what had happened.

~❧ ❧~

"Are you feeling sick again?" Ella asked when she entered the living room and found her mother lying on the sofa.

Mama yawned and pulled herself to a sitting position. "I'm not sick, just a bit tired and shaky this afternoon."

Ella was tempted to suggest that Mama make an appointment to see the doctor, but that subject had been discussed too many times, and Mama wouldn't budge. Loraine's mother had come by a few days ago and almost insisted that Mama see the doctor, but it was to no avail. Ella wondered what it would take for Mama to realize that she needed to have some tests run in order to find out why she was tired and shaky so much of the time. Mama had also begun to put on some weight, and she seemed to be thirsty a lot.

"Should I start supper now, or do you want me to wait awhile?" Ella asked, turning her focus to their immediate need.

"Guess you'd better wait until Charlene and your daed are ready to quit work for the day. When your daed came in for lunch, he said they'd probably be working late since they're getting behind and didn't have Lonnie's help again today."

Ella's eyebrows squeezed together. "I wish we'd get some word on how Lonnie's doing."

"Have you been out to the phone shed lately to check the answering machine?" Mama asked. "Maybe someone from his family has called and left a message."

Ella nodded. "I checked for messages before I came into the house, and there was no word from the Hershbergers."

The back door opened and banged shut. A few seconds later, Larry raced into the room.

"Did ya hear the news?"

"What news?" Ella and Mama asked at the same time.

Larry's eyes were wide, and his face was flushed. "Joe Beechy fell off the roof of his house and was rushed to the hospital this afternoon!"

"Oh, dear Lord," Mama moaned. "Not another tragedy in our community."

~≫ ≫~

"Jake, there's a phone call for you!"

Jake turned toward his boss's wife, wondering who'd be calling him in the middle of the day. "Can you take a message for me, Peggy?" he called in return.

She leaned over the porch railing and waved the dishrag in her hand. "I think you'd better take the call!"

Jake grunted as he wiped the sweat from his forehead. He'd been working in the corral with a difficult horse and didn't want to let up until he'd made some progress. But he figured if he didn't take the phone call, Peggy would keep hollering and waving that piece of cloth.

Maybe it's someone from home, Jake thought as he made his way up to the house. When he'd left Indiana and returned to Montana after Wayne and Loraine had told him they were in love and wanted to get married, he'd given his boss's phone number to Mom and Dad so they could keep in touch.

"Who is it, do you know?" Jake asked, stepping onto the porch.

Peggy nodded. "It's your mother. She said it was important and that she needs to speak to you right away." Peggy opened the back door and motioned to the kitchen. "You can take the call in there."

Jake hurried into the kitchen and picked up the phone. "Hi, Mom, it's Jake."

"Oh, Jake, I—I'm so glad you're there." Mom's voice trembled when she spoke. "There's been an accident. You need to come home!"

CHAPTER 11

As Jake's truck approached Middlebury, anxious thoughts filled his mind. When he'd talked to Mom on the phone, she'd said Dad's injuries weren't critical, but that he had two broken legs, some broken ribs, and lots of bumps and bruises. Dad would be laid up for several months, unable to work. As much as Jake hated the idea of taking over Dad's horseshoeing business, he felt obligated to do it. He didn't really mind shoeing horses; he just didn't want to do it full-time. Someday when the time was right, he hoped to have his own business—raising and training horses. He knew he wouldn't make the kind of money shoeing horses for Dad that he made back on the ranch in Montana, but he'd only be here a few months, and then he could head back to Montana, where he was accepted for the person he was and there were no painful memories from the past.

Jake's thoughts went to Loraine and Wayne. He hadn't seen them since he'd returned to Montana over a year ago, but he'd kept in touch by phone a few times. At least no one could say he'd run off to do his own thing and forgotten about his family and friends, the way he'd done the first time he'd left Indiana. He could still see the look of sadness on Loraine's face when he'd told her was leaving for Montana that first time, and his mind took him back to the past. . . .

～✖ ✖～

"Loraine, there's something I need to tell you."

"What is it, Jake? Why are you looking at me so seriously?"

Jake directed his horse and buggy to the side of the road and reached for Loraine's hand. "I–I'm planning to go away for a while."

"Go away?"

He nodded. "My cousin Sam, who used to live in Illinois, moved to Montana a few months ago, and. . .uh. . .I thought I'd spend the summer with him."

"Which Amish community in Montana did Sam move to?"

"None of them. Sam's working on a ranch in Montana for an English man who raises horses." Jake swallowed so hard that his Adam's apple bobbed up and down. "I want to try out the English way of life for a while—before I make a decision about joining the church." He paused and swiped his tongue across his lower lip. "The wages the man is offering per week are more than I can make working for my daed in a month, so I really can't pass on this opportunity."

Loraine's mouth hung slightly open. "What?"

"I said—"

"I heard what you said. I just can't believe you said it."

"It's not like I'll be gone forever. Probably just for the summer, that's all." He squeezed her fingers and smiled. "You'll wait for me, won't you?"

Loraine sat, staring at him.

"Say something, Loraine. Will you wait for me or not?"

Tears welled in her eyes. "For how long, Jake?"

"Until I come back to Indiana." Jake pulled her into his arms and kissed her on the mouth. "Just a few months, that's all," he whispered.

Loraine drew in a shaky breath and nodded slowly. "Jah, Jake. I'll wait for you."

⚯

As Jake's mind snapped back to the present, he shook his head. He'd really blown it with Loraine by not coming back soon enough or staying in contact with her while he was in Montana. Truth was, he probably wouldn't have returned to Indiana the first time if he hadn't heard about the terrible accident Loraine and her cousins had been involved in.

After he'd returned home, he'd tried to reestablish his relationship with Loraine, but when he finally realized she was in love with Wayne, he'd given them his blessing and returned to Montana. It hadn't been easy for Jake to leave home the second time, but in his heart, he felt it was the right thing to do.

After Jake had returned to Montana, it had taken several months for him to come to grips with the fact that Loraine would never be his. He'd told himself that he'd done the right thing by giving Loraine and Wayne his blessing, and in time, Jake's broken heart had begun to heal. Any romantic feelings he'd had for Loraine were now just a pleasant memory. While Jake had no interest in anyone at the moment, he was prepared to follow his heart should the right woman come along.

Jake's thoughts shifted as his folks' place came into view. He grimaced. *I hope Dad's going to be okay, and I hope he appreciates my coming home to help out and doesn't criticize everything I do.*

He pulled his truck up near the barn, turned off the engine, and stepped out.

When Jake entered the house, he found Mom in the kitchen, stirring a pot of something on the stove. She turned to face him, a grim expression on her face. *What, no "It's good to see you, Jake; I'm so glad you're home"?* This wasn't like Mom at all. She usually gave Jake a hug and said how much she'd missed him.

He stepped forward and slipped his arms around her waist. "It's good to see you, Mom. How's Dad doing?"

"He's hurting real bad and not one bit happy about being laid up." Her voice cracked, and she cleared her throat. "It could be some time before he's able to work again."

"I'll take over for him until he's better. You know I will."

Mom's bottom lip quivered. "Then you'll leave again." Her words were crisp and to the point.

Jake only shrugged and turned toward the door. "I'd better go see Dad. Is he in his room?"

"Jah, but he's asleep right now. I'd rather you didn't wake him."

"Oh, okay." Jake turned back around. "Where are my brothers and sisters? Are they still at school?"

"Jah. They should be here soon, I expect." Mom motioned to the table. "Why don't you take a seat and we can visit while I finish making my stew. I'd like to hear what you've been up to lately."

Jake pulled out a chair and sat down. "Pretty much the same old thing. . .breaking horses. . .and doing lots of chores around my boss's ranch. Oh, and I've starting training some horses to pull buggies and wagons."

Her eyebrows lifted as she handed him a cup of coffee. "Are there Amish in Montana?"

"There are a few small Amish communities, but the horses we've been training are to pull carriages and wagons at a dude ranch not far from my boss's spread."

"What's a dude ranch?"

"It's a place where folks go to relax, hike the trails, and have some good clean fun. At this dude ranch, a person can take horseback riding lessons, and they also offer hayrides and buggy rides."

"Do you like it better in Montana than here?"

Jake took a sip of coffee as he contemplated her question.

"Did you hear what I said, Jake?"

"I heard. Just wasn't quite sure how to answer."

She grunted. "It's a simple enough question. Do you like it better in Montana than you do here?"

"I like some things about it, but I miss some things about Indiana, too."

"Since you haven't come back and joined the church, I assume that means you're planning to stay English." Mom's comment was more of a statement rather than a question.

Jake gnawed on his lower lip as he watched her slice carrots and drop them into the pot of boiling stew. Part of him had wanted to return to Indiana and join the Amish church, but the longer he'd stayed away, the harder it had been to come back. He'd originally wanted to open his own business right here, but that was when he thought he'd marry Loraine. If he stayed in Indiana now and tried to open his own business, he wondered if Dad would give him a hard time and pressure him to give up the idea and shoe horses instead.

Lifting his elbows and flexing his shoulders, Jake stretched and yawned. He'd think about this some other time. Right now, he needed to concentrate on doing what was right by filling in for Dad and taking care of his family.

"Are you tired, son?" Mom asked.

"A little. It was a long drive."

"If you want to go lie down, I'll call you when supper's ready."

Jake shook his head. "If I lie down, I'll fall asleep and might not wake up until morning." He pushed away from the table. "Think I'll go outside and get my stuff out of the truck."

"You can put everything in your room," Mom said. "Kyle wanted to move in there when you left for Montana, but I told him no, that you might be back."

"Thanks, I appreciate that." Jake smiled at Mom then went out the door.

～≫✦≪～

Jolene trudged wearily up the stairs to her classroom. She'd just taught her first lesson in signing to Fern's class, and it hadn't gone well. The children who'd originally shown an interest in learning to sign hadn't acted interested at all. Jolene wondered if it had something to do with Kyle Beechy. She'd seen the way he looked at Irvin and

Sylvia today—like they had two heads or something. Kyle had made it clear that he wanted no part in learning how to sign. Even when Fern asked the class to be attentive as Jolene taught them to sign some simple words, Kyle had remained aloof and disagreeable.

When Fern tried to coax him to take part, the fire in Kyle's eyes and the firm set of his jaw had said it all. He would not even try to sign. And his constant interruptions with silly questions that had nothing to do with signing made it obvious that he was determined to see that the other scholars didn't learn signing, either.

Someone tapped Jolene's shoulder, and she whirled around. Fern stood on the step below her. "The children have gone outside for recess, and I was wondering if you'd like to join us in a game of ball." She spoke slowly while looking directly at Jolene.

Jolene shook her head. "I'm not in the mood to play ball right now."

Fern followed Jolene upstairs to her classroom and leaned on the front of the desk when Jolene took a seat. "You look upset. Is it because the scholars didn't catch on to what you were trying to show them?"

Jolene gave a slow nod.

"I think you just need to give it some time. Signing is new to the children." Fern shrugged. "I had trouble following along with what you were trying to teach us, too, but I'm sure with some practice I'll be able to learn."

"Anyone can learn to sign if they want to," Jolene said. "I'm just afraid that some— especially Kyle Beechy—don't want to learn."

Fern traced an ink stain on the desk with her finger then looked up at Jolene and frowned. "Kyle's my most challenging student, but these last few days, he's been more difficult than usual. I think he's probably upset about his daed falling off the roof."

Jolene suspected there was more going on with Kyle than just his dad's accident. He'd been mean to Irvin before that had happened. The boy obviously had a chip on his shoulder, and he seemed to enjoy causing trouble. Well, Jolene couldn't worry about that right now. She had her own students to teach, and that's where she needed to keep her focus. Irvin, while cooperating a little better the past few days, still wasn't staying focused on his lessons the way she felt he should be. If Kyle kept tormenting Irvin, Jolene planned to speak with Kyle's parents. Today, however, she wanted to stop by the stamp shop and pick up a few things on her way home. She planned to make some get-well cards—one for Jake's dad, and one for Lonnie Hershberger.

~ ~

Lonnie lay in his hospital bed, staring at the ceiling. He'd just been told by the doctor that the damage to his auditory nerves was severe and had caused complete hearing loss. It was a shocking blow, and Lonnie felt as if his whole world had caved in. He couldn't imagine spending the rest of his life in total silence. It would be like being trapped in a cave with no way out. He couldn't imagine not being able to hear his own voice. . .the warble of birds. . .a cat's meow. . .or the tinkle of wind chimes. There were so many things he would miss.

Pop tapped Lonnie on the shoulder, and he turned his head, barely able to swallow around the lump stuck in his throat. Pop picked up the notepad lying on the table beside Lonnie's bed and wrote something on it. His lips moved silently as he handed the notepad to Lonnie.

Lonnie's eyes had trouble focusing due to the tears he felt. He tried to blink them away as he read Pop's message: *There is one positive thing in all this. Jolene Yoder's here, and she'll be able to teach you how to read lips and talk with your hands.*

Lonnie said nothing; he just stared at the food on his meal tray that he hadn't touched.

Then Mom took the tablet and wrote something. *I know you're disappointed, and so are we.*

Angry words rolled around in Lonnie's head, and he gripped the edge of his sheet until his fingers turned numb. "You got that right," he mumbled. At least he thought his words had come out mumbled. Since he couldn't hear his own voice, he couldn't be sure how he'd sounded.

Disappointments are like weeds in the garden, Mom continued to write. *You can let them grow and take over your life, or you can rout them out and let the flowers sprout.*

Another wave of anger swept over

Lonnie, and he slammed his fist on his meal tray so hard that the glass of milk toppled over and the silverware tumbled to the floor. "I don't want to talk with my hands or think about flowers and weeds! I want to hear with my ears!"

CHAPTER 12

What's this?" Lonnie asked when his mother handed him an envelope shortly after he'd returned home from the hospital several days after his accident.

Mom's lips moved, but he had no idea what she'd said.

Lonnie gripped the edge of the sofa where he lay with his head propped on two pillows. "What? You know I can't hear you!" Irritation welled in his soul. Oh, how he wished he could change what had happened to him. If he could just turn back the hands of time, he'd never have gone anywhere near that propane tank. But then, if he hadn't checked on it and discovered the leak, someone else, maybe Mom, might have been hit by something from the explosion.

Mom pointed to the return address on the envelope, and Lonnie's heart gave a lurch. It was from Carolyn. The last few days had been a blur—more like a terrible nightmare, really. In the confusion and frustration of learning that he'd lost his hearing, he'd forgotten that Carolyn was supposed to be here in a few days. As anxious as he was to be with her again, he wasn't sure he wanted her to see him like this.

With an unsteady hand, Lonnie tore open the envelope and read Carolyn's note.

> **Dear Lonnie,**
> I would have called and spoken to you on the phone, but I knew you wouldn't be able to hear me. When your mamm called to let us know that you'd been in an accident and had lost your hearing, I was shocked. I can't imagine what it must be like not to be able to hear. I hope you're not in a lot of pain.

Speaking of pain. . .Mama came down with a bad case of shingles, and she's really miserable. She has so much itching and nerve pain that she can hardly function. Under the circumstances, I think it's best if I don't come to see you right now. It'll give you a chance to rest up and heal without feeling that you have to entertain me. As soon as my mamm's feeling better, I'll come there. In the meantime, get plenty of rest and write me back when you feel up to it.

As always,
Carolyn

Lonnie let the letter fall to the floor. A mixture of relief and disappointment flooded his soul. He wasn't ready to face Carolyn right now, so in some ways he was glad she wasn't coming. He didn't know how she'd react to him being deaf, and he wasn't prepared to ask her to marry someone who couldn't hear a word she said. Even so, he wondered if her decision not to come meant she didn't want to see him. Maybe she couldn't deal with the idea of having a boyfriend who was deaf.

Mom wrote something on the tablet and handed it to Lonnie. *What did Carolyn have to say?*

Lonnie handed the letter to Mom and waited until she'd had a chance to read it. When she finished, he said, "I can't help but wonder if Carolyn's not using her mamm's shingles as an excuse not to come."

Mom's eyebrows furrowed as she scrawled a reply. *Why would she do that?*

"Because I can no longer hear."

I'm sure that's not the reason. Carolyn's a good daughter and obviously feels that her mamm needs her right now. I'm sure she'll be out to see you as soon as she can.

Lonnie tossed the tablet aside and closed his eyes. "I'm tired. Wake me when it's time for supper."

The last thing Lonnie remembered before drifting off to sleep was Mom gently stroking his cheek, the way she'd done when he was a boy and didn't feel well.

※ ※

As Jolene and her family gathered on the front porch to sing and visit after their signing lesson, Jolene felt suddenly out of place. Everyone but her could hear the words to the songs. Everyone on the porch knew exactly what the others were saying without having to read their lips.

Now don't start with the self-pity, she berated herself. At least her family had taken an interest in learning to sign, and they hadn't acted disinterested or belligerent about it like Kyle and some of the other scholars at school. Andrew had surprised her by saying that if he learned to sign well enough he might be able to use sign language at church when the sermons were preached. Jolene was pleased about that. Not only would the signing benefit her, but it would help her two deaf students as well.

Andrew bumped Jolene's arm, interrupting her thoughts. To her surprise, he signed some of the words to "Amazing Grace."

Jolene smiled and signed along with him, showing him and the others the way to sign for each of the words. Soon everyone joined in, and they were all signing and singing "Amazing Grace."

Jolene found herself beginning to relax, and for the first time since she'd come home, she felt like part of the family again.

Just as they were finishing up the song, a horse and buggy entered the yard. It pulled up to the hitching rail, and Ezra Hershberger climbed out of the buggy.

When he joined them on the porch, he said a few words to Dad then moved over to where Jolene sat and stopped in front of her.

"As you may have heard, our son Lonnie has lost his hearing. My *fraa* and I were wondering if you'd be willing to teach him how to sign and read lips."

Jolene gave a nod. "If Lonnie's willing, I'd be happy to teach him."

Ezra grimaced. "I'm not sure my son's willing to do much of anything right now, but he's gotta be able to communicate, so like it or not, he'll learn."

❧ ❧

After supper that evening, Lonnie felt the need to be alone. It had been awkward watching his folks carry on a conversation with his sister, Sharon, and having no idea what any of them had said. Well, at least none of his married sisters had come to supper this evening. They'd have probably hovered over Lonnie and tried to baby him, the way Mom had done since he'd come home from the hospital.

No one seemed to notice when Lonnie grabbed the walking stick he'd been using to help with his temporary loss of balance and headed out the back door. Mom and Sharon were in the kitchen doing dishes, and Pop had gone to the living room to read the newspaper.

Lonnie took a seat in one of the wicker chairs on the porch. He closed his eyes and leaned his head back. A vision of Carolyn popped into his head, and he swallowed around the familiar lump in his throat. Would it be fair to ask Carolyn to marry a man who couldn't hear? What kind of husband would he be? Could he provide for a wife and family?

Sure won't be able to tune wind chimes anymore, he thought with regret. *Fact is I need my hearing for most any kind of work I might want to do.*

Someone tapped Lonnie's shoulder, and his eyes popped open. Wayne Lambright stared down at him. Of course, Lonnie hadn't heard Wayne's horse and buggy come into the yard, and that only fueled his irritation.

Wayne's mouth moved, but Lonnie had no idea what he was saying.

"Can't hear you. Can't hear a thing anymore!" Lonnie reached for the tablet and pen sitting on the small table on the porch and handed it to Wayne.

Wayne wrote something and handed it back to Lonnie. *I heard you were home from the hospital and I wanted to see how you were doing.*

"I've been better."

Wayne took the tablet and wrote something else: *I was sorry to hear about your accident. After losing my leg, I think I know a little of how you must be feeling right now.*

Lonnie grunted. At least he thought it was a grunt.

Wayne seated himself in the chair beside Lonnie. *Is there anything I can do to help?* he wrote.

Lonnie shook his head. "Not unless you can give me back my hearing."

I can't do that, but I can help by offering my support and listening when you need to talk about your feelings.

"My feelings?" Lonnie popped a couple of knuckles. "I'll tell you how I feel. I feel like my life's over. All the plans I'd made are shot to ribbons."

What plans have you made?

"I'd planned to propose to Carolyn, but I don't see how I can expect her to marry me now that I can't hear."

You shouldn't let your disability stand in the way of your happiness, Wayne wrote.

"That's easy enough for you to say. You've still got two good ears."

That's true, but I've only got one good leg, and when I first lost it I was angry, bitter, and full of self-pity. Because of my foolish pride, I almost lost Loraine to her old boyfriend, Jake Beechy.

"I'm not worried about anything like that," Lonnie said. "There is no one like Jake in Carolyn's life. I just don't see how I can expect her to marry a man who can't hear or provide a decent living to support a wife and family."

You may not be able to tune wind chimes anymore, but I'm sure there's something you can do without being

able to hear. You can still help your daed raise hogs, you know.

"Puh!" White-hot anger boiled in Lonnie's chest. If the only job he could do was raise smelly pigs, then he didn't care if he ever worked again!

CHAPTER 13

Jolene's heart pounded as she directed her horse and buggy down the road after school the following afternoon. She had two stops to make before going home, and she dreaded them both. When she'd tried to give Fern's class another signing lesson today, she'd had problems with Kyle again. Not only had he been unwilling to learn, but he'd convinced two of the other boys to ignore her as well. If that hadn't been enough, during recess Jolene had caught Kyle poking at Irvin with a stick, and he'd written Irvin a note saying he was a dummkopp who had no ears.

Jolene's first response had been to want to tell Kyle to stop tormenting Irvin, but after taking a few minutes to think things through, she'd decided it was best if she said nothing to Kyle. If he'd been one of her students, she would have punished him on the spot. Instead she'd spoken to Fern about the problem and had left it up to her to discipline the boy. But after thinking about it the rest of the day and seeing how Irvin had pulled further into his shell, she'd made a decision. Before going over to see Lonnie, she would stop at the Beechys' place and talk to Kyle's folks. Jolene hoped they would do something about their son's antagonistic attitude. If not, she didn't know what she would do.

Jolene's thoughts shifted to Lonnie. She hoped he'd be open to the idea of her teaching him total communication, but after the comment Lonnie's dad had made the other evening about Lonnie not being willing to do much of anything, she figured he might offer some resistance.

Guess I'd better wait and see how it goes and just deal with things as they come, she told herself as she turned up the Beechys' driveway. She'd just pulled her horse up to the hitching rail when Jake stepped out of the barn. He seemed surprised to see her, and the crimson color that spread across his cheeks let her know that he was either embarrassed or a bit uncomfortable in her presence. Maybe he'd never been around a deaf person before. Or maybe he was uncomfortable about the fact that he'd obviously chosen not to join the Amish church and had become part of the English world.

Hoping to put Jake's mind at ease, Jolene smiled and said, "How's your daed doing, Jake? I understand you came home to help out while his legs are healing."

Jake nodded and shifted from one foot to the other, as though he was nervous.

"I'm sure your help is appreciated."

"I have nothing to write on. Can you read my lips?" he asked.

"As long as you look directly at me when you're talking, I'm able to read your lips."

Jake seemed to relax a little as he leaned on the hitching rail.

Jolene glanced toward the house then back at Jake. "Is your mamm at home? I'd like to speak to her about something."

He shook his head. "Dad's sleeping and Mom went over to see the bishop's wife today. I think her and some of the women are having a *Gluckin*, because Mom took some of her sewing along to join the others as they spend the day visiting and doing whatever handwork they brought along. Is there something I can help you with, Jolene?"

She quickly related how Kyle had been acting toward Irvin and ended it by saying that Kyle didn't want to learn how to sign and had convinced some of the other children not to participate, either.

Jake's lips compressed as he squinted. "No point in bothering my folks about this; I'll take care of the situation."

"I know we can't force Kyle to learn how to sign, but I do want him to stop picking on Irvin."

"Maybe if I were to learn how to sign, Kyle would take an interest."

"I'd be glad to teach you."

"Would you have time for that?"

"I'll make the time. You can come by the schoolhouse some afternoon, whenever you're ready to begin."

❦

Lonnie had just taken a seat on the sofa when his mother entered the living room with Jolene Yoder.

Mom wrote a message on the notebook she carried then handed it to Lonnie.

Lonnie grimaced as he read: *Jolene's here to talk with you about learning to read lips and talk with your hands.*

"Not interested," he said, handing the notebook back to Mom.

With a look of frustration, Mom handed Jolene the notebook and left the room.

Jolene took a seat on the other end of the sofa, wrote something on the notebook, and handed it to Lonnie. *As I'm sure you know, I've been hired to teach Irvin and Sylvia Troyer. Besides their regular studies, one of the things they'll be learning from me is total communication, which includes signing and lip reading. I was wondering if you'd like to learn as well.*

He shrugged. "What for?"

Jolene wrote something else: *So you can communicate with others. Lip reading's especially important when you're with people who can hear, and signing's important when you communicate with those who are deaf. On the job, out shopping, and doing business. . .those are all things we do, and we need to be able to interact with people.*

Lonnie shook his head. "I have no job, so I won't be interacting that much. I can't tune wind chimes now that I can't hear!"

Our deafness doesn't have to be a disability, she wrote.

He slouched against the sofa and folded his arms. "It's a disability when I can't do the kind of work I enjoy." Lonnie thought about Job 2:10, which Pop had showed him after breakfast that morning: *"Shall we receive good at the hand of God, and shall we not receive evil?"* He knew there were others, like Job, who'd suffered and faced trials worse than him, but his deafness was still a bitter pill to swallow.

There are other jobs that don't require you to hear, Jolene wrote.

He shook his head stubbornly. "I don't want any other job!"

Jolene scrawled something else on the notebook, handed it to Lonnie, and left the room.

Lonnie stared at what she'd written and the words blurred on the page: *Believe it or not, I understand how you feel. If you change your mind, please let me know.*

CHAPTER 14

As Jolene pedaled her bike to school the next day, she thought about her visit with Lonnie. Didn't he realize that he'd never be able to live a normal life unless he could communicate with others? He was bitter and angry right now, but then she'd felt that way, too, after she'd lost her hearing. She'd come to accept her disability, and learning total communication from her aunt had not only changed her way of thinking, but it had also opened up a whole new world for her.

I think I'll stop by the Hershbergers' after school again today, Jolene decided.

Maybe I can get Lonnie to change his mind about letting me tutor him.

Jolene's thoughts turned to other things. Fern had reminded her class at the close of school yesterday that today would be pet day where anyone could bring a pet to share with the class. Irvin and Sylvia were invited to bring their pets, too, and Jolene hoped it might spark an interest in Irvin. She'd seen several cats at the Troyers' place, as well as a dog, so she figured the children might bring one of those.

As Jolene entered the schoolyard, she spotted Kyle and his brother Elmer trudging across the yard, each holding one end of a birdcage. A colorful parrot flapped its wings against the cage and hopped up and down. It seemed like an unusual pet for boys as rambunctious as Kyle and Elmer. Jolene pictured them having a big shaggy dog that liked to bark and make a nuisance of itself. Several children had gathered around Kyle and Elmer and were pointing at the parrot. Both boys beamed, obviously enjoying the attention.

Maybe that's all those two need, Jolene thought as she parked her bike and headed across the yard. *With their daed laid up and their mamm extra busy right now, Kyle and Elmer might not be getting much attention at home. When I see Jake again, I'll mention it to him.*

Jolene was almost to the schoolhouse when she saw Irvin and Sylvia sitting on the porch. Sylvia had a kitten in her lap. Irvin had just removed a turtle from the cardboard box sitting near his feet.

"Good morning," Jolene signed. *"I'm glad to see that you brought your pets."*

Sylvia nodded enthusiastically and signed, *"My kitten's name is Mittens. She has four white paws."*

Jolene smiled. *"Mittens is a cute kitten."* She looked at Irvin. *"What's your turtle's name?"*

He tipped his head and stared at her like he didn't have a clue what she'd signed.

Jolene signed again. *"What's your turtle's name?"*

Irvin stared straight ahead.

Sylvia nudged Irvin's arm, but he ignored her. She looked up at Jolene and signed, *"The turtle's name is Tommy."*

Jolene was sure Irvin was just being stubborn by refusing to respond to her question. She was tempted to tell Sylvia to let her brother speak for himself, but she decided not to make an issue of it. She pointed to the schoolhouse and signed, *"Let's go inside. You can put your pets in their carriers and bring them upstairs. When the other class is ready for show and tell, we'll go downstairs and join them."*

Sylvia put the kitten inside its carrier, and Irvin put the turtle back in the box. Then Jolene followed the children up the stairs to their classroom.

As the children approached their desks, Sylvia stood in front of Irvin with her back to Jolene. She stayed like that a few seconds before she finally turned and faced Jolene. *"I told my brother that he'd better pay attention and do his lessons today."* Her forehead wrinkled as she pursed her lips. *"Said I'd tell Papa if he didn't."*

Jolene bit back a chuckle, and then she told the children that it was time for them to sign the Lord's Prayer.

Sometime later as Jolene was about to give the children their arithmetic lesson, Fern entered the room, looking quite distraught. Jolene moved closer so she could read Fern's lips.

"My helper, Becky, isn't feeling well, and I need to take her home," Fern said. "Would you mind taking over my class while I'm gone?"

Jolene's mouth went dry. "You—you want me to teach the scholars?"

"You won't have to teach—just have them show their pets while I'm gone." Fern touched Jolene's arm. "It won't take me long to drive Becky home, and I'm sure you'll do fine while I'm gone."

Jolene gave a slow nod. If all she had to do was oversee the children as they showed their pets, it shouldn't be too hard.

"Get your pets; we're going downstairs," Jolene signed to the children. Sylvia jumped right up and got her kitten, and Irvin, though moving slowly, picked up the box with his turtle inside. They both tromped down the stairs ahead of Jolene.

As soon as Fern left with Becky, Jolene went to the blackboard and wrote: *Those of you who brought small indoor pets can show them now. Afterward, we'll go outside to see the bigger pets.*

Before Jolene had the chance to explain that they would take turns showing their pets, Elmer Beechy raced across the room where his parrot's cage sat on a shelf. He fumbled with the latch but was unable to open it.

Kyle leaped out of his chair, pushed his brother aside, and pulled the latch open. The parrot hopped out, flapped its wings, and swooped over the children's desks.

Pandemonium broke out as most of the girls ducked down on the floor, while several boys leaped out of their seats and chased after the bird. Jolene clapped her hands, trying to get the scholars' attention, but she was completely ignored. While the parrot continued to fly around the room, Kyle, wearing a smug expression, took a seat at his desk and stared straight ahead as though nothing out of the ordinary had happened.

Jolene stood in front of Kyle's desk. "Please catch the parrot and put him away!"

He cupped his hands around his ears. "What was that? I can't hear you."

Jolene gritted her teeth. In her previous years of teaching, she'd never encountered such a difficult child. Even though Kyle had been in her class two years ago, he'd been much younger then and had never given her any problems. The way he acted now made no sense, but it had to stop!

Suddenly, Irvin jumped out of his seat, raced to the back of the room, and jerked the door open. The parrot made another circle of the room and flew out the door. Kyle leaped out of his seat and chased after it.

Jolene was tempted to go after Kyle but decided it was best to let the boy go and try to get the rest of the class under control. She motioned to Sylvia and signed, *"Why don't you show us your kitten?"*

Sylvia left her seat and was about to open her pet carrier when Kyle burst into the room, riding his pony. He stopped in front of the blackboard, leaned down, scooped up a piece of chalk and wrote in big letters: *MY PONY'S NAME IS SHADOW.*

Jolene's hand shook as she pointed to the door. "Take that animal outside! The schoolhouse is no place for a horse!"

"It's not a horse; it's a pony," Kyle said, looking at her defiantly.

Jolene groaned; her patience was gone. Why did this young boy have to be such a challenge? Determined not to let Kyle know how upset she was, Jolene grabbed the pony's bridle and led him out the door. When she returned to the classroom, she found a stool and told Kyle he had to sit in the corner until Fern returned. She'd be glad when school was over for the day and she could go home and collapse on the sofa. Then she remembered her decision to see Lonnie. She hoped that visit would go better than the rest of her day.

~≈ ≈~

When Eunice pulled up to the hitching rail at the Yoders' place, she spotted Andrew talking to a young, dark-haired man she'd never seen before.

Andrew smiled when Eunice stepped down from her buggy, and her heart skipped a beat.

"Have you met Jake Beechy?" Andrew asked.

Eunice shook her head. She knew Jake's parents and siblings, but she'd never met him.

"Jake was in Montana when you moved to Indiana, but he's back now, taking care of his daed's business." Andrew motioned to Jake. "He came over to shoe a couple of our horses."

"I see." Eunice smiled at Jake. "It's nice to meet you."

"Nice to meet you, too," Jake said as he pulled some tools from the back of his pickup.

Eunice couldn't help but notice the dimple in Jake's chin. His dark hair and deeply set blue green eyes were in sharp contrast to Andrew's light brown hair and hazel-colored eyes. While both men were nice looking, Jake was far more handsome. But then, good looks weren't everything. Eunice was attracted to Andrew's easygoing, soft-spoken ways.

"I came by to deliver the candles your mamm ordered at the party she hosted awhile back," she told Andrew.

"Want me to get them out of the buggy for you?" he asked.

"I'd appreciate that." Eunice went around to the back of her buggy and motioned to the box full of candles.

Andrew whistled. "Mom sure ordered a lot!"

"Oh, they're not all hers. Most of them are what the other women who came to her party ordered."

"Sounds like you had a successful party."

Eunice smiled. "I did."

Andrew reached into the buggy and lifted the box with ease, and then he headed across the yard with Eunice following on his heels. When he reached the house, he set the box on the porch and turned to face her. "My mamm's not here right now, but I'll make sure she knows these are here as soon as she gets home."

"What about your sister? Is she at home?"

"Nope. She's still at the schoolhouse."

"Oh." Eunice hesitated, wondering if she should invite Andrew to her house for supper one night next week, but she changed her mind. When she'd been trying to win Freeman Bontrager's heart last year, she'd become too pushy and had sent him straight into the arms of Katie Miller. She wouldn't make that mistake again.

"Tell your mamm and schweschder that I'm sorry I missed them," she said.

"I will."

Eunice hurried across the yard. When she reached the place where Jake had begun shoeing one of the horses, she paused. "I'll probably see you again soon because my daed has a couple of horses he needs to have shoed."

"No problem," Jake said as she untied her horse. "Tell him to give me a call."

"I will." Eunice stepped into her buggy and gathered up the reins. When she reached the end of the driveway, she glanced over her shoulder and saw Andrew waving at her. She smiled. *If I don't chase after him, maybe he'll chase after me.*

~❦~

Lonnie gripped the stick he was using to steady himself and kicked a pebble, sending it flying up the driveway. He'd been sitting on the front porch and had seen the mailman go by, so, despite his equilibrium being off some due to his loss of hearing, he'd walked down to pick up the mail. He'd hoped that there would be another letter from Carolyn, but there'd been nothing but a stack of bills. On the one hand, he was disappointed that there was no letter from her. On the other hand, he felt a sense of relief. If Carolyn didn't write, he wouldn't have to write back. What was there to say? She already knew he'd lost his hearing, as well as his job. Without a job, he couldn't offer her a future. Without a job he enjoyed, he'd never be truly happy.

Wayne had suggested that he didn't

need his hearing for every kind of job. But what job could he do that wouldn't require him to hear? Jobs were scarce here in Indiana, and even if he could find something he was able to do with his hearing loss, he didn't want just any old job. He wanted a job he enjoyed, like the one he'd had making wind chimes.

When Lonnie stepped onto the porch, he dropped the mail on a little table and flopped into one of the wicker chairs with a groan. He was surprised when he glanced toward the road and saw Jolene pedaling her bike up the driveway. She pushed it near the house, climbed off, and pulled a notebook from her backpack. Then she stepped onto the porch and handed the notebook to Lonnie.

He squinted at the words she'd written: *I've been thinking about you and wondering if you'd reconsider and let me to teach you how to sign and read lips.*

He surprised himself when he gave a slow nod. "When can we begin?"

I can't do it today, she wrote, *but if you can come by the schoolhouse after school lets out tomorrow, I can start teaching you then.*

"I'll be there." *But I don't have to like it,* he told himself.

❧ ❧

Jake had just finished cleaning the barn when he spotted Kyle riding up the driveway on his pony.

"How'd it go at school today?" Jake asked after Kyle halted his pony near the barn and climbed down.

The boy frowned. "It was baremlich."

"What was so terrible about it?"

"I got in trouble for somethin' I didn't do—least not on purpose, anyway."

"What was that?"

"I was tryin' to get the parrot's cage open so Elmer could show the dumm bird, and the crazy critter hopped out and scared the scholars when it flew around the room. Then that daab *buwe*, Irvin, opened the door, and the bird flew outside. Jolene blamed me for the whole thing." Kyle's forehead wrinkled as he squeezed his eyebrows together. "I always get in trouble for things that ain't my fault."

"Did you tell Jolene that you didn't let the parrot out on purpose?"

"Jah, but she didn't believe me. Made me sit in the corner facing the wall while the other kids showed their pets." Kyle grunted. "Had to sit that way for half an hour."

Jake frowned. "That doesn't seem fair to me. Would you like me to have a talk with Jolene about this?"

Kyle shook his head vigorously. "I'd be in more trouble if you did that."

Jake leaned against the barn door and thought. "How come Jolene was the one who punished you? I thought she was hired to teach the deaf children, not your class."

"Becky got sick, so Fern took her home." Kyle shuffled his feet a few times. "Jolene took over until Fern got back, but instead of teachin', she asked us to show our pets."

"So didn't you get to show yours?"

"Huh-uh. Sat in the corner the whole time."

"That doesn't seem right to me. You took your pony to school to show it to the scholars, and you should have had the right to do so. Think I'll go over to the schoolhouse right now and have a talk with her about this." Jake moved toward the back of the barn where his truck was parked. He'd get there quicker if he didn't take the time to hitch his horse to a buggy.

Kyle grabbed the sleeve of Jake's jacket. "She ain't there. Left as soon as school was out."

"Then I'll head over to her house and talk to her."

"She ain't there, neither. Heard her tell Fern that she was goin' over to see Lonnie Hershberger after school."

Jake was tempted to head over to Lonnie's and have a talk with Jolene but figured it'd be best if he spoke to her privately. He'd wait an hour and then go over to Jolene's house. He needed to get to the bottom of this before the day was out.

CHAPTER 15

Jolene eased herself onto the sofa and closed her eyes. She'd been fighting a headache most of the day, and by the time she'd left Lonnie's, the headache had gotten worse. She hadn't argued when Mom suggested that she rest awhile before it was time to start supper. Maybe a short nap would soothe her jangled nerves and relieve the headache. She'd been planning to stop by the Beechys' place and talk to Jake about his brother's antics with the pony but had decided it could wait until after supper. Maybe by then, she'd have a better idea of what to say.

Jolene was on the verge of drifting off when Mom entered the room.

"Sorry if I startled you." Mom's lips moved slowly. "Jake Beechy is on the porch. He says he needs to speak to you right away."

"That's good, because I need to speak with him, too. Please tell him to come in." Jolene swung her legs over the side of the sofa and sat up. A few seconds later, Jake entered the room. The frown on his face made Jolene wonder if Kyle had already told him about the pony episode.

"My brother Kyle came home from school pretty upset today," Jake said before Jolene could open her mouth. "I'd like to know why you assumed he'd intentionally let Elmer's parrot out of its cage."

Jolene squinted as she rubbed her forehead. "I didn't assume that at all."

Jake's brows drew together. "Then why'd you punish him for it?"

"I didn't. I—"

"I don't think it was fair that you made him sit in the corner while the others showed their pets."

Jolene shook her head. "Letting the parrot out of its cage is not why I punished

Kyle. I made him sit in the corner after he rode his pony into the schoolhouse."

Jake's eyes widened. "What?"

"It's true. Kyle went outside, and when he came back in, he was riding his pony."

A muscle in Jake's face quivered as he lowered himself into the nearest chair. "Kyle never said a word about riding his pony into the schoolhouse. No wonder you made him sit in the corner. Now that I know the truth, I'll make sure he's punished."

Jolene thought a minute as she formulated her words. "I wonder if Kyle might be taking his frustrations out at school because he's not getting enough attention at home."

"What makes you think that?"

"The boy seems so angry all the time, and it's gotten worse since your daed's accident."

Jake thumped the dimple in his chin a few times. "Guess you could be right. Now that Dad can't do any of his chores, Kyle's expected to do more than he normally did. He doesn't have much time for play these days, and whenever anyone says something to Kyle, they're usually asking him to do another chore."

Jolene was about to comment when Ella stepped into the room. She took one look at Jake and halted. Then she quickly looked at Jolene. "Sorry, I didn't realize you had company."

"Didn't you see my buggy outside?" Jake asked.

"I did see a buggy, but I didn't know it was yours." Ella said something else to Jake, but since her head was turned, Jolene couldn't make out what it was. Jake said something then, but his head was turned now, too. Even without hearing what Jake and Ella were saying, Jolene knew by their body language that something unpleasant was going on.

Jake rose from his seat and stood in front of Jolene. "I'll be heading for home now, but you can rest easy—my brother won't be riding his pony into the schoolhouse ever again." He glanced at Ella and hurried from the room.

"What was going on between you and Jake?" Jolene asked Ella after the door had closed behind Jake.

Ella's face flamed. "That man makes me so mad!"

"Did he say something to upset you?"

Ella flopped onto the sofa beside Jolene and said something, but her head was turned toward the window.

Jolene tapped Ella's arm. "I can't understand what you're saying unless you look at me."

Ella turned toward Jolene. "Sorry. You speak so well that I keep forgetting you can't hear what I'm saying."

Jolene smiled, appreciating the compliment. "Since I can't hear, I never know if I'm speaking clear enough or at the correct volume. Sometimes I find it hard to concentrate on reading lips, too."

"I imagine it would be hard."

"It's really a lot easier for me if someone signs."

"I suppose it would be, but signing seems difficult to me."

"It's not that hard to learn. There are four of us in this community now who can't hear, so for the benefit of us all, I'm hoping more people will learn how to sign."

"I'd like to learn." Ella smiled. "Can I be one of your first adult students?"

"Actually, I've already begun teaching Mom, Dad, and Andrew. And starting tomorrow, I'll be giving Lonnie lessons after school's out for the day. If you'd like to come to the schoolhouse, you can have your first lesson with him."

"Won't that make it harder, having two of us to teach at the same time?"

"Not really. Lonnie seemed a little nervous about learning to sign, so maybe having someone else in the room who wants to learn will help put his mind at ease."

"I guess we could give it a try. If Lonnie seems uneasy with me being there, maybe we can figure out some other time for you to teach me."

"That'll be fine." Jolene touched Ella's arm. "Getting back to Jake—did he say something to upset you?"

Ella frowned. "Said he was surprised I wasn't married and raising a family by now."

"Why would that upset you?"

"I think he was trying to rub it in that I'm still an old maid."

"You're not an old maid."

"Jah, I am. I'm twenty-four years old and don't even have a boyfriend."

"I don't have one either, and I'm more of an old maid than you are because I'll probably never get married."

"Why do you say that?"

"Think about it, Ella. What man would want to marry a woman who can't hear what he says to her?" Jolene massaged her forehead. "Even if I were to marry, I'm afraid of becoming a *mudder.*"

"How come?"

"What if one of my kinner were to hurt himself and cry for help? Unless I was in the same room and saw it happen, I'd never know that he'd been injured."

"Lots of deaf people marry and have kinner," Ella said. "I'm sure they have ways of learning to cope."

"Maybe so, but it wouldn't be the same as if I could hear." The throbbing in Jolene's head increased. "It doesn't really matter, because I'm happy teaching my students. I don't need to get married and have kinner of my own."

"Me neither. I've learned to accept the fact that I'm destined to be an old maid."

"Wouldn't you like to meet a man and fall in love?"

Ella shrugged. "Maybe, but I don't know who it'd be."

"What about Lonnie or Jake? They're both single and nice looking."

"In case you've forgotten what I told you

the other day, Lonnie has a girlfriend in Illinois." Ella wrinkled her nose. "And I'd never consider Jake as a boyfriend."

"Why not?"

"Besides the fact that Jake will no doubt head back to Montana as soon as his daed's on his feet, he can't be trusted to keep his word about anything!"

"Are you referring to something in particular?"

"Sure am. When he and Loraine were going out, he made all kinds of promises about them having a future together, but then he ran off to Montana and didn't bother to keep in touch."

"That's in the past, Ella. Loraine's been over Jake for a long time, and she's happily married to Wayne."

"But Jake lied to Loraine. He let her believe that he loved her and was coming back."

"Jake wasn't much more than a teenager when he went to Montana the first time, and what he did then doesn't mean he can't be trusted now."

"It's not the only time Jake has lied. He lied to—" Ella's cheeks turned pink and she abruptly stopped talking.

"What were you going to say?" Jolene asked. "Who'd Jake lie to?"

Ella shrugged. "It doesn't matter. The point is, Jake's not the right man for me."

"I'm sure the right man will come along when the time is right." Jolene yawned, struggling to keep her eyes open.

"I'd better go and let you rest. When I first arrived, your mamm said you had a headache and had come in here to lie down." Ella patted Jolene's arm in a motherly fashion.

Jolene smiled with gratitude. She really did need to rest, as the throbbing in her head had gotten worse. "I'll see you tomorrow afternoon."

Ella nodded and hurried out the door.

⚜

By the time Jake got home from Jolene's, he'd worked himself up pretty good. He had half a notion to find Kyle, haul him out to the woodshed, and give him a spanking for saying that Jolene had punished him for letting the parrot out. "He should have told me the truth about riding the pony into the schoolhouse," Jake mumbled as he led his horse to the barn.

Even after Jake had put the horse in its

stall and brushed him down thoroughly, he was still fuming. He didn't want to deal with Kyle but knew someone had to. Dad wasn't up to it, and Mom had enough on her plate, trying to keep up with household chores and caring for Dad and the children.

Jake fed his horse some oats, left the barn, and walked slowly to the house, knowing he needed to calm down before he spoke to Kyle. He found Mom in the kitchen, peeling potatoes in front of the sink.

"Where's Kyle?" he asked. "I need to speak to that boy!"

"He's in the living room, doing his homework."

Jake started in that direction but halted when Mom called, "What's going on? You look *umgerennt*. Has Kyle done something wrong?"

Jake turned to face his mother. "I *am* upset, and I'll tell you why as soon as I've spoken to Kyle." He hurried from the room.

Jake discovered Kyle sprawled out on the sofa, reading a book. "I thought you were supposed to be doing your homework. At least that's what Mom thinks you're doing."

Kyle rolled over on his side and glared

at Jake. "For your information, I'm finished with it."

"Then you ought to be outside doing your chores."

"I'll do 'em after supper."

Jake marched across the room and halted in front of the sofa. "Sit up. I want to talk to you."

Kyle made no move to get up.

Jake nudged Kyle's leg. "Sit up and move over so I can sit down."

Kyle grunted and pulled himself to a sitting position.

Jake took a seat beside him and cleared his throat.

"What's wrong? Have ya got somethin' stuck in your throat?"

Jake squinted at Kyle. "I just talked to Jolene, and I want to know why you lied to me about the reason you were punished at school today."

Kyle's cheeks flamed, and he dropped his gaze to the floor.

"Answer me, Kyle. Why didn't you tell me that you'd ridden your pony into the schoolhouse?"

Kyle shrugged. "Figured you'd blab it to Mom, and then I'd be in trouble with her."

"I can't speak for our mamm, but you're in big trouble with me! Not only for pulling such a crazy stunt with the pony, but for lying about the reason you were punished." Jake grimaced. "Not to mention making me look like a fool for accusing Jolene of wrongly punishing you." He rose to his feet. "Come with me to the barn. I've got some extra chores for you to do."

"I don't have to do what you say!" Kyle's face darkened. "You ain't my daed!"

"That's true, but Dad's not in any shape to be doling out punishment right now, so I'm filling in for him until he's back on his feet." Jake motioned to the door. "Now get on out to the barn and be quick about it!"

Kyle sat with his arms folded.

Jake was out of patience. If this was what it was like to be a father, then he was in no hurry to settle down and get married. "You'd better do as I say, little brother!"

"You ain't my boss."

"I am until Dad's better, so get off that sofa and get out to the barn!" Jake's hand shook as he pointed to the door. No wonder Jolene had put Kyle in the corner. She should have kept him after school and given him a bunch of chores to do at the schoolhouse.

Just then, Dad rolled into the room in his wheelchair. The top of his nearly gray hair stood on end, and his clothes were wrinkled, like he'd just woken up. "What's all the yelling about?" Dad's eyes narrowed as he stared at Jake.

Jake debated whether he should tell Dad about Kyle's antics at school. He didn't want to upset him, but he guessed Dad had the right to know what had gone on. He quickly related the whole thing and ended it by saying, "I think Kyle needs to be punished, so I'm sending him out to the barn to do some extra chores."

"It's your mamm's and my place to punish our kinner, not yours," Dad said gruffly. "You need to stay out of things that are none of your business."

Jake's fingers curled into the palms of his hands until his nails dug into his flesh. "Everything around here's my business these days."

Dad leveled him with a look that could have stopped a run-away horse. "What's that supposed to mean?"

Jake sighed deeply. "As soon as I heard that you'd been hurt, I left my job in Montana to come back here and take over shoeing horses for you, not to mention doing all the chores you used to do around here." He pointed to Kyle, who still sat slumped on the sofa. "I think that gives me the right to dole out punishment to my contrary little brother whenever it's needed, don't you?"

"No, I don't! And as far as you leavin' Montana to come here, I'm sure that you're only here out of obligation." Dad glanced down at the casts on his legs. "If I was a bettin' man, I'd bet that as soon as I'm able to work again, you'll trot right on back to Montana to play cowboy with a bunch of wild horses!"

"What's going on in here?" Mom asked as she entered the room. She looked first at Jake and then at Dad.

"I'm settin' our oldest son straight on a few things," Dad mumbled. "He seems to think him coming home to help out gives him the right to punish our kinner."

"Just Kyle right now." Jake repeated the story of the day's events to Mom. "A few extra chores won't kill the boy, and I figured I was doing you and Dad a favor by taking over."

Mom slowly shook her head. "You should have told me about this sooner and let me handle the discipline of Kyle."

"That's right," Dad interjected. "If you knew so much about discipline, you would have disciplined yourself and not run off to Montana like you did!" Sweat beaded on his forehead. "Ever since you turned sixteen, you've been nothing but rebellious."

"I'm not rebellious. I'm just trying to—"

Dad clapped his hands. "Don't interrupt me when I'm speaking, boy! You need to think things through, set your priorities straight, and decide what's the right thing to do."

Jake had listened to about as much as he could take. "Do what you will with my spoiled brother, but I'd appreciate it if you stopped trying to make me feel guilty for all my decisions!" He whirled around and stalked out of the room. He could hardly wait for Dad's legs to heal so he could head back to Montana!

CHAPTER 16

Jolene dismissed her class of two to go home and smiled when Irvin gave her a nod and signed, *"See you tomorrow, Teacher."* Things had gone better today, and for that she was grateful.

She glanced at the rules she'd written on the blackboard that morning:

1. **Pay attention.**
2. **Don't bother others.**
3. **Behave in class.**
4. **Use total communication (signing, finger spelling, speech, and lip reading).**

5. **Remember to do your homework and bring it to school.**
6. **Cooperate and share with others.**

Consequences for Not Obeying:
1. **Name on the board—warning.**
2. **One check—stand against the wall.**
3. **Two checks—parents will be told.**

Jolene had made it clear to both Irvin and Sylvia that she expected them to follow those rules. She figured the children's folks had made a few rules, too, for Sylvia, who'd cooperated from the beginning, had been even more attentive today, and Irvin had actually done most of his work. She had a hunch that Sylvia had told on Irvin, and he'd probably been punished at home for not paying attention in class and refusing to do what Jolene asked.

Jolene had just taken a notebook and pen from her desk when she felt a swish of air. She looked up and saw Lonnie step into the room. When the door swung shut, he said, "I'm here for my lesson."

Knowing that the school desks were too small for Lonnie's tall frame, Jolene pulled out the chair at her desk and motioned for him to sit down.

He hesitated then asked, "Where are you going to sit?"

Jolene moved over to the blackboard and wrote: *I'll stand for now.* Then she wrote the letter *A* and turned to face Lonnie. She made the hand gesture for *A*, with her fingers balled into the palm of her hand and her thumb facing up. Next she wrote the letter *B* and made the hand gesture, with all four fingers facing up and the thumb pulled inward across the palm of the hand. She continued writing the letters of the alphabet and making the proper hand signs until she'd done each one.

Lonnie looked at her with an eyebrow quirked and a perplexed expression. Was it really that hard to understand, or didn't he want to learn?

Maybe I'm going too fast, Jolene decided. She pointed to the letter *A* and made the hand sign for it again. Then she wrote on the blackboard and asked Lonnie to make the same hand sign she'd just made.

He did as she requested but without much enthusiasm. Then she showed him again how to make the hand signs for the letters

B and *C*. They practiced each of those several times then moved on to the letters *D*, *E*, and *F*. Jolene was about to start with the letter *G* when Ella stepped into the room.

"Sorry I'm late," she said, looking at Jolene. "I went with my daed to run some errands, and it took longer than we expected. He dropped me off here and suggested I go home with you after my lesson. He has a few more errands to run here in Topeka, so he'll pick me up at your place later this afternoon."

"That's fine," Jolene said, "but we'll have to walk to my house because that's how I came to school today."

Ella smiled. "That's okay. It's a nice day, and I'll enjoy the walk."

Jolene motioned to the blackboard and explained to Ella what she'd taught Lonnie so far. "Why don't you have a seat at one of the scholars' desks and follow along?"

Ella pulled out a chair and took a seat. The desk was a bit small for her, but she was short and fit in the chair a lot better than Lonnie would have.

Ella smiled at Lonnie, but he sat stony faced with his arms folded.

Jolene went to the blackboard and

wrote: *Ella wants to learn how to sign, so I invited her to join us today.* She pointed to the letter *A*. When she made the hand sign for it, Ella did the same.

"I wish I hadn't come," Lonnie said.

"What was that?" she wrote on the board.

"Nothing."

Jolene thought Lonnie had said he wished he hadn't come, but she couldn't be sure because toward the end of his sentence, he'd lowered his head. She continued to show Ella how to make the letters *B, C, D,* and *E*; then she pointed to the letter *F* and made the sign for that, but Lonnie didn't respond.

A few seconds later, he jumped to his feet. "I'm going home."

Before Jolene had a chance to respond, Lonnie raced out the door. She groaned and flopped into the chair where he'd been sitting. *"Es is mir verleed."*

"Why are you discouraged?" Ella asked.

"I'm not a good teacher. I feel like a failure."

Ella left her seat and stood in front of Jolene. "You need to stop questioning everything you do and quit blaming yourself for things that aren't your fault. It's obvious that Lonnie doesn't want to learn."

Jolene blinked back the tears stinging her eyes. "I think Lonnie's discouraged and probably a bit overwhelmed because there's so much to learn."

"Maybe I should bake him a loaf of friendship bread and attach a verse of scripture like I've done for several others in our community when they've gone through trying times."

"That's a thought. I don't know if he'll appreciate it, though." Jolene motioned to the blackboard then looked back at Ella. "Do you want to continue with the lesson, or are you ready to head for home?"

"You look tired and stressed," Ella said. "Maybe we should put the lesson on hold and start walking to your house."

Jolene nodded and pushed away from her desk. She was beginning to feel another headache coming on.

⚜

As Ella and Jolene walked along the shoulder of the road, the afternoon sun shone in a crystal blue sky. Despite the chilly fall weather they'd been having, the sun had shone nearly every day that week.

A slight breeze lifted the ribbon ties on Ella's head covering, while it whispered through the nearly bare trees that were close to the road.

Ella glanced at Jolene as she walked by her side. What a shame she couldn't hear the wind or any of nature's other sweet sounds. Ella couldn't imagine what it must be like for her cousin. It would be horrible to lose one's ability to hear. Yet Jolene seemed to be coping fairly well. *Better than I would be if I'd lost my hearing,* Ella thought.

They hadn't gone far when a hefty white goose waddled down the driveway of an English farmer's house, honking as it went.

Ella nudged Jolene's arm and pointed to the goose. "Looks like there's trouble heading our way."

"What was that? I can't tell what you're saying unless you look at me."

The goose gave a loud *honk* and started running toward them.

"It's a goose! Probably a mean goose!" Ella shouted, making sure that Jolene could see her face.

As the goose grew closer, it headed for Jolene. She gasped and started running in circles.

Suddenly the goose stopped, turned, and ran after Ella. She gave it a nudge with her foot. The goose stood still a few moments, but then it started after her again. Her heart pounding, Ella nudged the goose again, with a little more force. It turned and waddled a few steps toward home, but then it did a sudden U-turn and came after Jolene again.

Jolene and Ella started running down the road, but the goose was much faster than Ella anticipated and soon overtook them. She screeched to a halt and gave the goose a sterner nudge with her foot, which sent the goose rolling in the tall grass along the shoulder of the road. But it quickly got back up and came after her again, honking and raising a ruckus.

Jolene took hold of Ella's arm. "Have you noticed that the goose hasn't actually bitten either one of us?"

Ella drew in a shaky breath and shook her head. "The only thing I've noticed is that it won't quit running after us."

"Hold still, Ella. I think this silly old goose just wants to walk with us."

Ella froze. Sure enough, the dumb goose came right up, leaned into her leg, and looked up at her like she was a long-lost friend.

Ella leaned over so she was eye to eye with the goose. "I'm sorry for rolling you with my foot and anything else I did that might have traumatized you."

Like an obedient dog, the silly goose proceeded to waddle alongside Ella. Finally, at Jolene's suggestion, they turned back toward the farmhouse the goose had come from. When they got there, Ella walked the goose back to its yard, where it honked a farewell and waddled off like nothing had ever happened.

Ella joined Jolene at the end of the driveway, and they both started laughing. Jolene laughed so hard that tears rolled down her cheeks. Ella smiled as they headed back down the road. Jolene had seemed so down after Lonnie left the schoolhouse in a huff. It was good to see her relax and find some humor in what had started out to be a very stressful event. Maybe that's what they all needed these days—to look for the humorous side of things.

❦

As Lonnie drew close to home, a feeling of guilt washed over him. He'd acted like a spoiled brat and knew he should have stayed and finished his lesson. For some reason, though, having Ella there had made him feel nervous. Maybe it was because she seemed so capable. Maybe it was because he didn't want her to see how stupid he was. He'd had a hard enough time concentrating on what Jolene had shown him, and remembering the finger positions had been no easy task. At the rate he was going, he'd never learn to sign the entire alphabet, much less be able to sign any words.

Lonnie guided his horse up the driveway and halted near the barn. After he unhitched the horse, he spent some time brushing the animal down. This gave him the opportunity to think things through a bit more. By the time he was done, he'd made a decision. After supper, he'd go over to Jolene's and apologize for his childish behavior.

When Lonnie headed for the house, he saw Mom sitting in a chair on the back porch, peeling potatoes. When he stepped onto the porch, she wrote something on the tablet that had been lying beside her and handed it to him. It read: *You're home sooner than I expected. How'd your first lesson with Jolene go?*

"Not good. There's too much to learn." Lonnie chose not to elaborate.

It'll get easier with time and practice. Mom smiled and continued to write. *As soon as you learn how to sign, your daed and I will ask Jolene to teach us.*

Lonnie shrugged.

Mom wrote something else on the tablet. *I think I know something that will lift your spirits.*

"What's that?"

There's a letter for you on the table. It's from Carolyn.

He hurried into the house and tore open the envelope, but he'd only read a few words when his heart started to pound:

Dear Lonnie,
    This is hard for me to say, but I won't be coming to see you after all. I've met someone, and. . .

The words blurred on the page, and Lonnie blinked against the unexpected tears behind his eyes. He sank into a nearby chair. Carolyn wasn't coming; she'd found someone else. Was it because she didn't want to be stuck with a man who couldn't hear?

What was the use in learning to sign or read lips if he couldn't have Carolyn? Without her, his life had no meaning. So much for that time when she'd told him she thought God had brought them together!

Lonnie lifted his gaze toward the ceiling and railed at God for the injustices He allowed. "It's not fair! Nothing in my life is fair anymore!" He sprang from the chair, knocking it to the floor. He was glad he couldn't hear the *crash*.

Lonnie dashed across the room and jerked open the back door with such force that he felt the vibration when it hit the wall.

When he stepped onto the porch, he drew in a couple of shaky breaths. Then, taking the stairs two at a time, he headed straight for the barn. This day couldn't be over soon enough to suit him!

CHAPTER 17

How are things going at school?" Loraine asked Jolene when they met at the hardware store in Shipshewana the following afternoon.

Jolene shrugged. "Things are a little better with Irvin and Sylvia, but Lonnie doesn't seem to want to learn."

"Oh that's right, you had. . ." Loraine turned her head as she reached for a stack of baby blankets.

Jolene tapped Loraine's arm. "What did you say? I couldn't see your lips."

Loraine's cheeks colored as she faced Jolene. "Sorry."

"Reading lips is the only way I can know what others are saying, unless they know how to sign."

"Speaking of signing," Loraine said. "I understand that you're going to be teaching Ella."

"That's right. She had her first lesson yesterday and another one this afternoon. Lonnie was supposed to have another lesson with us today, too, but he didn't show up."

"Maybe he got busy with something at home."

"I hope that's all it was. He seemed upset when he left the schoolhouse yesterday, and I was concerned that he might not come back today."

"I'm sure he'll be back for more lessons. He won't be able to communicate without learning to sign and read lips."

"You're probably right. I'll give him a few more days, and if he doesn't show up, I'll go over to his house and talk to him about it." Jolene motioned to the blanket Loraine held. "Are you getting ready for the big day?"

Loraine smiled. "I can hardly wait until the boppli's born this spring."

"I'm happy for you."

"I've been concerned about our finances, but Wayne's begun making wooden items, and he's already sold a few things to some of the furniture stores in the area, so I think we'll be okay."

"What about Ada and Crist? Are they getting by on what Crist makes in his taxidermy shop?"

"So far, but Wayne will be taking less money from the business now that he's found a way to supplement our income, so Crist will earn most of the profits."

"I guess Ada could always look for a job if she needed to."

Loraine shrugged. "Maybe, but she likes being at home."

"She might find something she could make and sell from her home like some folks in our community have done."

"I'm sure she'll help out if she needs to, so I'm trying not to worry about it."

Jolene swallowed hard. It was a challenge not to worry about a lot of things these days.

❧ ❧

As Ella approached the Hershbergers' place, her breath caught. The sun peeked out between fluffy white clouds, casting a golden light on the pastures surrounding their farm. The fields of drying corn rustled, and birds chirped a happy chorus in the trees overhead. Fall was a beautiful time of year.

Ella secured her horse to the hitching rail and reached inside the buggy to get the friendship bread she'd made for Lonnie. Then she sprinted to the house and knocked on the door. A few moments later, Lonnie's mother, Irene, answered her knock.

"I came to see how Lonnie's doing and to give him a loaf of friendship bread." Ella handed the bread to Irene. "There's a verse of scripture attached to the wrapping."

"That's nice of you. I'm sure Lonnie will appreciate the gesture." Irene opened the door wider. "Come inside, and we can chat awhile."

Ella followed Irene into the kitchen, and Irene placed the loaf of bread on the counter. "Please, have a seat," she said, motioning to the table.

When Ella sat down, she noticed the late-afternoon shadows bouncing off the walls. The days were getting shorter, and soon it would be dark by late afternoon— a sure sign that winter was coming.

"Would you like a cup of coffee or some tea?" Irene asked.

"No, thanks."

"How are things at your place? Is your daed keeping busy in his shop?"

"Since he hasn't found anyone to take Lonnie's place, he's busy enough, but it's mostly with out-of-state orders right now."

"Lonnie misses his job tuning wind chimes. He's been miserable ever since he lost his hearing." Irene sighed deeply. "Now, with Carolyn breaking up with him, he feels worse than ever."

"When did that happen?"

"He got a letter from her yesterday, saying she'd met someone else. He's convinced that she broke up with him because of his disability. Now he's despondent and doesn't want to learn how to sign or read lips."

"Is Lonnie at home now?" Ella asked. "I'd like to speak to him."

"He's out in the barn." Irene took a tablet and pen from the desk in the kitchen and handed it to Ella. "You'll need this so you can communicate with him."

"Okay." Ella left her seat, plucked the scripture verse off the loaf of friendship bread, and scurried out the door.

She found Lonnie in the barn, sitting on a bale of straw, staring at the rafters. When she touched his shoulder, he jumped.

"Sorry if I startled you."

"Huh?"

Using the tablet and pen Irene had given her Ella scrawled a note and handed it to Lonnie. He read her words with a look of disinterest. *I went to the schoolhouse this afternoon for another signing lesson and was disappointed that you weren't there.*

"I changed my mind about learning to sign."

How come? Ella wrote in reply.

"Carolyn broke up with me. Nothing matters anymore now."

Ella saw the anger and pain on Lonnie's face, even heard it in his voice. She wished there was something she could say to make him feel better. It was never fun to be jilted.

Ella wrote again on the tablet: *I brought you a loaf of friendship bread with a verse of scripture attached. I think the verse might help you understand that God has a plan for your life.*

"Some plan! There's no way you could understand what I'm going through. You still have two good ears."

That's true, but I've suffered losses. Ella squeezed onto the bale of straw beside him. *You're not the only one who's lost your hearing. Jolene lost hers in the accident we were in, and she's learned to cope with her handicap. She doesn't sit around feeling sorry for herself because she can't hear, either.*

"It's not just my loss of hearing that's got me down. It's the fact that Carolyn broke up with me because of it." He slowly shook his head. "I can't understand why God allows people to do such hurtful things."

People aren't puppets, and I don't think anyone really understands why bad things happen to good people. Ella lifted her pen as she thought about what more she should say. *God has a plan for your life, and I think you should let Jolene teach you to communicate through signing and lip reading so that others don't have to write everything down.* She handed Lonnie the verse of scripture that had been attached to the bread: *"I will instruct thee and teach thee in the way which thou shalt go: I will guide thee with mine eye. Psalm 32:8."*

He read the verse but gave no response.

If Jolene's willing to give up her time to teach you, don't you think you ought to quit feeling sorry for yourself because life's handed you a harsh blow and learn from her?

His face blanched then quickly turned pink. "I guess both Jolene and I share a great loss."

Ella nodded.

"My miserable situation isn't her fault, and I guess she only wants to help me."

Does that mean you'll come back for more lessons? Ella wrote.

"I guess so."

That's great. I'll see you at the schoolhouse tomorrow afternoon.

~≪ ≫~

For the last fifteen minutes, Jake had been sitting at the kitchen table, drinking a cup of coffee and visiting with his mother while she prepared supper.

He enjoyed this quiet time, watching her slice carrots and potatoes into the pot of vegetable soup. While he was living in Montana and sleeping in the bunkhouse, he'd missed times like this. There'd always been such an easy camaraderie between him and Mom.

Not like me and Dad, Jake thought ruefully. *We've never seen eye to eye on much of anything.* Jake still hadn't gotten over Dad hollering at him for trying to discipline Kyle.

Stretching his arms over his head, Jake yawned.

"If you're tired, why don't you go lie down?" Mom suggested. "I'll call you when supper's ready."

Before Jake could reply, Dad wheeled into the kitchen. "Thought I heard voices in here." He looked over at Jake. "How come you're not outside doin' the afternoon chores?"

"They're done already."

"Oh." Dad maneuvered his wheelchair up to the table and reached for the coffeepot. "So, Jake, how's business been going this week?" he asked as he poured coffee into the cup Mom handed him. "Are you managing to keep up?"

"I'm doing fine."

"Are you making sure to get the horses' hooves cleaned and trimmed real good before you put on their shoes?"

Irritation welled in Jake's chest. "I know how to shoe a horse, Dad."

"Jah, well, you haven't been helping me for some time."

"I did plenty of shoeing at the ranch in Montana, along with lots of other things that involved horses."

"Humph!" Dad folded his arms and glared at Jake. "All you ever seem to talk about is Montana."

A muscle in Jake's jaw quivered. Wouldn't Dad ever let up?

"If you had a lick of sense, you'd forget about Montana, stay here, and join the church."

Jake didn't like the way this conversation was going, and he was afraid if he stayed much longer, he and Dad would end up in a full-blown argument. He pushed his chair away from the table, dumped his coffee into the sink, and strode across the room.

"Where are you going?" Mom called.

"I've got a few more chores to do in the barn."

"I thought you said you'd done all the chores," Dad said.

Jake just hurried out the door.

Once outside, he leaned against the porch railing and watched the horses grazing in the pasture. He probably had enough money saved up to put a down payment on a place of his own if he had a mind to, but he wasn't sure whether he wanted to settle in Indiana or Montana. If he stayed here, there might be more conflict with Dad than there already was. If he went back to Montana, Mom would be hurt.

At one time, Jake had thought he was ready to join the Amish church, but now he wasn't sure it would be the right thing for him to do. He didn't want to make a lifelong commitment to something just because it's what his folks wanted. The decision to be Amish or not was between him and God, not him and Dad.

A spark of anger and a flare of determination settled over Jake. He'd made up his mind a long time ago that he would make his own decisions. Dad would just have to deal with whatever he decided. Jake knew he couldn't do anything until Dad's legs healed sufficiently. In the meantime, he would keep out of Dad's way as much as possible and try to stay busy.

CHAPTER 18

The following day, Ella finished her work in Dad's shop early and headed to the schoolhouse for another signing lesson. The scholars were just leaving when she arrived, and she greeted Fern, who stood on the porch. "Is Jolene in her classroom? I came for my signing lesson."

"She's still here. She gave the children in my class another lesson today, too."

"I didn't realize they were learning to sign. Was that your idea or Jolene's?" Ella asked.

"Both. We thought it would help Irvin and Sylvia if they could communicate with the other children." Fern motioned to Kyle Beechy, who was about to climb onto his bike. "He's given Irvin a hard time about not being able to hear, so I think learning to speak with his hands will be a good thing for him. It'll give him a better idea of what it's like for people who are deaf."

"I hope it helps." Ella moved toward the stairs. "Guess I'd better get up there before Jolene thinks I'm not coming." When she reached the first step, she turned back around. "Will you be at the young people's volleyball game on Friday night at the 850 Center?"

"I don't know," Fern replied. "I hadn't really thought about going. I'm really not much of a volleyball player."

"You should go. I'm sure it'll be a lot of fun, even if you just sit and watch."

Fern smiled. "If I do go, then I'll go by myself. Freeman and Katie will probably go, and I'm sure they'd like some time alone as they travel to and from the game. It'll be difficult enough for them after they're married and living in the same house with me."

"They do want you to continue living there, right?"

"I believe so, but even though Grandma

left the house to both Freeman and me, I offered to move out so he and Katie can have the house to themselves after they're married." A stiff breeze blew under the eaves of the porch, and Fern pulled the collar of her jacket tighter. "Freeman insists that the house is half mine and says he wants me to stay on."

"What does Katie say about it?"

"She agrees with Freeman—even said she enjoyed my company."

"Then I'm sure everything will be fine."

"Thanks. I'll see you later," Fern added as she stepped out the doorway. "I need to get home and start supper before Freeman closes his bike shop. He's usually hungry as a mule by the end of the day."

Ella chuckled as she hurried up the stairs. When she entered Jolene's classroom and saw no sign of Lonnie, she was disappointed.

She stepped up to Jolene's desk. "I'm sorry to see that Lonnie's not here. I stopped by to see him yesterday, and he said he'd be coming today."

"Did he say why he missed the last lesson?" Jolene asked.

Ella was on the verge of telling Jolene

that Lonnie's girlfriend had broken up with him, when the door swung open and Lonnie stepped into the room.

"I'm sorry for missing yesterday's lesson," he said.

Jolene wrote a message for him on the blackboard: *You're here now; that's all that matters. Since you and Ella want to learn how to sign, I think it would be good if you both come here a few days a week for signing, and then since Lonnie will also need to learn lip reading, maybe he can come on a different day just for that.*

"That's fine," Lonnie said.

Ella agreed, too. She was glad Lonnie had come, but his somber expression told her that it would be awhile before he got over being jilted by Carolyn.

Jolene erased the board and had just written the first five letters of the alphabet, when the door opened and Jake stepped in.

He walked up to Jolene and said, "I heard you were giving a lesson on signing here today, and I wondered if I could join you."

She smiled. "You're more than welcome to join us."

"Oh, great," Ella muttered.

Jolene glanced over at Ella, and she must have noticed the scowl on her face, for she quickly added, "Of course, if you'd rather come by my house for lessons on the evenings I'll be teaching my family how to sign, you're welcome to do that."

"I just might," Jake said, "but I'm here now, so I may as well get in on this lesson."

~⁂~

Ella felt relieved when the lesson was over and Lonnie and Jake had gone. It was hard for her to be in the same room with Jake. Watching the way he'd kept flirting with Jolene made her sick to her stomach. At least it had seemed like flirting.

"What's wrong with you today?" Jolene asked. "For someone who said they wanted to learn how to sign, you didn't show much interest. Every time I looked your way, you were scowling."

"Jake isn't to be trusted."

Jolene's brows puckered. "What's Jake got to do with it?"

"Nothing. I mean, it irritated me that he was here, and I had trouble concentrating."

"Why would you feel irritated because Jake wants to learn how to sign?"

"I don't care whether he learns to sign or not. What riles me is the way he always manages to worm his way into people's lives. Then he jerks the rug out from under them as soon as they start to have feelings for him."

"Are you referring to the fact that Jake hurt Loraine when he took off for Montana and didn't keep in touch with her, or do you have feelings for Jake?"

Ella's face heated. "Of course not! The only feelings I have for Jake are feelings of irritation."

"Did you ever think that maybe Jake going to Montana and leaving Loraine in the lurch was a blessing?"

"How could it be a blessing?"

"Loraine and Wayne wouldn't be happily married right now if Jake hadn't left."

Ella grunted. "No, Loraine and Jake would be happily married."

"You don't know that. They might not have gotten married even if Jake had stayed in Indiana. And if they had gotten married, it doesn't mean they would have been as happy together as Loraine and Wayne seem to be."

"You could be right." Ella pursed her lips.

"But since Jake left Indiana twice, then I'm sure he's bound to leave again."

"Maybe he will go back to Montana when his daed's doing better, but that's Jake's decision. It's no reason for you to sit here with a long face and ignore everything I was trying to teach today."

"You're right. I shouldn't have let my feelings about Jake affect my desire to learn signing." Ella touched Jolene's arm. "Can I offer you a bit of advice?"

"What's that?"

"Don't let Jake get too close to you, and don't listen to any promises he makes."

"What are you talking about?"

"Couldn't you see the way he was flirting with you this afternoon?" Ella asked. "If you're not careful, he'll break your heart, the way he did Loraine's."

Jolene's mouth hung slightly open. "Did you just say what I thought you said—that Jake was flirting with me today, and that he might break my heart?"

Ella nodded. "That's exactly what I said."

"You're kidding, right?"

"No, I'm not. The whole time you were showing us what finger positions to use for certain letters and words, Jake sat there grinning like a lovesick *hund*. He even winked at you."

Jolene shook her head. "I think he was just being friendly. And hopefully he enjoyed the lesson."

"People don't wink at the teacher because they're enjoying the lesson. You didn't see Lonnie winking, did you?"

"Well, no, but—"

"You'd do well to heed my advice and stay as far away from Jake as possible."

"You're serious, aren't you?" Jolene's cheeks had turned a deep rosy pink, matching the color of her dress.

"I am serious. You need to watch out for Jake and keep hold of your heart so he doesn't break it."

"Yes, Mother."

"I mean it, Jolene. Jake's not to be trusted."

"I'm glad Lonnie came back today," Jolene said, abruptly changing the subject. "I was worried that I'd said something to upset him the other day."

"It wasn't you that kept Lonnie from coming yesterday; it was his girlfriend, Carolyn."

"What do you mean?"

"When I stopped by his place yesterday, I found out that he'd gotten a letter from Carolyn saying she'd found someone else and was breaking up with Lonnie."

Deep wrinkles formed across Jolene's forehead. "No wonder he seemed so sullen today. I'm surprised he came here at all."

"He wasn't going to, but I gave him a little pep talk and shared a verse of scripture with him."

"I'm sorry to hear he was jilted like that, but maybe in the long run it'll work out for the best."

"What do you mean?"

"Maybe God has someone else in mind for Lonnie—someone who'll make him happier and be a better wife than Carolyn."

"That could be, I suppose."

"Maybe that someone will be you."

Ella's eyes widened. "I have no more interest in Lonnie than I do Jake. Besides, it's too soon for Lonnie to show an interest in anyone." She twirled the ends of her head-covering ties around her fingers. "If and when Lonnie does take an interest in someone, I'm sure it won't be me."

"How do you know?"

"Because we have nothing in common."

"Jah, you do. You both like wind chimes, and you and Lonnie used to work together in your daed's shop."

"That's true, but Lonnie can't work there anymore, and the fact that we both like wind chimes isn't reason enough for him to be interested in me."

"One never knows how things will go."

"Changing the subject," Ella quickly said, "are you planning to go to the volleyball game on Friday evening?"

"I don't think so."

"It'll be like old times."

Jolene nibbled on her lower lip. "I wouldn't be comfortable there."

"Why not?"

"I'd feel out of place, like I didn't fit in."

"You can sit on the sidelines with me, and we'll be out of place together. How will that be?"

"Well, maybe I'll go if Andrew does." Jolene rose from her chair. "In the meantime, I need to get home and help Mom start supper. Our lesson went longer than I'd planned."

"Then I took up more of your time by talking about Jake and Lonnie."

Jolene glanced at the clock. "It's okay. I'll still be home in plenty of time to help with supper."

⚓⚓

Andrew had just pulled his horse and buggy up to their hitching rail when he saw Jolene's buggy pull in behind him.

"How come you're so late?" he asked when she stepped down from her buggy.

"I had another lesson to teach; only this time Ella wasn't the only one there. Lonnie and Jake came, too."

"It makes sense that Lonnie would come, but why was Jake there?"

"He thinks if he learns to sign, his brother Kyle might take more of an interest in what I'm trying to teach Fern's class."

"Guess that makes sense."

"Do you really think Jake will go back to Montana once his daed's doing better?"

Andrew shrugged. "With Jake, who knows?"

"Ella doesn't trust Jake. She thinks he'll break someone's heart and then leave for Montana again."

"Who's heart does she think he'll break?"

"Mine."

Andrew's eyebrows lifted high. "How's

he gonna break your heart? You're not in love with him, are you?"

"Of course not! I haven't been back from Pennsylvania very long, so when would I have had the chance to fall in love with anyone?"

"Good point."

Jolene clutched the folds in her dress. "Ella seems to think that Jake was flirting with me today. After the lesson she warned me about him and said I shouldn't be alone with him."

Andrew unhitched Jolene's horse then turned to face her. "I think Ella's right about Jake leaving again, but I doubt he'll be around long enough to make a move on you or anyone else. But I do think it would be best if you don't have any of your lessons alone with him."

"Surely you don't think I have anything to worry about where Jake's concerned."

"Probably not, but I'd feel better if you didn't put yourself in a compromising position."

"I won't. He'll either have his lessons with Lonnie and Ella, or he'll come over here and learn with our family." She smiled. "I invited him to join us some evening."

"I guess that'd be okay. At least that way I can keep an eye on him."

She nudged his arm. "Changing the subject, I was wondering if you're planning to attend the volleyball game on Friday night."

"Definitely. Wouldn't miss it for the world."

Jolene quirked an eyebrow. "I've never seen you so excited about a social before. What's up?"

"Nothing. I've been working hard lately, and it'll be nice to let down and have some fun."

"There wouldn't be someone special you're looking forward to seeing, would there?"

Andrew was relieved when Jake pulled up in his buggy just then. He wasn't ready to talk about his interest in Eunice. Besides, some things about Eunice bothered him, and unless she changed, he wouldn't begin a serious relationship with her.

"I've been thinking about what you said at the schoolhouse," Jake said to Jolene when he joined them.

"What was that?" she asked.

"About coming over here for lessons." Jake shook his head. "I don't think I ought to go to the schoolhouse for lessons if El-la's going to be there."

"How come?" Andrew asked before Jolene could respond.

"I fooled around a lot this afternoon during our lesson, thinking it might put Ella at ease, but she seemed irritated and edgy the whole time. I know Ella doesn't like me, although I don't know why." Jake kicked a pebble with the toe of his boot then looked back at Jolene. "Can I come over here for lessons instead?"

She nodded. "That's fine with me. Everyone in the family is busy with other things for the rest of this week, but on Monday evening we'll have another lesson. Could you come over then?"

"Sure." Jake smiled at Jolene. "Will I see you at the game on Friday night?"

"We'll both be there," Andrew was quick to say. *And I'll be watching out for my sister.*

CHAPTER 19

Jolene sat on the sidelines, watching the game of volleyball that had begun a short time after she and Andrew had arrived. Andrew, who enjoyed any kind of ball, had joined the game right away. Jolene, already feeling out of place, had opted to sit and watch. It would be hard to play volleyball, knowing she wouldn't be able to hear what her teammates were shouting to each other. Reading lips would be nearly impossible with everyone running and jumping after the ball.

Jolene glanced around the building to see if Lonnie had come, but there was no sign of him. He'd probably decided not to come, knowing he wouldn't be able to communicate with anyone without the use of a tablet and pen. It would probably be some time before Lonnie felt ready to attend a social event such as this. Jolene looked forward to teaching him how to sign and read lips and hoped he'd catch on quickly now that they'd begun regular lessons.

She glanced back at the volleyball players and was surprised to see Ella and Jake playing on the same team. As much as Ella disliked Jake, it made no sense that she'd be on his team. Maybe she'd had no choice as to which side she played on.

Someone touched Jolene's shoulder, and her head jerked to the right. Fern smiled down at her. "Mind if I join you?"

"Of course not; have a seat." Jolene motioned to the folding chair beside her then turned to face Fern when she sat down. "It sure is a nice evening," she said. "Not cold and windy like it's been the last few days."

Fern smiled. "Sometimes when the fall weather turns warm we get a surprise cold snap with snow." She rubbed the bridge of her nose as her smile was replaced with a frown. "I hope winter doesn't come early this year, because I'm in no hurry for snow."

"Your scholars will probably like it, though," Jolene said. "Most kinner love playing in the snow."

"That's true. I enjoyed making snowmen and sledding down the hill behind the schoolhouse when I was a girl." Fern touched Jolene's arm. "How are things going with the lessons you've been giving after school? Are your adult students catching on to signing as easily as some of the kinner in my class seem to be?"

Jolene shook her head. "Children learn new things easier than most adults, but I'm sure that, given a little time, Lonnie and Ella will catch on."

"What about Jake? I hear that he came over to the schoolhouse to sit in on a lesson on signing from you, too."

"He came once, but he's decided to take part in the lessons I'm giving my family." Jolene debated about telling Fern that Ella felt uncomfortable around Jake but decided it'd be best not to say anything.

"I guess Jake's keeping busy shoeing

horses and doing his daed's chores. Taking evening lessons will probably be easier for him."

Jolene nodded and was about to say something more when she spotted Eunice heading their way, holding a bag of ice against her left hand.

～≈ ≫～

Eunice flopped down on the chair beside Fern and groaned. "I'm never playing volleyball again!"

"How come?" Fern asked.

Eunice held up her hand and grimaced. "I was trying to hit the ball over the net, when Matthew Stoltzfus got in my way and knocked me down. When I landed, my left hand took the brunt of the fall, and I think I may have sprained my wrist."

"Are you sure it's not broken?" Fern asked with a look of concern. "Maybe you should go to the hospital and have it x-rayed."

"If it was broken, I don't think I could do this." Eunice lifted the bag of ice and wiggled her fingers, and then she turned her hand palm up. "It does hurt, though."

"That's exactly why I decided not to play. Volleyball can be a dangerous sport." Fern nudged Jolene's arm, and Jolene turned to look at her. "Have you ever gotten hurt playing volleyball?"

"A few times. But I haven't played since I lost my hearing."

"There must be lots of things deaf people can't do," Eunice said.

Jolene pulled back like she'd been stung by a bee. "There are lots of things deaf people *can* do."

Eunice's face heated. "I didn't mean you couldn't play. I just meant. . ."

Jolene stood, smoothing the wrinkles in her dress. "I think I'll go see if there's any more hot apple cider." She hurried away.

So much for trying to befriend Andrew's sister. Eunice turned to Fern. "It was sure rude of Jolene to walk off like that. She didn't even let me finish my sentence."

"She probably couldn't see your lips and didn't realize you were speaking. Whenever you speak to Jolene, you need to look directly at her."

"I forgot."

"Maybe you should learn how to sign. Jolene's been giving lessons after school."

"I really don't have time for that right now. I've been busy hosting candle parties in the evenings and making soap deliveries during the day, and there's not much time for anything else." Eunice flicked a piece of lint from her dress. Truth was, signing seemed difficult to her. She'd never been good at learning new things and was afraid that she wouldn't be able to learn how to sign. If she messed up, she didn't want to embarrass herself in front of anyone.

"I know you're busy," Fern said, "but tell me who isn't busy these days?"

Eunice was relieved when Katie showed up and started a conversation with Fern. If Fern had kept pressuring her about learning to sign, she might have ended up telling her that she was afraid to try. It wasn't easy for Eunice to admit that she felt like a failure. With the exception of Fern, Eunice had never been able to keep a friend. She knew that because of her shiny blond hair and vivid blue eyes, some men thought she was pretty. Yet even though she'd had several boyfriends, she hadn't been able to keep one. Maybe she wasn't smart enough. Eunice had struggled with reading and math when she was in school, and she had no artistic skills whatsoever. About the only thing she had ever succeeded at was her new soap and candle business.

"Are you okay?"

Eunice jumped at the sound of a man's voice. She looked up and saw Andrew staring down at her, his dark eyes revealing the depth of his concern. "When I saw you fall, I was worried that you may have broken a bone or something."

Eunice smiled, despite the pain in her wrist. "I think I just sprained my wrist, so I'm not going to play ball anymore tonight."

"Are you sure? Maybe you should have it x-rayed."

"I'm fine, really. What I would like, though, is something to drink."

"I'll get you a glass of apple cider." Andrew started to walk away, but Eunice, feeling left out of the conversation between Fern and Katie, decided to join him. As they headed to the refreshment table, loud voices erupted from the players. The game had stopped. Jake and Ella were standing nose to nose.

~≈ ≈~

"Would you please stay out of my way?"

Ella planted both hands on her hips and

stared up at Jake, wishing she wasn't so short so she could look him directly in the eye. "I was not in your way; you were in my way!"

"No, I wasn't."

"Jah, you were. Seems like every time I reach for the ball you step in front of me."

"That's because you've been reaching into my playing space."

Ella gritted her teeth. It wasn't her choice to play on the same team with Jake, but they'd both been chosen to play on this side of the net, so she'd decided to make the best of it. She'd figured as long as he stayed out of her way, everything would be fine.

"Are we playing or what?" someone hollered.

Ella took her position as Jake picked up the ball and served it over the net. Things went okay until the ball came her way again. She leaped for it just as Jake rushed forward, ducking his head. *Smack!*—their foreheads collided with a sickening thud.

"You did that on purpose!" Ella winced and rubbed her forehead.

"Did not."

"Jah, you did!"

"No, I didn't, Ella." Although looking a bit perturbed as he rubbed his forehead, Jake kept his voice calm.

Ella's hand shook as she pointed at him. "You—you—oh, never mind!" She whirled around and marched off the court.

"Are you okay?" Jolene asked when Ella joined her at the refreshment table and quickly poured herself a glass of apple cider. "Looks like you've got a good-sized bump on your forehead."

Ella touched the bump and winced. "Jah, and it sure does hurt."

"Want me to get some ice for you?"

Before Ella could reply, Jake sauntered up. "You okay, Ella? Need me to get you some ice?"

"I'll live." Ella figured that, as much as her head hurt, Jake's must hurt, too, but she was so irritated with him that she didn't bother to ask.

"You sure?"

"Sure that I'll live or sure that I don't need any ice?"

Jake chuckled. "I was talking about the ice."

"I'm fine. If I need any ice, I'll get it."

"Suit yourself." Jake turned to Jolene,

wearing that same goofy grin he'd had at the schoolhouse the other day. He said something, but his voice was so low, Ella couldn't make out what he'd said.

Ella edged a bit closer to Jolene, hoping she could pick up on their conversation. If Jake even suggested that he give Jolene a ride home tonight, she was prepared to intervene.

"I'm looking forward to next Monday night," Jake said to Jolene, his smile widening. "I think it'll be easier for me to learn signing with your family than it would if I came over to the schoolhouse."

Ella was glad to hear that Jake wouldn't be joining her and Lonnie at the schoolhouse, but she wished he wouldn't spend any time with Jolene. At least they wouldn't be alone.

Jake and Jolene continued to visit, and Ella continued to fume. Once, Jake glanced over at Ella with a strange expression, but then he looked quickly away. Was he deliberately trying to irritate her by talking to Jolene?

Ella was about to interrupt their conversation when someone called her name. She turned. Cara Cummings, one of her

English neighbors, was racing across the room.

"Your dad collapsed in your living room, and your mom asked me to come get you right away!"

CHAPTER 20

I hope whatever happened to my uncle Rueben isn't serious," Andrew said to Eunice as he watched Cara Cummings's car pull away. "Ella's neighbor sounded desperate to take her home, and from the look I saw on Ella's face, I think she feared the worst."

"Maybe it's nothing serious. Maybe Ella's neighbor is just overly alarmed. Some people get that way when someone passes out, you know." Eunice was trying to show Andrew that she was concerned, but he gave her a blank stare and shook his head.

"I don't think Cara was overly alarmed.

She wouldn't have driven clear out here to get Ella if she didn't think the situation was serious." He glanced over to where Jolene sat with Katie and Fern. "I'm going to see if Jolene wants to go over to Ella's with me. If something terrible has happened to her daed, then she'll need our support." Before Eunice could respond, Andrew hurried away. She wished she could have visited with him longer but appreciated the fact that he was so concerned about his family. Andrew would probably make a good husband someday.

～ ※ ～

"I'm glad you suggested that we go over to Ella's," Jolene said to Andrew as their horse and buggy left Topeka and headed down Highway 5. "When I saw Ella leave with Cara in such a hurry I was worried."

Andrew turned in his seat so he was facing her. "I have a hunch Ella's going to need our support."

"Are you saying you think Uncle Rueben might die?"

"Let's just hope for the best." There were deep wrinkles etched in his forehead.

"Instead of hoping, I'd rather pray."

"Jah, we need to do that, too."

Jolene closed her eyes and prayed, *Heavenly Father, please be with Uncle Rueben and the rest of his family.*

⚹⚹

When Cara Cummings's car pulled into the yard, Ella's heart leaped into her throat. A beam of light from the ambulance parked near her house flashed crimson against the barn. Whatever had happened to Papa must be serious, or an ambulance wouldn't have been called.

Ella leaped from the car and raced to the house with her heart hammering so hard she could hear it echo in her head.

When she stepped into the living room, a scream tore from her throat. Papa lay on the floor, pale and unmoving. Two paramedics stood nearby, talking to Charlene, while Mama knelt beside Papa, sobbing as if her heart would break. Ella looked at Larry, who stood beside their younger sisters as though in a daze. "Wh–what happened?" she rasped.

"Papa came into the house after doin' some chores and said he felt kinda funny. Then all of a sudden he clutched at his chest and. . .and he fell on the floor." Larry motioned to the paramedics. "They think

Papa had a heart attack." He swiped at the tears running down his flushed cheeks and sniffed. "They told Mama that Papa is dead."

Ella felt the blood drain from her face. She tried to speak but couldn't make her lips move. A jumble of thoughts tumbled around in her head like a windmill going at full speed. This couldn't be happening. Papa couldn't be dead. There must be some mistake!

CHAPTER 21

Despite Ella's resolve not to break down during Papa's graveside service, salty tears mixed with tepid raindrops and rolled down her cheeks. She sniffed deeply and glanced at Mama, who stood between her and Charlene. Poor Mama's body shook as she leaned on Ella and sobbed. Ella knew that when Papa died, a part of Mama had gone with him. They'd been together over twenty-five years. In all the years Ella had been alive, she'd never heard either of her parents say an unkind word about each other, and only a few times had she heard them disagree on anything.

Ella thought about how Lonnie's uncle, Bishop James Hershberger, and his wife, Sadie, had stopped by their house the other day to offer condolences. *"One generation comes, another passes away,"* the bishop had said. *"Many people miss out on great blessings because they don't understand why God allows certain things. They question Him rather than accepting His will."*

While Papa's casket was being lowered into the ground, Ella prayed. *Lord, I don't know why You took my daed, but please be with us in the days ahead, and help me to accept this as Your will.*

As the seriousness of the situation settled fully into Ella's mind, troubled thoughts tumbled around in her head. Larry wasn't old enough to take over Papa's business, and she didn't know anything about running it except how to do the books. She couldn't expect Charlene to take over everything Papa had done. Mama knew nothing about making wind chimes. Besides, it was all she could do to keep up with household chores and care for the younger children. None of them could take over Papa's wind chime business, so how in the world were they going to support themselves?

Even though many folks from their community had rallied around these past few days, bringing in food and offering to do whatever was needed, it wouldn't be right to expect help from others indefinitely. Not when she was able-bodied and ought to take responsibility for her family's welfare. Charlene was old enough to work outside the home. Maybe if they both got jobs, they could earn enough money to take care of Mama and their siblings. Trouble was, someone really needed to be at home helping Mama and making sure she didn't overdo. Maybe it would be best if Charlene stayed home and Ella found a job.

Ella glanced over at Jolene and Andrew, who stood nearby with their family. She'd been ever so grateful when they'd shown up at her house the night Papa died. Mama had needed her support, and with Andrew and Jolene taking over the responsibility of the children, Ella had been able to concentrate on helping Mama make the necessary arrangements for Papa's body to be taken to the funeral home.

Ella blinked as the crowd of mourners moved away from the gravesite. She'd been so caught up in her thoughts that she hadn't even realized the service was over.

Mama's chin quivered and her eyes glistened with tears as she looked at Ella. "I. . .I know that death is a part of living, but it–it's such a terrible thing."

Ella squeezed Mama's hand. First Raymond had been taken from them, and now Papa. She wondered how much more her family could bear.

Bishop Hershberger, holding a large black umbrella, stepped up to them. *"Da Herr sei mit du."*

The bishop's wife, Sadie, nodded in agreement. "Jah, may the Lord be with you."

He's going to have to be, Ella thought as they moved away from the gravesite. *Because I sure can't take care of my family alone.*

As Ella and her family approached their buggy, she saw Jake, whose rig was parked nearby, glance her way. She wondered if his look of sympathy was genuine or the result of doing what he thought was expected of him.

Turning away, Ella grabbed the reins and backed up her horse. As she led the procession of black buggies toward their house, where the funeral dinner would be served, she made a decision. Tomorrow morning she would look for a job.

❧ ❧

Jake flicked the reins to get his horse and buggy moving and watched the Yoders' rig up ahead. His heart went out to Ella and her family. It couldn't be easy losing someone so close to you. Even with the disagreements that often took place between him and Dad, Jake couldn't imagine not having Dad around.

As he clucked to his horse to make him go faster, Jake made a decision. Even though he and Ella were not on the best of terms, he would find some way to help her family.

CHAPTER 22

The following night, Ella sat on the front porch steps, watching the stars come out. The rain had stopped several hours ago, and dusk had settled over the land like a soft pink blanket.

She drew in a deep breath and released it with a shuddering sigh. With Papa gone, nothing would ever be the same. It didn't look like they'd be able to support themselves. She'd spent most of the day going from store to store in Topeka, looking for a job. She'd been told by each of the store managers that there were no openings. Then she'd gone to Middlebury but found no work there, either. Should she put a notice in places like *The Budget* or *The Connection* and hope to sell off Papa's wind chime supplies? If she did, it could be awhile before she had any response. Since she'd had no luck finding a job in the places she'd been to today, tomorrow she would go to Shipshewana and try her luck there.

She swallowed hard as she stared up at the night sky. "What am I going to do, Lord? If I can't find a job, how am I going to take care of my family?"

She heard only the whistle of the wind under the eaves of the house and the singsong *ribbet, ribbet* of the frogs living near the pond out behind their place.

The screen door creaked, and when Ella glanced over her shoulder, she saw Charlene.

"What are you doing out here by yourself?" Charlene asked, taking a seat beside Ella on the step.

"Just sitting. . .thinking. . .trying to figure out some way to support this *familye*."

"God will take care of our family; you'll see."

Ella choked back a sob and reached up

to touch her head covering. She was sure it was still held firmly in place and needed no adjusting, but it gave her something to do with her hands.

"It's okay to cry, you know. God gave us tear ducts for a reason."

Ella nodded. Her freckle-faced teen-age sister with her big blue eyes and innocent smile suddenly seemed more mature than she was.

Ella's gaze went to Papa's shop at the end of the driveway. "It's hard to understand why God takes some and leaves others." She swallowed hard and drew in a shaky breath. "I mean, Papa always seemed so healthy. For some time now, Mama's been the sickly one. It makes no sense why God took Papa."

"Are you saying you think God should have taken Mama instead?"

"*Nee*, of course not! I just meant that it doesn't make sense the way Papa's heart gave out on him when he seemed so healthy."

"Guess only God knew Papa's heart was weak." Charlene touched Ella's arm. "Do you think Papa's in heaven with Jesus?"

"Jah, I do. Papa was a God-fearing man. He believed in Jesus and tried to live a good Christian life. I'm sure he's in heaven right now, walking the streets of gold and listening to the angels sing."

"I miss him so much. I know Mama does, too." Tears welled in Charlene's eyes, and she sniffed a couple of times. "What'll we do if we can't find jobs, Ella?"

"We'll find something. At least one of us needs to, and I think it ought to be me."

"How come?"

"Because I'm the oldest, and it's my job to take care of our family. Mama needs your help here, doing chores and taking care of the kinner."

Charlene stood, smoothing the wrinkles in her dress. "Can we talk about this later? Right now I think we should go inside and see if Mama needs us for anything."

"You go ahead," Ella said. "I'll be in shortly."

"Okay, but don't sit out here too long. It's getting colder by the minute."

"I'll be fine. Tell Mama I'll be in soon."

The door clicked shut behind Charlene, and Ella went back to brooding. She needed to trust God to take care of them, but she couldn't sit around idly and wait for an answer.

~⚜~

Lonnie paced between his horse's stall and the wall behind him, where he and Pop had placed a stack of hay earlier in the week. It was hard to believe that Rueben Yoder was dead. Lonnie had just seen Rueben a few days ago, when he'd stopped by the hardware store in Shipshewana. Rueben had looked and acted just fine.

It must be hard for Ella and her family to have lost Rueben. He'd been a good man, kind and fair in his business dealings, and he'd never said a harsh word to Lonnie during the time he'd worked for him. *Not like Pop, who's always criticized me.* Lonnie grimaced. *Guess I shouldn't be thinking that way about my own daed. But for the grace of God, it could have been Pop who'd died of a heart attack. Besides, since my accident, Pop has been nicer to me. Maybe it's because he feels sorry for me because I'm deaf.*

Lonnie wondered why it often took a tragedy to make people show kindness and compassion to one another. *Doesn't the Bible teach in John 13 that we are to love one another as Christ loved us? Maybe I haven't been kind enough to Pop. Maybe I should force myself to take more interest in his smelly pigs.* He slowly shook his head. *That doesn't mean I want to help raise and butcher hogs for the rest of my life, though.*

I wish I could find some kind of work that I'd enjoy as much as I did making wind chimes. I wonder what will become of Rueben's business now that he's gone? Lonnie knew that Ella did the books and Charlene worked on assembling the wind chimes, but someone needed to run the operation and tune the chimes.

If I still had my hearing, I could help Ella run the business. Lonnie sank to a bale of hay and slumped against the wall, questioning God yet again as to why he'd lost his hearing.

Suddenly an idea popped into Lonnie's head. Was it a whisper from God or his own wishful thinking? *Maybe I could assemble the chimes, and then Charlene could learn how to tune and cut pieces of pipe. Ella could keep doing the books, and if she needed help ordering parts and supplies, I could help with that, too.*

Lonnie hoped Ella would be open to the idea. He knew how stubborn and independent she could be.

Think I'll stop by and see Ella tomorrow morning, he decided. *Hopefully she'll like my idea.*

CHAPTER 23

After a restless night, Ella decided that the first thing she needed to do after breakfast was to go over Papa's books to get an accurate estimate of where they were financially. Before Papa died, she'd kept the receipt book from their customers' orders up to date, as well as the lists of supplies they had in the shop and supplies they needed to order. Trouble was, only Papa had known exactly how much he actually made and how much was in the bank. Ella needed to be sure they had enough money to live on until she was able to find a job.

"I'll be out in Papa's shop if you need me for anything," Ella said to Charlene.

"Okay," Charlene called as she hurried down the hall, carrying a breakfast tray for Mama.

Ella glanced out the kitchen window. Seeing that it was still raining, she slipped into her jacket and grabbed an umbrella. As she opened the back door, a blast of cold wind hit her in the face. She shivered and decided against opening the umbrella, which would no doubt have turned inside out.

Pulling the collar of her jacket tightly around her neck, Ella dashed across the yard. She entered the shop and had just turned on the gas lights and propane stove, when a deep sense of loss flooded her soul. This was Papa's place. It didn't seem right that he wasn't here, sitting at his workbench with a smile on his face. He'd loved making wind chimes and had taken great care crafting each one.

Tears clouded Ella's vision, and she covered her mouth to stifle a sob. If she missed Papa this much, how must Mama feel?

"I need to get myself under control," she

murmured. "It'll do no good to sit here feeling sorry for myself." Taking a seat at her desk, she opened the bottom drawer and retrieved the ledger, which she hadn't seen since the day before Papa died.

Ella's eyebrows furrowed as she scanned the places of business that carried their wind chimes. "Order Canceled" had been written next to half of the names.

Ella scratched her head. How could that be? She hadn't seen any cancellations when she'd last gotten the mail.

She squinted at the ledger and realized that "order canceled" had been written in Papa's handwriting. Sometime before Papa's death, maybe that same day, he'd picked up the mail and discovered the canceled orders.

Ella's gaze traveled around the room, and she spotted the wind chimes that had already been finished. Maybe it was a good thing some places had canceled their orders, because they didn't have nearly enough chimes to fill all the orders she'd thought they had.

She grimaced. It wouldn't matter if they had one hundred orders; they couldn't fill them—not just her and Charlene. Besides, even if Papa hadn't died, sooner or later he'd have probably lost his business. In these hard economic times it seemed that not so many people wanted wind chimes. Papa had mentioned that their business was slacking off, and he'd been concerned about having enough money to pay all his bills.

Ella let her head fall forward, resting it on the wooden desk. *Dear Lord, please show me what to do.* She stayed like that for several minutes, thinking, praying, and fighting back tears of frustration. She hated being in a situation that seemingly had no answers. She hated feeling so helpless.

Ding! Ding!

Ella jerked her head up and turned. Lonnie stood by the door.

"I hope you weren't busy," he said, speaking louder than usual, she assumed, because he couldn't hear his own voice.

He handed Ella the tablet he'd pulled from inside his jacket, and she quickly wrote him a note: *I came in here to go over the books.* She wished they knew how to sign well enough so that she wouldn't have to write everything down.

"I didn't get to talk to you much at the funeral the other day," Lonnie said. "You were busy with others, and I didn't want to intrude." He paused a few seconds. "With your daed gone, I know things will be difficult for you financially, and I have an idea I wanted to share with you."

Ella swallowed hard. Their financial situation was even worse than he could imagine. *What's your idea?* she wrote.

"I thought maybe I could take over Charlene's job and she could tune the chimes."

That's a nice thought, but it won't work.

"Is it because I can't hear? Because if that's the reason—"

She shook her head and scrawled another note. *Papa's business is in trouble. There are more bills than we have money for, and several places of business have canceled their orders. I'm afraid Papa's business will have to be sold.*

Lonnie's eyebrows drew together. "I'm sorry to hear that. Aren't there some other places you could contact about selling your daed's chimes?"

I don't know of any others, Ella wrote. *Even if there were any who'd be willing to place an order, the three of us could never keep the business going.*

"How can you be sure?"

For one thing, Charlene's tone deaf. She can't even carry a tune when she sings, so she'd never be able to tune the chimes.

"Maybe she could do the books and you could tune the chimes."

That wouldn't work, either. Charlene's not good at math. She'd mess up the books for sure.

He scratched his head. "There has to be someone you could hire who has a good ear for tuning chimes."

We don't have enough money to pay anyone. We've been struggling financially for some time, and now that we've lost several orders, we're in worse shape than ever. Ella stopped writing and squeezed her eyes shut, hoping the action would keep her persistent tears at bay. When she opened them again, Lonnie was staring at her in a curious way. Was it compassion she saw on his face, or something else?

I appreciate your offer, she wrote, *but there's only one thing for me to do.*

"What's that?"

I'm going to send out the wind chimes to the people who have already placed orders, and then I'll have to close the shop and sell everything.

"Then what'll you do? How will your family survive?"

I'll be heading into Shipshe as soon as I'm done here to look for a job.

"Jobs are hard to come by these days."

Ella grimaced. She didn't need that reminder. *I'll find something. I have to.*

～✻～

"Where are you off to in this nasty weather?" Jake's mother asked when he slipped into his jacket and started for the back door.

"I've got a horse to shoe over at Crist Lambright's. Then I'm planning to stop by and see Ella on my way home."

Mom's eyebrows furrowed. "Why would you need to see her?"

"I didn't get to speak with her at the funeral the other day, and I want to offer my condolences." Jake pulled his stocking cap on his head. "Thought I'd ask if they have any chores that need to be done while I'm there."

"I'm sure Ella's family is taking care of

their chores. She does have several siblings, you know."

Jake couldn't believe his mother's clipped tone. "Ella only has five siblings who are living, and they're all younger than her. The little ones can't do heavy chores. Besides, with the exception of Charlene, the kinner will be in school all day."

"I realize that," Mom said with a huff, "but there are others in the community who will help out. With your daed laid up, you've got enough to do right here."

Jake stared hard at his mother. "What's wrong, Mom? You act as though you don't want me to help Ella's family. Doesn't the *Biwel* teach that we're to help our neighbors?"

Mom pursed her lips. "Don't quote scriptures to me, young man. If you had any interest in what the Bible says, you would have joined the church by now!"

Jake jerked his head, feeling as though he'd been slapped. "Now you're talking like Dad. I thought you understood why I haven't made up my mind about becoming Amish yet."

She shook her head. "I've never said I understood it. I've just chosen not to say too much, hoping that if I didn't push you too hard you'd make the right decision."

"The right decision being that I join the church, you mean?"

She shrugged.

"At one time I thought moving home and joining the church was what I wanted, but when Loraine married Wayne—"

"We've been over this before. You can't base your decisions about getting baptized and joining the church on whether someone agrees to marry you." Mom's voice raised a notch, and her cheeks colored to a deep crimson. "It's a commitment to God and to the ways of the church you've grown up in—the church our ancestors of old gave their lives for in martyrdom."

"I know all that, and someday, when I feel the time's right, I'll make my decision about whether to join the church or not." Jake put his hand on the doorknob. "In the meantime, I'm going over to shoe Crist's horse. After that, I'll be heading to the Yoders', and if they need any chores done, I'll do 'em."

"What if Ella won't let you?"

Jake turned to face his mother. "Why wouldn't she let me?"

"Do I need to remind you that every time you and Ella are anywhere near each other, you end up in an argument?" She took a step toward Jake. "Think about it, son. Ella doesn't like you, and I don't think it's a good idea for you to put yourself in a position that could lead to another argument with her—especially when she and her family are grieving for Rueben."

"I won't say anything to upset Ella or anyone else in her family. I just want to let them know that I'm available to help out."

Mom turned her hands palm up, clinging to a dishcloth. "Do as you like, but don't be surprised if Ella says no."

CHAPTER 24

When Ella entered the hardware store in Shipshewana, she spotted her friend Esther behind the counter. Forcing a smile, she stepped up to Esther and said, "I need a job. Is there anything available here right now?"

"I'm afraid not," Esther said with a shake of her head. "I doubt we'll be hiring until spring, and that's only if the economic situation takes a turn for the better."

"Oh, I see." Ella swallowed around the lump in her throat. She was beginning to think she'd never find a job.

"Have you checked at any of the restaurants in town to see about working in the kitchen or waiting tables?" Esther asked.

"I've checked just about everywhere, for every kind of job." Ella turned away from the counter. "I'd better go." She hurried off before Esther could respond.

She'd just entered the corridor between the hardware store and the fabric store, when she saw Katie heading her way.

"I'm surprised to see you out shopping today," Katie said. "I know your mamm took your daed's death pretty hard, and I figured you'd be home with her."

"Charlene's staying with Mama so I can look for a job."

"But you have a job selling wind chimes."

Ella shook her head. "Even if Papa were still here, we'd soon have to close the shop."

"How come?"

Ella explained about the canceled orders and Lonnie's offer to trade jobs with Charlene. "But you see," she said, "even if Charlene could tune the chimes, we can't continue to operate if we can't find places to buy and sell our chimes." She rubbed the bridge of her nose and blinked. She would not give in to her tears.

Katie slipped her arm around Ella's waist. "Are you okay?"

"I'm afraid I won't be able to find work and that I'll let my family down."

"Whenever I get frightened and think I might have another panic attack, I remind myself that these are just feelings and that they'll soon pass. I know that the sooner I focus on God and His power, the faster I'll see relief from my fears." Katie gently patted Ella's back. "God will give you the strength for each new day. Remember, you don't have to bear your burdens alone. Your family and friends are here to help in any way we can. One of the reasons we Amish survive is because we rely on God and one another."

Ella sniffed and dabbed at her eyes. "I appreciate that reminder."

"I thought I'd go to the Blue Gate for lunch today. Would you like to join me?" Katie asked. "It might lift your spirits a little."

"Danki for the offer, but I've been gone quite awhile and need to get home and check on Mama. When I left home this morning, she was still in bed and hadn't eaten any breakfast."

"I'm sure it'll take some time for her to

come to grips with your daed's death." A look of sadness passed over Katie's face, but it was quickly replaced with a smile. "When Timothy died, I thought my life was over, but now I have Freeman, and we're very happy."

"Are you suggesting that my mamm will fall in love and get married again?" Just the thought of Mama being with some other man made Ella's skin prickle.

Katie shook her head. "I'm not saying that at all. I just meant that in time the pain won't be so intense and your mamm will be able to laugh again."

Ella sighed. "It's not just Mama grieving over Papa that worries me. She's struggled with health issues ever since Raymond died, and stress seems to make it worse."

"I know what you mean about that. One thing you need to remember is that God doesn't want you to worry. He wants you to trust Him in all things."

"Sometimes that's easier said than done."

"One of the scriptures that helped me the most when I was having panic attacks is Isaiah 41:10: 'Fear thou not; for I am with thee: be not dismayed; for I am thy God: I will strengthen thee; yea, I will help thee; yea, I will uphold thee with the right hand of my righteousness.'"

Tears sprang to Ella's eyes despite her resolve to remain in control. "Danki for those words. I'll try to remember."

~≪ ≫~

As Jake neared the Yoders' place, he rehearsed what he was going to say to Ella. He hoped she'd be cordial when he offered his help. After their encounter during the volleyball game, he wasn't sure what to expect.

Maybe I won't have to talk to Ella, Jake thought. *Maybe she'll be busy with something and her mamm will answer the door.*

As Jake turned his horse and buggy up the Yoders' driveway, a giant puddle came into view. When the water splashed up, his horse whinnied and tossed its head.

"Aw, quit acting like a boppli," Jake hollered. "You've been through plenty of mud puddles before."

The horse whinnied again and plodded up the driveway as if he was in no hurry to get where they were going.

"I'd have been better off if I'd left you at

home and driven my truck today," Jake mumbled. To keep the peace at home he'd parked his truck behind the barn and had been driving the horse and buggy most places. If he had to travel any farther than fifteen miles, he used the truck, regardless of how Dad felt about the vehicle. He also used it whenever he had to go anywhere to shoe a horse. It was easier and cheaper than hiring a driver to haul him and his shoeing tools around.

Jake didn't understand the way Dad carried on over him owning a truck. Many young people in their community who hadn't joined the church owned cars and trucks. Jake figured Dad's irritation had more to do with his having moved to Montana than it did with him driving a motorized vehicle.

When Jake entered the Yoders' yard, he spotted Charlene hanging clothes on the line. He stopped the horse, tied it to the hitching rail, and sprinted across the yard to join her. "Is your mamm at home?" he asked.

Charlene nodded and motioned to the house. "She's in bed, though, and I don't want to disturb her."

Jake figured after the ordeal Verna and her family had just been through she was probably exhausted, but it did surprise him to hear that she was still in bed this late in the day. "Is Ella here?" he asked.

"Huh-uh. She went to Shipshe to look for a job."

"Won't she continue to work in the wind chime shop?"

Charlene shook her head. "Not with Papa gone. We could never keep the place going on our own. Is there something I can help you with?"

"Actually, I'm here to help you." Jake cleared his throat a couple of times. "I mean, I was wondering if you need my help with anything."

Charlene gave a slow nod and pointed to the barn. "The horses have been fed already, but their stalls need to be mucked out."

"No problem. I'll take care of that right now. When I'm done, if there's anything else you need me to do, just say the word."

"That's so nice of you, Jake. There's a lot we could use help with around here." Charlene smiled sweetly. "I think my sister's wrong about you."

Jake was on the verge of asking Charlene to be specific about what she'd meant but changed his mind. He already knew what Ella thought of him, so he didn't need to hear whatever Charlene might say that would confirm the fact. Instead of asking any questions about Ella, Jake headed determinedly for the barn.

～⋇～

As soon as Ella pulled into her yard, she spotted a horse tied to their hitching rail with an open buggy parked nearby. *Who'd be using an open buggy in this chilly weather?* she wondered.

She glanced around the yard but saw no sign of anyone. A line full of clothes flapped in the breeze, so Charlene had done what she'd been asked and gotten the laundry done. She must be inside, visiting with whoever had come to pay them a call.

Ella unhitched her horse, Pet, from the buggy and led her to the barn. When she drew near the horse's stall, she halted. Jake was inside, spreading fresh straw on the floor.

"What are you doing here?" Ella's voice came out in a squeak.

"Came to help out." Jake reached for Pet's bridle and led her into the stall before Ella could respond.

She flopped onto a bale of hay inside the stall and stared at the floor. "Who said we needed your help with anything?"

"Charlene did. When I told her I came to help, she said the stalls needed to be mucked out."

"We can manage the chores on our own, Jake."

His boots stopped in front of her, and she was forced to look up. "Not to worry; I'll help whether you want me to or not because I know things have to be really hard for you right now." He stepped forward as if to comfort her, but she leaned away.

Jake grunted and took a step back. "What's your problem, Ella?"

She lifted her hand in exasperation. "Don't you understand? We don't need your help!"

"Sure you do." He moved close to the stall door and made a sweeping gesture of the barn. "Lots of chores need be done here, not to mention other areas around your place."

"We'll get them done without your help."

Ella's cheeks burned like fire. No one had ever been able to get under her skin the way Jake did.

"Look, Ella, I just want to be your friend."

"Jah, right. False friends are like dandelions—they're found everywhere."

Jake held his palms down, as if trying to calm a nervous horse. "I'm not a false friend."

Ella tapped her foot as her impatience mounted. "Just leave, Jake. I'm getting tired of saying this. We don't need your help! We can manage on our own!"

Jake didn't budge. As he stared at her, the silence between them grew thick like a heavy blanket of fog.

After several moments of deafening quiet, Ella spoke again. "If you won't leave, then I will." She stood up so quickly that she lost her balance. *Thunk*—she bumped her head on Jake's chin.

"Yeow!" they both hollered.

Ella grimaced and rubbed the top of her head. "The last bump you gave me is barely healed, and now I've got another one!"

Jake stuck out his tongue and swished it from side to side. "Why don't you watch what you're doin', Ella? You made me bite my tongue!"

"Sorry," they said in unison.

Jake reached out as if he might touch her, but then he quickly jumped back. "Are—are you okay?"

"I'm fine. You'd better go now, before any more damage is done."

He shook his head and folded his arms. "I'm not leaving. I started a job, and I aim to finish it."

Ella exhaled a puff of frustration. "Fine then, do whatever you like!" With her back straight and her head held high, she left the stall and walked out of the barn.

❧ ❧

Jolene glanced at the clock on her classroom wall. The school day would be over soon, and she felt frustrated because there was so much more she wished to teach. Both Sylvia and Irvin had been quite attentive today. She was pleased at how well they were learning to read lips. As she'd prepared her lesson for the children, she remembered what her aunt had taught her about a deaf person being very alert to the expression of people. Jolene knew she'd have to remember to make her facial

expressions be one of the ways she com-
municated with the children. When she
said, "Sit down" or "Pay attention," it had
to show on her face.

Today she had worked on voiceless
consonants: *h*; *wh*; *p*; *t*; *k*; *ca*; *co*; *cu*; *ck*,
which to her surprise, the children had
seemed to understand quite well. A few
minutes ago, she'd given them each an
easy-reading fiction book. They seemed
quite content, and Sylvia even giggled
when she read something humorous.

When Jolene saw Irvin chuckle, she was
even more surprised. She left her desk
and went to see what he thought was so
funny.

Wearing a big grin, Irvin looked up at
her then pointed to a page in his book and
said, "There are many black cows, but
they all give white milk."

"Good job, Irvin." Jolene signed as she
spoke. She smiled and patted the top of
his head. It was so good to see that he
was not only learning, but actually seemed
to enjoy being in school. Now if she could
just get through to Jake's brother Kyle.
When she'd given Fern's class another
lesson on signing this morning, Kyle still

hadn't participated. But at least he hadn't made any trouble. She guessed that was something to be grateful for.

When Jolene dismissed Irvin and Sylvia to go home a short time later, she reached into her desk and pulled out a hand mirror. Lonnie would be coming by for another lesson today, and since she was sure Ella wouldn't be here, she decided to work with Lonnie on lip reading.

Jolene had just placed the mirror on her desk when Eunice entered the room.

"Hello, Jolene. I was wondering if you could do something for me."

"What's that?"

Eunice's cheeks colored. She leaned on Jolene's desk, as if needing it for support. "Well, you see. . ." She paused and moistened her lips with the tip of her tongue. "I'd like to learn how to sign, but I don't want anyone to know about it—especially Andrew."

"How come?"

The crimson color that had splashed over Eunice's cheeks deepened. "I. . . uh. . .want it to be a surprise. Would you be willing to teach me to sign and not tell anyone?"

Jolene didn't understand Eunice's reason for wanting to keep it a secret, but she nodded and said, "If you'd like to come by here on Friday afternoon, we can begin then."

"And you won't tell anyone?"

"It'll be our little secret."

A look of relief flooded Eunice's face. "Danki, Jolene."

Eunice turned and was almost to the door when Lonnie stepped in. Jolene didn't know whether Eunice had said anything to him or not, because Eunice's back was to her now.

When Eunice left the room, Jolene moved aside so Lonnie could sit at her desk. Then she smiled and pointed to the blackboard, where she'd written him a message: *Today, we're going to begin learning how to read lips, since you'll need that in order to communicate with others who can hear.*

Apprehension flickered in Lonnie's eyes. "Not sure I'm ready for that."

Yes, you are, she wrote. *If you're going to communicate with hearing people, then you need to be able to read lips.* How many times had she told him this already?

Was he just being stubborn, or didn't he get it?

"I stopped by to see Ella today and suggested that I do Charlene's job of putting the wind chimes together so Charlene could tune and cut the pipe," Lonnie said, suddenly changing the subject. "Ella said that won't work because Charlene's tone deaf and can't tune chimes. She also said her daed's business is in trouble and will have to close, so she's going out to look for a job today."

Jolene grimaced. In these hard times, things were bad enough, but now with Uncle Rueben gone, Ella had a lot of responsibility on her shoulders. What she really needed was a job that would keep her at home where she could look out for her mother. But what kind of a job could it be?

CHAPTER 25

When Lonnie entered Freeman's bike shop to see about getting a new tube for the flat tire on his bike, Jake was talking to Freeman. Not wishing to interrupt, Lonnie dropped to his knees and began to pet Freeman's dog, Penny. Every time Lonnie visited the bike shop, the cocker spaniel was either sleeping on the braided rug near the door or making a pest of herself with the ball she kept dropping at the customers' feet.

Lonnie glanced over at Freeman and Jake and wondered what they were saying. Since Jake was turned toward him, he tried to read his lips. It was good practice to do so. Jolene had told him that during one of their lessons. Lonnie was no expert on lip reading yet, but he was pretty sure Jake had said something about Jolene. He kept watching Jake's lips. Had he said something about asking Jolene out?

Lonnie wondered if he should try to discourage Jolene from seeing Jake. While Jake seemed like a nice enough fellow, Lonnie had heard that Jake had trouble staying in one place. Lonnie was just beginning to get to know Jolene, and she seemed like a nice young woman. If she was interested in Jake, then she'd be hurt if he left Indiana.

A few more customers entered the shop, and Lonnie began to feel uncomfortable about watching Jake's lips. *Guess it's really none of my business what Jake says or does,* he decided. *I have enough of my own problems to deal with.*

Penny's tail swished against Lonnie's arm, so he turned his attention to her again. The dog's mouth opened, and as she pressed her body against him, Lonnie actually felt the vibration of her bark. This surprised him, because until he'd lost his hearing, he'd taken for granted the things he could feel, taste, smell, and see. When he'd first found out he was deaf, one of his nurses had told him that his other senses would become stronger. He guessed she'd been right.

The dog swished her tail again, snatched Lonnie's stocking cap, and tore across the room. Lonnie couldn't let the mutt have his hat; it had been a Christmas gift from Mom. He took off after the dog, waving his hands. "Give me back my cap!"

Penny zipped to the left, and then to the right, with Lonnie right on her heels. Freeman stopped talking to Jake and got in on the chase. Round and round the room they went, until the dog darted in between a row of bikes. Lonnie made a lunge for his cap, which was still hanging from the dog's mouth. He missed, and the bikes toppled over, landing on the floor.

Lonnie's face heated. "I'm so sorry, Freeman. I hope nothing broke."

Freeman said something, but Lonnie couldn't tell what. All eyes seemed to be on him, which made him feel even more embarrassed than he already was. He leaned in between the bikes, grabbed his cap, and raced out the door.

❧ ❧

For the last several days Ella had kept so busy doing chores and trying to help Mama cope that she hadn't had time to continue looking for a job. She'd gone to the bank the other day and now knew that it wouldn't be long until they were out of money. They might have to start selling off things like she'd seen some other people do because of a job loss.

Ella removed the tea kettle from the stove and took a seat between Mama and Charlene at the table. As much as she dreaded it, they needed to discuss a few things.

"I need to tell you something, Mama," Ella said as she handed her mother a cup of tea.

Mama looked at Ella with a pained expression. "Not more bad news, I hope."

Ella swallowed around the lump in her throat. She wished she didn't have to tell Mama the truth about their financial situation. "I'm afraid it is bad news. After looking through Papa's books the other day, I discovered that several wind chime orders had been canceled. Since then, I've been to the bank and discovered that we have very little money left in our account." Ella blinked hard to keep her tears from flowing. "Between that and the fact that Charlene and I can't run the shop by ourselves, I've come to the conclusion that after we send out the few orders we have, we'll need to close the shop."

Mama sat staring at her cup. Ella wondered if she'd even heard.

Charlene's face turned crimson, and she slammed her hand on the table so hard that it jiggled their cups. "It's not fair that we lost Papa so unexpectedly! Do we have to lose his business, too?"

"Lots of things in life aren't fair, but. . ." Mama paused and blew her nose on her napkin. *"Mer muss ausbeharre bis ans end."*

"Why must we bear it until the end, Mama?" Charlene's eyes flashed angrily, no longer the calm young woman she'd been the other evening. "Why doesn't God bring only good things to the people who follow Him?"

Lines of strain etched Mama's face as

she reached over and touched Charlene's arm. "God didn't promise that His people would never suffer. Tribulations are part of living in this sinful world."

Ella marveled at her mother's wise remark. Despite the grief Mama had been dealing with, she was ministering to her hurting daughter. Mama truly was a remarkable woman, and that made Ella even more determined to take care of her and the rest of the family. Until she found a job, Ella would find it difficult to be hopeful, but she knew for her family's sake that she must remain positive.

She pushed away from the table. "I think I ought to get the dishes done. We can talk about our financial situation some other time."

"I believe you're right. If we all think about this for a while, maybe one of us will come up with a plan." Mama stood. "It's a chilly evening. I think I'll take my tea and go to the living room so I can sit by the fire." She walked out, leaving Ella and Charlene alone.

Ella moved over to the sink and pulled a dirty kettle into the water where she'd placed some other dishes to soak. As she scrubbed the pot vigorously, soapy water cascaded over her hands and dripped back into the sink. It felt good to keep busy. It was the only thing that kept her from breaking down in a puddle of tears.

"You want me to dry, or are you gonna let the dishes drain?" Charlene asked.

Ella shrugged. "It doesn't really matter. If you'd like to join Mama in the living room, that's fine with me. Just be sure you don't say anything that might upset her."

Charlene thrust out her lower lip as she frowned. "I'm not gonna do or say anything to upset Mama, and you need to quit bein' so bossy."

"Someone has to be in charge now that Papa's gone. As the oldest, it's my job to look out for Mama and see that our family is taken care of."

Charlene opened her mouth like she might say more, but then she closed it and left the room.

Ella grabbed another kettle and sloshed the sponge around as she blinked back tears of anger and frustration. *Oh, Papa,* she silently cried. *I miss you so much.*

The back door banged, causing Ella to jump. Either Charlene had gone outside, or someone had come into the house.

❦

When Jolene entered her aunt's kitchen with Loraine and Katie, she wasn't surprised to find Ella in front of the sink with a sponge in her hand. Ever since Jolene could remember, Ella had always kept busy. Even when they were young girls, Ella thought she needed to be working when she should have been playing. She was the kind of person who always seemed to put other people's needs ahead of her own.

"We came to see how you're doing," Jolene said, stepping up to Ella so she could see her face. Loraine and Katie moved close to the sink, too.

"I'm doing as well as can be expected." Ella's smile appeared to be forced; there was no laughter behind her eyes. "If you'd like to have a seat at the table, I'll pour us some tea."

Everyone took seats, and Ella served the tea, along with a loaf of freshly baked friendship bread.

Jolene's fingers curled around the handle of the warm cup. It felt like old times, the four cousins sitting together. Only they weren't innocent young girls anymore. One of them was married and expecting a baby; one was on the brink of marriage; and the other two had a lot of responsibility on their shoulders.

Loraine transferred her cup from one hand to the other, while Katie blotted her lips with a napkin. "This bread is really good, Ella. You're better at baking than anyone I know."

"Danki." Ella smiled, although again, it appeared to be forced. She was obviously putting up a brave front, but Jolene knew her cousin was hurting.

"Is there anything we can do to help you?" Loraine asked. Jolene was glad everyone faced her, even when they spoke to Ella.

Ella's eyes filled with tears. She blinked rapidly, as though trying to keep herself from crying. "Guess the thing we need most is a lot of prayer, because short of a miracle, we'll soon be out of money."

"What do you mean?" Katie asked.

Ella told them about her dad's business and how there was no way she and Charlene could keep it going. "So I need to find a job," she said. "Unfortunately, none of the places I've been to so far are hiring right now."

Everyone agreed that they would pray for Ella's family, and then they sat quietly together, drinking their tea and eating the friendship bread.

Soon after Jolene had taken a second piece of bread and covered it with butter, an idea popped into her head. "I think I know a way you can make some money," she said, smiling at Ella.

"What's that?" Ella asked, slouching in her chair.

"Why don't open a home-based bakery? You could sell fresh baked goods to others in our community and to the tourists."

Ella blinked a couple of times and sat up straight. "You really think I could do that?"

"I don't see why not."

"I agree with Jolene," Loraine said. "With your baking skills, I'll bet in no time you'd have all kinds of business."

"Oh, I don't know. There are so many things I'd have to do first, and there's really no place for a bakeshop in the house."

"Maybe you could use your daed's shop," Katie suggested. "It'll be empty after you sell off your daed's things."

Ella tapped her fingers along the edge of the table. "The building would need a lot of work to turn it into a bakeshop. We'd have to buy an oven, a refrigerator, a bakery cabinet, and so many other things."

"You'd also need to have the place inspected by the health department and get the proper license," Loraine put in. "It would take some doing, but if it's God will, then I'm sure it'll all work out."

Ella tugged her earlobe. "I'm not sure it would work, but I'll give it some thought."

"And don't forget to pray," Jolene said with a smile. "Remember now, we'll all be praying with you."

CHAPTER 26

Ella filled the sink with hot water and added some detergent. A glint of light shone through the kitchen window from the full moon outside. She was relieved that the day was almost over. She was eager to get the dishes done and head upstairs to her room. She would need to rise with the call of the rooster tomorrow morning, for there'd be plenty of chores waiting for her to do before breakfast. She and Charlene would keep busy the rest of the day, painting the barn.

"I don't know about you, but I'm all done

in," Charlene said as she pulled a clean dish towel from the drawer.

Ella nodded. "I've always enjoyed baking before, but since I opened the bakeshop two weeks ago, it seems like all I do is bake and wait on customers."

"But your business is doing well, and it's already making us some money. Isn't that so?"

"Jah, and I'm grateful for the money that some in our community donated so I could buy everything I needed to get the business going. The only problem is, I'm kept so busy with the bakeshop that I can't keep up with all the chores that need to be done around here, which is why I'll be closing the shop tomorrow in order to paint the barn." Ella smiled at Charlene. "I appreciate the way you've taken over so many of the household chores, waited on customers, and have even helped with some of the baking. If Mama felt better, I'm sure she'd do more, too."

Charlene's nose crinkled. "Do you think there's something seriously wrong with Mama? Should we insist that she see the doctor?"

Ella dipped her hands into the soapy water and picked up another dish. "I don't think we can insist that Mama do anything. But we do need to keep praying about the matter, and I may ask Aunt Priscilla to speak with Mama again, too."

"Good idea. Let's hope she'll listen this time."

⁓ ❧

Several buckets of white paint sat in the driveway along with a bucket of water for cleaning brushes and rollers. Ella had put Larry and Amelia in charge of the younger siblings so Mama could rest. Charlene would paint the lower half of the barn, while Ella climbed the ladder and did the upper half, since Charlene was afraid of heights.

"It's too cold to be doing this," Charlene complained. "I'd rather be inside where it's warm and toasty."

"You'll warm up once you start working." Ella motioned to the bucket of paint near Charlene. "Now get busy and stop complaining."

Charlene frowned. "You're bossing me around again, and I don't like it!"

"I wouldn't boss you at all if you did what you're supposed to do." Ella grabbed her paint bucket and a brush and then scurried up the ladder. Truthfully, she didn't like the idea of painting the barn any more than Charlene, but it needed to be done. Complaining wouldn't help. If Papa hadn't died, he'd have had the barn painted already. Just a few days before his death, he'd told Ella that he wanted to get the painting done before winter set in.

Ella swallowed around the lump that seemed to be clogging her throat a good deal of the time these days and forced herself to concentrate on what she was doing. With each stroke of the brush, she reminded herself that she was doing this for Papa.

Ella had just started painting around the opening of the loft when she heard the familiar rumble of buggy wheels. She looked down and saw Jake climb out of his buggy. He tied his horse to the hitching rail, walked toward the barn, and looked up at her. "What are you doing up there?" he hollered.

"What's it look like?" she called in return.

"Looks like you're tryin' to paint the barn."

"I'm not trying; I *am* painting the barn."

"You should have asked for help."

"Charlene's helping me."

Jake looked around. "She's not here now."

"She probably went to the house for a few minutes."

"If you'll come down off that ladder, I'll take your place."

Ella stiffened. Jake had no right to tell her what to do. She clamped her teeth tightly together and kept painting.

"If you won't come down, then I guess I'll do some painting down here, 'cause it looks to me like Charlene didn't finish what she started."

Ella clenched the paintbrush so tightly that her fingers turned numb. Did Jake really want to help, or was he just trying to irritate her? She slapped another blob of paint on the barn and didn't look down.

"You've got a lot on your shoulders these days," Jake called. "I know it can't be easy, and you shouldn't be expected to do everything alone."

Ella ignored him and kept painting until Charlene showed up and hollered, "Mama's up from her nap, and she set some doughnuts and hot coffee on the table.

Why don't you take a break and come inside for a while?"

"In a minute. I want to finish what I started up here before I take a break."

"Does that invitation for doughnuts and coffee include me?" Jake asked.

"Jah, sure," Charlene said sweetly. "You're more than welcome to join us, and I appreciate you taking over my job of painting."

Ella almost gagged. Why was Charlene being so nice to Jake? Didn't she realize he couldn't be trusted? More than likely, he'd come over here to make himself look good in his folks' eyes. He probably thought his dad would be nicer to him if he knew Jake had come here to help. Well, if Jake was going in the house, then Ella was going there, too. She couldn't take the chance that he'd say or do something to upset Mama—or that he'd flirt with Charlene. It seemed as if Jake liked to flirt with every young woman he knew—everyone but Ella. Well, that was fine with her! If Jake ever tried to flirt with her, she'd be quick to put him in his place.

When Ella finished painting around the

opening of the loft, she shifted her paintbrush to the other hand and slowly descended the ladder. She'd only gone down
a few rungs when her foot slipped. She
lost her grip on the bucket, and it fell. When
she tried to catch hold of it, the ladder
wobbled. Ella shouted for Charlene to hold
it steady, but it was too late—Ella and the
ladder tumbled to the ground.

CHAPTER 27

Sprawled on the ground, with one foot wedged against the ladder and wet paint running down one arm, Ella stared up at Jake with a bewildered expression. "Wh–what happened?"

"The ladder toppled, and you fell. I tried to catch you, but your foot hit me in the head, and I lost my balance." Jake dropped to his knees beside her. "Are you hurt? Do you think anything's broken?"

She gave a noncommittal grunt and winced as she tried to sit up. "My. . .my head's throbbing, and so's my arm."

Jake held his hand gently against her

shoulder. "Don't move. You might have a broken bone."

"Jake's right; your arm—especially your wrist—is beginning to swell, and I'll bet it's broken." Charlene bent close to Ella, her eyes huge.

"It can't be broken." Tears glistened in Ella's eyes. "How am I supposed to bake if my arm is broken?"

"Let's not put the buggy before the horse," Jake said. "We need to get you to the doctor so we know if it's broken. Then you can worry about how you're going to do any baking." He reached up to rub his forehead.

"Are you okay?" Charlene asked, bending close to Jake.

"It's nothing; just a little bump is all." He looked at Ella and said, "I'm starting to get used to bumps on the head."

Just then, Verna, Ella's mother, came running out of the house. "Ach! What happened to you, Ella? I looked out the kitchen window and saw you lying on the ground."

"She fell off the ladder," Jake explained. "Her wrist is really swollen, and I think her arm might be broken."

The look Ella shot Jake was as chilling

as the crisp fall air. "I can speak for myself, Jake Beechy."

Verna looked up at the barn then back at Ella. "I knew this painting job was too much for my girls. I should have insisted that we ask some of the men we know to paint the barn for us."

"I'll take Ella into the house, and we'll get some ice to put on her arm," Jake said, looking at Verna. "If you or Charlene will go out to your phone shed and call one of your drivers to take us to the hospital, Ella can have her arm looked at."

Verna bobbed her head. "That's a good idea. I'm glad you're here, Jake. You're thinking more clearly than the rest of us right now." She patted Ella's shoulder. "I'll call Marge Nelson and see if she's free to take us to the hospital."

Without hesitation, Jake bent down, scooped Ella into his arms, and started across the yard.

"What do you think you're doing?" she screeched.

"I'm taking you to the house."

"Put me down! It's not my leg that's broken. I'm perfectly capable of walking to the house by myself."

"You're full of *hochmut*, you know that?"

"I am not full of pride. Now put me down!"

"No, I'm going to carry you."

"No, you're not!"

Ella's lips may have told Jake no, but he could tell she was in no shape to walk on her own, so he kept hold of her as he continued walking toward the house.

"Did you hear what I said?"

"I heard you, but I'm not putting you down." Jake quickened his steps. "You had a nasty bump on the head, and you might get dizzy and pass out if you try to walk."

"Jake's right," Charlene agreed as she hurried along beside them. "You hit your head pretty hard, and you could have a concussion like the one you had when you were in that horrible van accident."

Ella opened her mouth like she might say something more, but then she quickly clamped it shut. When Jake felt her body begin to relax, he smiled and stepped onto the porch.

~⚹~

Jolene hauled several braided throw rugs out to the porch and draped them over the railing. She'd just picked up the broom to beat the dust from the rugs when a pickup truck barreled up the driveway. It stopped near the house, and Jake got out. Why was he driving his truck instead of his horse and buggy?

"Hello, Jake," Jolene said when he stepped onto the porch. "I'm surprised to see you this afternoon."

"I came by to tell you about Ella."

"What about her?"

He leaned against the porch railing, but when his hip touched one of the rugs, he pulled quickly away. "Ella fell off the ladder when she was trying to paint her daed's barn."

Jolene gasped. "That's baremlich! Is she hurt badly?"

"Not as bad as she could have been, but the terrible thing is she did break her arm." Jake's eyebrows pulled together. "When Verna couldn't get ahold of their driver, I went home and got my truck so I could drive Ella to the hospital. Then I waited there with Verna until Ella had her arm set in a cast." He thumped his chin a couple of times. "Ella's really worried about how she'll keep up with that bake-shop of hers now that she only has the use of one hand."

"Maybe I can help out after I'm done teaching in the afternoons," Jolene said.

Jolene's mother came out the door just then and stepped up to Jolene. "I heard what you said, and I think helping Ella would be too much for you."

"How come?"

"Because you're already overextending yourself with the signing lessons you're teaching after school." Mom touched Jolene's arm. "I've got more time on my hands than you do, so I'll go over to Ella's and help out with the baking a few times a week. I'm sure that once the word gets out, others will help, too."

"I hope Ella's more receptive to their help than she was with mine today. If she'd gotten off that ladder when I asked her to and let me paint the upper part of the barn, she wouldn't have fallen." Jake grimaced. "She's the most stubborn, determined woman I know." He motioned to Jolene. "Nothing at all like you."

"I don't know about that," Jolene replied.

"I can be pretty determined and stubborn, too—just in a different way than my cousin."

~❦ ❦~

Ella struggled to keep her eyes open as she reclined on the sofa. The prescription pain medication made her drowsy. It was hard to focus on Mama, Charlene, and the younger children who were gathered around her, wearing anxious expressions.

"Does your arm hurt a lot?" Sue Ann asked.

Ella forced a smile, not wishing to frighten her six-year-old sister. "Not so much." But her whole arm had throbbed until the medication had taken effect.

Mama took a seat on the sofa beside Ella and motioned to her cast. "I'm awfully sorry that you fell and broke your arm, but I'm grateful you weren't seriously hurt. Don't think I could deal with another tragedy in this family."

"Me, neither," Charlene put in. "Our family needs some happy times."

Ella blinked back stinging tears. Because of her carelessness in coming down the ladder, she'd almost brought more grief to her family. She thanked the Lord that she hadn't been seriously injured. "I'm sorry. I should have been more careful."

"You shouldn't have been paintin' the barn at all," Larry chimed in. "I'll bet Jake would've helped sooner if you'd asked, and so would some of the other men in our community."

Ella grimaced. She didn't want to rely on others for help, and she didn't want Jake hanging around. The next time they needed help, if she couldn't do it, she'd ask someone else.

CHAPTER 28

The days sped by with the delicate shifting of fall into winter. Ella had finally resigned herself to the fact that she needed to accept help from her family and friends. Everyone but Jake, that is. Her irritation mounted every time he came over and offered his help. Charlene said Ella ought to be willing to accept anyone's help no matter how she felt about them personally. Ella knew her sister was right, but it was hard to accept help from Jake when she knew he'd be going back to Montana soon and would leave his family in the lurch.

Ella was also afraid that Jolene might

have fallen into Jake's trap. Due to the signing lessons, Jolene had seen a lot of him lately and had told Ella that she was excited about the possibility of Jake and Andrew taking turns signing the message for the deaf people at church. Obviously, Jolene didn't realize that Jake wouldn't be sticking around. He'd probably fed her a bunch of lies, the way he had Loraine. The sparkle in Jolene's eyes whenever she talked about Jake was enough to make Ella sick. He had her believing he was a nice person, but she didn't really know him. Not the way Ella did.

"I wish he'd leave Indiana right now," Ella fumed as she opened the oven to check the bread she had baking. The intense heat from the oven hit her in the face and made her feel dizzy. Seeing that the bread wasn't done, she quickly shut the door. She was glad that she had the cast off her arm now and could at least do more things on her own.

Tap. Tap. Tap.

"Someone's at the door!" Charlene hollered from the living room, where she'd gone to dust and clean windows.

Ella dropped her potholders to the counter and went to answer the door. When she opened it, she was surprised to find Jake standing on the porch, holding a purple and white African violet with lacy edges.

"Guder mariye. Figured I'd catch you here before you opened your bakeshop for the day." Jake grinned and handed Ella the plant.

"Morning." She stared at the African violet. "Who's this for?"

"I bought it for you. Charlene said you liked African violets, so I figured you might like this one."

Ella's brows puckered. Was Jake trying to butter her up? Did he think she might put in a good word for him where Jolene was concerned?

"That frown you're wearing makes me think you don't like African violets," he said.

"It's not that. I just wondered why you'd buy me a plant."

"Just told you—Charlene said you liked African violets. You've been so down lately, and I figured it might put a smile on your face."

"Okay, well—danki." Ella took the plant and started to close the door, but Jake stuck the toe of his boot inside, which kept the door from closing. "It's cold out here. Aren't you going to invite me in for a cup of hot coffee?"

Ella contemplated his request. She wanted to tell him to head for home, but that would be rude. Besides, she'd have to answer to Mama if she sent Jake off in this chilly weather without something warm to drink.

She brushed some flour from her apron and opened the door wider. "Follow me."

When they entered the kitchen, Ella set the plant on the counter and took two cups down from the cupboard. By the time she'd placed a pot of coffee on the table, Jake had removed his jacket and stocking cap and taken a seat.

He sniffed the air. "Something sure smells good in here. Have you got something baking in the oven?"

"It's friendship bread. I sell more of that than anything else in my bakeshop." She motioned to some loaves cooling on the counter. "Would you like some to go with your coffee?"

"Sure, that sounds good, but let me cut it for you." Jake jumped up, cut several slices, placed them on a plate, and set it on the table.

"Danki," Ella mumbled, and then she took a seat two chairs away from him.

~⋇⋇~

Jake picked up a piece of the bread, and his mouth watered when he took the first bite. "Umm. . .this tastes *wunderbaar.*"

"I'm glad you like it," Ella mumbled, staring at the table. Why did she always avoid looking at him?

They sat silently as the minutes ticked by. If Jake had known what to say, he would have offered more conversation.

Finally, Ella pushed back her chair and hurried over to the stove. "I need to check on my bread."

"Need any help with that?"

"No, thanks. I can manage." Ella grabbed a potholder and opened the oven door. She removed some nicely browned loaves and placed them on the cooling racks she'd set on the counter.

"How come you're baking in here and not in your bakeshop?"

"I sometimes do my baking here in the mornings before going out to the shop. Having the oven on for a while helps warm the kitchen without having to light the stove we normally use for heat."

"Guess that makes sense. Is there anything you'd like me to do while I'm here?" Jake asked. "I've got a few hours before I have to be back home."

She shook her head. "I can't think of a thing that needs to be done."

Jake had a hard time believing that, but he decided not to push it. He glanced at the counter across the room. "I'd like to buy a loaf of that bread, and also some doughnuts if you have some to sell."

"I have some doughnuts in the shop," she said, "but there'll be no charge."

"How come?"

"With all the chores you've done around here in the last few weeks, I should pay you."

"No way! You need to make a living."

"We're getting along okay, and I won't take any money from you today."

Jake took a drink of coffee as he pondered things. Ella's fierce independence both amused and irritated him. He wondered what was behind her unwillingness to accept his help or his money. Was she

like that with everyone or just him? Whenever he said anything to her, she acted so
defensive, and he was getting tired of it.
"Ferwas bischt allfat so schtarkeppich?"
he asked.

Her lips puckered as she glared at him.
"Why am *I* always so stubborn? You're the
one who's stubborn. Stubborn and. . ."

"Jah, well, I'm stubborn because my
daed taught me to be that way. He's the
most stubborn man I know."

She smiled, but he suspected she was
gritting her teeth and wishing he would go.

"I'll tell you what," he said, carefully
choosing his words. "I'll accept the bread,
but I insist on paying for the doughnuts."

To his relief, Ella gave a quick nod then
quickly launched into telling him about the
success of her bakeshop.

Jake was happy to talk about the bakeshop. It seemed to put her at ease. She
seemed almost like the old Ella he'd known
when they were children.

They talked about the bakeshop a few
more minutes, and then Jake made a huge
mistake. He mentioned Ella's dad, and
what a nice man he'd been.

Unexpected tears spilled over and dribbled down Ella's cheeks. She quickly grabbed a napkin and blotted them away.

Oh, great, now I've made her cry. Jake left his seat and sat in the chair beside Ella. "I'm sorry. I shouldn't have mentioned your daed. I wasn't thinking about how it'd make you feel."

She blinked a couple of times, and the heavy sadness in her face finally lifted. "It's okay. I can't allow myself to fall apart every time my daed's name is mentioned. He's gone and he's not coming back, so I may as well get used to the idea."

"It still has to hurt," Jake said. "I know I'd feel awful if something happened to either one of my folks."

She nodded slowly. "It does hurt, but I can't waste time feeling sorry for myself when there's so much work to be done. I need to focus on taking care of my family."

"You're right, family's important, but you have to think of yourself, too."

She didn't reply.

"My daed's legs have taken much longer to heal than the doctor had hoped, but he'll finally be getting his casts off tomorrow,"

Jake said, moving their conversation in another direction. "Then he'll begin physical therapy."

"How long will it be before he's able to shoe horses again?"

Jake shrugged. "Can't really say. Guess it all depends on how well he responds to the therapy."

She opened her mouth like she might say something more, but then she closed it again. It seemed like she'd been doing a lot of that lately—at least whenever Jake was around.

After several more minutes of silence, Jake pushed back his chair and stood. "Guess I'll head out now, so if you'll get the bread and doughnuts for me, I'll be on my way."

The look of relief that came over Ella's face told Jake all he needed to know. She still didn't like him and probably never would.

He followed Ella out to her shop, and as soon as she'd put the bread and doughnuts in a paper sack, Jake paid her. He'd just opened the door to leave when Lonnie stepped into the bakeshop. He seemed to

be coming around here a lot lately. At least
he'd come by nearly every time Jake had
been here. It made Jake wonder if something was going on between Lonnie and
Ella. Well, if there was, it was none of his
business.

CHAPTER 29

Ella had just begun mixing the batter for some gingerbread when the bell on the door of her bakeshop jingled. She hurried into the front room just in time to see Jake step through the doorway.

"Wie geht's?" he asked.

"I'm fine; just busy is all."

"Guess that's nothing new for you, is it?" Jake smiled and moved over to the glass-topped display case where the baked goods were kept. "I came here to buy a few things, and I insist on paying for everything this time."

"What do you need?"

He touched his chin dimple as he eyed the baked goods. "Let's see now. . . . I'll take three loaves of bread, a dozen glazed doughnuts, and two packages of dinner rolls."

"Anything else?"

"Think that'll be all for this time."

Jake had been making a habit of coming by for baked goods at least twice a week, and Ella wondered if his family really needed that much or if he just bought things in order to help them out financially. Since she hadn't let him do too many chores for them, she had a hunch he was trying to make up for that by buying bread, cookies, and pies. It didn't make sense why he insisted on helping, though. Especially when the two of them didn't get along that well.

She hurriedly packaged up the items he'd requested, and then after he'd paid her, she moved toward the back room. "If you'll excuse me, I have some gingerbread I need to finish mixing."

"Mind if I tag along? Maybe we can visit for a few minutes."

With a brief nod, she said, "You're welcome to come along, but I don't know how much talking I'll be able to do. If another customer comes in, I'll have to drop what I'm doing and wait on them."

"Where's Charlene? Doesn't she usually wait on customers when you're baking?"

"Charlene's not here right now. She went with Mama to a doctor's appointment."

"Is your mamm feelin' poorly?" Jake asked as he followed Ella into the kitchen.

"Mama hasn't felt well for a long time, and it's taken us this long to finally convince her to see the doctor. I hope he'll run some tests and that we'll find out what's wrong with her soon." Ella frowned. "She's really tired most of the time, and she's put on quite a bit of weight even though she doesn't eat very much."

"Hopefully it's nothing serious," Jake said. "Maybe she just needs more rest."

"It seems like all Mama does is rest." Ella sighed. "It's hard not to worry about her."

Jake leaned against the counter and watched as Ella started mixing the gingerbread dough. "Maybe you'll have some answers soon."

"I hope so." She stifled a yawn.

Jake moved closer to where she stood. "You talk about your mamm being tired, and yet every time I see you, there are dark circles under your eyes. Right now, you look like you're about to fall asleep." He nudged her arm. "As my mamm often says to me, *'Ich iwwerduh mich net.'*"

"I am not overextending myself, and I'm not going to fall asleep." Was Jake trying to start another argument? Was that the reason he'd come over here today—so he could needle her some more?

"Would you like me to give you some examples of how you overextend yourself?"

She tapped her foot out of frustration and shook her head.

Jake held up one finger. "You're working in the bakeshop six days a week." Another finger shot up. "You clean the house—"

"Charlene helps with that."

"Okay, Charlene helps, but I've seen you cleaning several times when I've come by to see if you needed my help with anything."

Ella clenched her teeth. *Then why don't you quit coming by?*

Jake held up a third finger. "You do outside chores that are meant for a man." A fourth finger joined the other three. "You're taking signing lessons from Jolene." He held up his thumb. "And I've seen you in town running errands and grocery shopping. If all that's not overextending yourself, then I don't know what is."

"I'll say it again," Ella spoke through tight lips. "I am not overextending myself. I do what I do because it needs to be done, and it's really none of your business how hard I work or how much I choose to do."

"Okay, okay, don't get so riled."

"I'm not riled."

"Jah, you are, and you seem so uptight. Maybe you ought to ask someone to give you a foot massage. My mamm used to give me foot massages when I was a buwe, and that always helped me relax."

Ella nearly laughed out loud, thinking how Jake must have looked getting a foot massage from his mother when he was a boy. "I don't need a foot massage," she mumbled.

Jake motioned to the table. "Well, then, I think you ought to sit down and take a deep breath or have something warm to drink. That can be relaxing, too."

The thought of taking a break did sound appealing, but Ella didn't want Jake to think she was taking his advice, so she shook her head and muttered, "I can't sit down; I've got more baking to do."

"Suit yourself, but if you're not going to take a break, then would you mind if I sit for a few minutes? It's mighty cold out this afternoon, and I'd like the chance to thaw out before I have to hit the road again."

"Feel free to have a seat. As soon as I get my gingerbread in the oven, I'll bag up your order."

"You did that already, remember?" Jake motioned to the sack on the counter.

Ella's face heated. "Oh, that's right."

Jake flopped into a chair.

Ella turned back to her job.

Jake popped his knuckles a few times and hummed a familiar tune.

Ella fanned her hot face with the corner of her apron and tried to ignore him. She really did wish he'd go home.

By the time Ella had put the gingerbread in the oven, she realized she needed a break.

"Would you like a cup of hot chocolate or some coffee?" she asked Jake.

He grinned like a little boy. "Hot chocolate sounds good."

She poured hot water into two cups and added some powdered cocoa mix. Then she placed the cups on the table along with some friendship bread, fresh butter, and a jar of homemade elderberry jelly.

"I'm glad to see you took my advice about taking a break," Jake said when she seated herself in the chair opposite him.

She picked up her cup and lifted it to her lips. One sip of the hot chocolate sent a ripple of warmth surging through her. She really had needed a break.

"Say, what's that on your nose?" Jake asked, leaning forward and squinting at Ella.

She lifted her hand. "Where?"

"Right there." Jake stood and moved quickly to the other side of the table.

As he started toward her, Ella shooed him away with her hands and then swiped at her nose. "Don't bother; I'm sure I can get it."

"Oh, great, now you made it worse." Jake bent down and reached his hand toward her face. Without thinking, she grabbed his hand, and in so doing, a strange prickly sensation zinged up her arm. She let go of his hand as quickly as she'd grabbed it.

A hint of a smile flitted across Jake's face, revealing the deep dimples in his cheeks. Was he laughing at her? Did he know about the strange sensation she'd felt? Had he felt it, too?

"I was just going to rub off that speck of flour on your nose, because you look really funny like that." Jake's eyes sparkled with laughter. "Now the whole side of your nose is white with flour."

Feeling rather foolish, Ella reached up to wipe her nose. "There, is that better?"

Jake stared at her, his placid expression unreadable. Several seconds went by, and then his face broke into a wide smile. "Jah, that's much better."

Ella was relieved when he returned to his side of the table and sat down. She drank her hot chocolate and pushed her chair aside. "I think I'd better get back to work now."

"Okay. I'll leave you to it, then." Jake grabbed his sack of baked goods and moved toward the door. "Thanks for the goodies," he called over his shoulder before the door banged shut.

Ella breathed a sigh of relief. Every time Jake came around, she felt flustered. She wished she could make him stay home, but knowing Jake's pattern, he'd probably be back in a few days to buy more doughnuts or bread.

Ella had just started to clean up the mess she'd made from the gingerbread when the back door swung open and Mama stepped into the room. "Was that Jake Beechy's buggy I saw leaving our place as we were coming in?" she asked.

Ella gave a quick nod. "He came by for some baked goods."

"Again? Seems like he was just here a few days ago." Mama gave Ella a knowing look. "He's been coming around a lot lately. Is there something going on between you two?"

Ella shook her head. "The only thing going on between me and Jake is a lot of tension."

"Maybe you feel irritated whenever he comes around because you're attracted to him."

WANDA E. BRUNSTETTER

"That's *lecherich*, Mama. There's nothing about Jake that I'm attracted to."

Mama gave Ella's arm a little squeeze. "It may not be as ridiculous as you think. I didn't like your daed all that well when we first met, either."

"I didn't just meet Jake. I've known him since we were kinner." Ella plopped her hands against her hips and frowned. *"Der Jake is en lidderlicher kall."*

"Despicable is a very harsh word to be calling Jake. You need to think about the way you speak of others, Ella. I doubt that Jake's as bad as you make him out to be." Suddenly Mama's eyes filled with tears. "Before your daed and I started going out, there were times when he irritated me to no end with his teasing."

"What'd he do?"

"Well, when we were young and still in school, he used to poke me in the ribs to make me giggle, and it hurt. And whenever he came over to visit my bruder, he used to sneak upstairs to my room and put straw in my bed." Mama chuckled. "I didn't realize it back then, but he only did those things to get my attention. It wasn't until we were teenagers that I began to realize your daed wanted to take me out."

"And you still wanted to go out with him after all the mean things he'd done to you when you were a kinner?"

"Oh, jah. I had a big crush on him, even though I didn't like most of the things he'd done. I knew he'd grow up someday, and I hoped when he did that he'd see me as a woman he could love and not just as someone to tease." Mama reached for a paper towel and blotted the tears clinging to her lashes. "I miss your daed so much and would give anything to have him here teasing me right now."

As Ella reflected on her mother's words, she felt a prickly sensation creep up her spine. She'd had a crush on Jake when they were children, but she'd never admitted it to anyone, not even her cousins. She'd never told a soul about the promise Jake had made when he'd walked her to school, carrying her books, either. She'd thought he liked her as much as she liked him. She'd thought he had really meant it when he'd promised to take her for a ride in his buggy when he turned sixteen. But no, the first time Jake took a girl for a ride, it had been Loraine, not Ella.

She shivered despite the warmth in the bakeshop. Jake was a liar; he wasn't to be trusted.

"Are you all right, Ella?" Mama asked. "You look umgerennt."

Ella blinked. "I'm not upset. I was just thinking."

"About what?"

"It was nothing important." No way could she tell Mama what she'd been thinking. Ella touched Mama's arm. "I should have asked right away. How'd it go at the doctor's?"

Mama shrugged. "Okay."

"Did he run any tests? Does he know why you're so tired and shaky?"

"Calm down, Ella. You sound like a screech owl."

Ella hadn't realized her voice had risen. "I'm sorry, Mama. I'm just worried about you. You've been feeling poorly far too long."

"The doctor thinks I either have hypoglycemia or diabetes. He's scheduled me for some blood tests on Friday."

Ella hoped Mama had hypoglycemia rather than diabetes, because she knew it could be controlled by a change in her diet. If Mama started eating regularly instead of picking at her food, and if she made sure she ate the right kinds of food, then hopefully, she'd feel better in no time.

~❧ ❧~

When Lonnie pulled his horse and buggy into the schoolyard, several children were heading for home, including Sylvia and Irvin. Irvin waved, and Lonnie waved back then signed to Irvin, *"Have a good afternoon."* He was pleased that he knew how to sign enough words to make sentences now. As his lessons with Jolene had continued, he'd begun to feel more confident that he'd soon be talking easily with his hands without feeling self-conscious or unsure of himself.

Lonnie's folks were taking signing lessons from Jolene as well, which made it easier for Lonnie to communicate at home. Mama had caught on so well that she and Lonnie could carry on a conversation without her having to write everything down.

Lonnie started across the yard and saw Eunice heading that way on her bike. She halted when she saw him, turned the bike around, and took off down the road.

Lonnie shrugged. He could never figure out why Eunice did any of the things she did. She was nothing like Jolene, that was for sure.

When Lonnie entered the schoolhouse, he nearly bumped into Fern, who was coming out the door. Her face colored, and she signed, *"Sorry."*

"Me, too," Lonnie signed back. He was glad Jolene had been teaching Fern and some of the children in her class how to sign. It made it easier than trying to read people's lips. Even so, he knew the day was coming when he'd have to rely on lip reading more than signing in order to get a job that took him outside his home.

Sure wish there was something I could do besides work with Pop's hogs. Lonnie grunted as he tromped up the steps to Jolene's classroom. *I wonder how hard it's going to be to find a job once I start seriously looking.*

Lonnie knew he could continue helping Pop with the hogs for as long as he wanted, and even though things seemed to be better between him and Pop, raising hogs wasn't the kind of work he cared to do. He needed something that was more of a challenge—not that pigs couldn't be challenging at times. What he wanted was something fun, something he'd really enjoy.

When Lonnie entered Jolene's classroom, he found her sitting at her desk, looking over some paperwork. She didn't look up, so he assumed she hadn't realized he'd come in. If she'd been able to hear, he would have cleared his throat loudly. Under the circumstances, he figured the best thing to do was to tap her on the shoulder.

He walked slowly up the desk, and when his hand connected with Jolene's shoulder, she jumped. He jumped, too, because for some unknown reason, a jolt of electricity had shot up his arm. He shrugged it off, attributing it to the fact that there must be static electricity in the air from the cold weather they'd been having.

Jolene patted her flushed cheeks and signed, *"Are you ready for another lesson on lip reading?"*

Lonnie bobbed his head, feeling suddenly nervous and shy in her presence. It made no sense; he'd been alone with Jolene several times and had never felt like this.

"Before we begin our lesson," Jolene signed, *"I'd like your opinion on something."*

"What do you need my opinion on?" Lonnie asked, hoping he'd understood what she'd said and had signed the right words.

"This is kind of lengthy, so I'm going to write it out." Jolene picked up the tablet on her desk and wrote: *I know you and Andrew have become friends, so I hope you won't repeat what I'm about to tell you.*

Lonnie shook his head and signed, *"I won't repeat."*

Jolene smiled and continued to write. *As you might know, Andrew has recently begun going out with Eunice Byler.*

Lonnie shrugged in reply. Who Andrew went out with was none of his business.

From some of the things Andrew has said to me, I know he has more than a passing interest in her.

"Maybe so," Lonnie signed.

I'm afraid Eunice might not be right for Andrew.

"How come?"

Because she likes to gossip. I spoke

with her yesterday, and she told me some things that were none of my business—things that, in my opinion, didn't bear repeating.

Lonnie frowned, and he spoke out loud. "I'm not much of an expert on love, but I think Andrew's smart enough to know whether Eunice is right for him or not. Of course, I misjudged Carolyn and thought she was the one for me." He groaned. "One thing's for certain. I'll never fall in love again."

"How do you know?"

"It'd be hard for me to trust another woman not to hurt me the way Carolyn did. Besides, what kind of husband and father would I make when I can't hear?"

Before Jolene could comment, Kyle Beechy rushed into the room. His lips moved fast as he waved his hands. Lonnie had no idea what the boy was saying.

❧ ❧

Seeing the urgent look on Kyle's face sent a wave of panic through Jolene. She put her fingers to her lips to shush the boy. "Slow down, Kyle. I'm not able to read your lips when you're talking so fast."

The color in the boy's blue eyes darkened like the night sky. "Irvin's been hit by a car. He couldn't hear it coming. I tried to warn him, but he couldn't hear me, either." Tears gathered in the corners of Kyle's eyes, and he blinked several times. "You've gotta come with me, Teacher. I think Irvin might be dead!"

Jolene jumped out of her chair, grabbed her coat, and raced down the steps behind Kyle. When she opened the schoolhouse door, a blast of frosty air stung her nose.

As she ran along the shoulder of the road behind Kyle, the frigid air caused her throat to ache from breathing too deeply. She turned once and saw Lonnie sprinting behind them. He caught up to her in a few long strides.

When they came upon the scene of the accident, Jolene's breath caught in her throat. A car was parked along the shoulder of the road, and a young woman stood beside it, tears streaming down her face. Several children, including Sylvia, were gathered around the small form lying on the ground near the car. Irvin was still breathing, but blood seeped from a gash in his head, and he wasn't moving.

In the whirlwind of confusion, one thing was clear: The boy was hurt and needed immediate medical attention.

CHAPTER 30

Stop crying, and tell me what's wrong," Jake said when he arrived home from Ella's and found his little brother sitting on the back porch, bawling like a wounded heifer.

Kyle looked up at Jake and choked on a sob. "Ir–Irvin's in the hospital. He might even be dead, and—and it's all my fault!"

Jake's forehead wrinkled. "What are you talking about?"

"If I knew how to sign, I could've warned him."

Jake set the sack full of bakery items on the porch and took a seat beside Kyle. "Tell me what happened."

Kyle gulped and sniffed a few times as he poured out the story of how Irvin had been hit by a car, and how he'd run to the schoolhouse to get help.

"Did you push Irvin in front of the car?" Jake asked.

Kyle shook his head.

"Then why do you think the accident was your fault?"

Kyle swiped at his tear-stained face. "I. . .I was teasin' him about not bein' able to hear, and he started runnin' real fast. He must not have been watchin' where he was goin', 'cause he ran in front of the car. I called out to him, but of course, he couldn't hear my warning."

"That's terrible, and I'm real sorry to hear it, but there's one thing I don't understand."

"What's that?"

"Since Irvin can't hear, and you haven't learned how to sign, how'd he know you were teasing him?"

Kyle's shoulders shook as he hung his head. "I. . .I poked him a couple of times. Then I guess he read my lips when I said he was a dummkopp who can't talk right and acts like a boppli."

Jake clenched his fists. "How many times have you been told not to tease?"

"A lot."

"And yet you keep doing it?" Jake glared at his brother. "What makes you keep teasing Irvin when you know it's wrong?"

Kyle leaned forward, letting his head drop into his hands. "I–I'm mad at you, and since I can't say what I want. . ." His voice trailed off as sniffling and hiccups took over.

Jake placed his hand on Kyle's head. "How come you're mad at me?"

Kyle mumbled something about Jake leaving, but Jake could only make out a few words because the boy was crying so hard.

"Sit up, dry your eyes, and tell me what's on your mind," Jake said, gently patting Kyle's back.

Several seconds went by before Kyle finally lifted his head. "I'm mad 'cause you moved to Montana. And—and then you keep comin' back."

"You don't like it when I come home?"

"It's not that—it's just that when you're gone, Dad's real cranky and moody. Mom cries a lot, too." Kyle gulped in a quick breath. "Then whenever you come back, Dad's crankier than ever, and Mom makes over you like you're her favorite son. I wish you'd make up your mind 'bout where you're gonna live and then stay put once and for all. Maybe if you decided to stay in Montana, Mom and Dad would accept the idea and stop frettin' over you all the time. Or better yet, if you stayed here, we'd all be happy."

Kyle's words jolted Jake to the core. He knew Mom and Dad weren't happy about him living in Montana, but until this moment, he'd had no idea it had affected his little brother so, or that Kyle had been carrying all this pent-up anger toward him.

Jake knew he'd have to work on improving his relationship with Kyle. He also needed to make a definite decision about whether he should stay in Indiana or return to Montana. Right now, though, they needed to find out how Irvin was doing.

❧ ❧

"Why are you getting home so late?" Mom asked when Jolene entered the kitchen. "It's way past time for supper, and I was beginning to worry."

Jolene slipped off her heavy woolen

shawl and hung it over the back of a chair. "Irvin was hit by a car after school, and I stayed with him at the hospital until his folks got there."

"What happened? Is Irvin badly hurt? Is he. . ."

Mom's lips were moving so fast that Jolene couldn't keep up. She held up her hand. "Please, one question at a time."

"Sorry. Sometimes I still forget that you're reading my lips."

Jolene motioned to the table. "Let's have a seat, and I'll tell you about it."

They both found chairs, and Jolene explained how she'd ridden in the ambulance with Irvin while Lonnie went to notify his folks. Then when Irvin's folks arrived at the hospital, Jolene had stayed with them until they'd gotten some word on Irvin's condition. Jolene drew in a deep breath. "We were so relieved when the doctor came out and said Irvin hadn't been critically injured, although he did require several stitches in his forehead, and his collarbone is broken."

Mom shook her head slowly. "It's a miracle that boy wasn't killed. What was he doing in the street, anyway?"

"I'm not sure. Kyle Beechy's the one who came and got me, and he was so upset, I couldn't get many details from him." Jolene paused and licked her dry lips. "With Irvin being deaf, I'm sure he didn't realize the car was coming."

"Is it any wonder that I worry when you take the horse and buggy out?" Mom touched Jolene's arm. "If a car honked its horn to warn you that it was passing, you'd never know it."

"I'm very cautious whenever I go out on the road. I watch my side mirrors and look over my shoulder often when I'm in the buggy. The rest I leave in God's hands."

"You're right, of course; we need to put every part of our lives in God's capable hands." Mom gave Jolene's arm a gentle squeeze. "But I'm a mudder, and I guess it's just my nature to worry about my kinner, no matter how old they are or how cautious they might be." She glanced toward the door then looked back at Jolene. "Someone's knocking, so I'd better see who it is."

Mom hurried from the room, while Jolene remained at the table. A few minutes later, Mom was back with Jake at her side.

"Do you have any word on Irvin?" he asked, taking a seat beside Jolene. "My little bruder's really worried about him."

Jolene explained everything that had transpired at the hospital.

"Kyle blames himself for the accident," Jake said, "because he was teasing Irvin, and then Irvin ran into the road in order to get away from him."

"I don't know how many times I've asked Kyle to stop tormenting Irvin," Jolene said, shaking her head. "Will he never learn?"

Jake's solemn expression lightened a bit. "I think he's finally learned his lesson. Right before I came here, he told me that if Irvin lives, he'll apologize for all the teasing he's done. He even said that he wants to get to know Irvin better, and believe it or not, he's now willing to learn how to sign."

"That's good news, and you can let Kyle know that Irvin will live, because his injuries are not life threatening." Jolene's shoulders lifted and then fell as she released a deep sigh. "Maybe God will take this near tragedy and bring something good from it."

CHAPTER 31

It had been two weeks since Irvin's accident. Due to the broken collarbone, when he returned to school he wore a sling to keep from lifting his arm, and there was still a red mark on his forehead where he'd been cut, but otherwise he looked pretty chipper. Even more amazing, it appeared as though Irvin and Kyle might actually become friends. When Jolene went downstairs to give Fern's class another signing lesson, Kyle had surprised her by participating. He'd even invited Irvin to sit beside him. By the time class was over, Kyle had learned how to sign a few words, including the word *friend.*

"Guess what, Teacher," Sylvia signed when she and Irvin entered Jolene's class-room after their lesson downstairs.

"What?"

"It's snowing!"

"Is that so?" Jolene went to the window and peered out. Sure enough, the ground was covered with a thin layer of white.

"Can we make a snowman during re-cess?" Irvin asked.

Jolene patted the top of his head. *"You're not supposed to use your right arm yet, and I don't think you can roll a snowball too easily with just one hand."*

"Irvin can watch while you and me make the snowman." Sylvia then turned to Irvin and signed, *"Would that be all right with you?"*

He tipped his head as though mulling things over. Finally, he gave a quick nod.

"Since that is all settled, are you two ready to begin your lessons?" Jolene asked.

Both children nodded and then hurried to the chairs at their desks. Jolene smiled. It was good to see her young students so well adjusted and eager to learn. Her adult students were catching on to signing, too. Last Sunday in church, Andrew had signed part of the bishop's sermon. Having him do that had given the worship service a lot more meaning for Jolene. After church, Jake had told her that he might like to try signing at the next service. Things were definitely looking up.

⊱ ⊰

Jake smiled as he listened to his horse's hooves crunch in the snow and watched the steam escaping his horse's nostrils. It had begun snowing earlier today, and the snowflakes were so big they looked like spun sugar. He'd always liked snowy weather and had enjoyed playing in the snow when he was a boy.

Wish I had time to play in it right now, Jake thought as he guided his horse up the Yoders' driveway. *Maybe when Kyle and Elmer get home from school, we can make a snow fort.*

When Jake hopped down from his buggy, the stiffening breeze ruffled the hair peeking out from under his stocking cap. Winter was definitely here, for it was getting colder every day.

Jake put the horse in the barn, and once

he had the animal settled in one of the stalls, he hurried toward the bakeshop. As Jake stepped onto the porch, wet snow fell from his boots in slushy clumps. He entered the shop, and the sweet smell of cinnamon and apples assaulted his senses.

He'd only been standing by the bakery counter a few seconds when Ella stepped out of the back room, carrying two pies. She blinked a couple of times and jumped back when she saw him. "Ach, I didn't hear you come in!"

"Guess the bell above your door isn't working," he said. "At least I didn't hear it ring when I opened the door."

Ella glanced up at the bell and frowned. "It's not there. Someone must have taken it down."

"Who'd do that?"

She shrugged. "I have no idea. It might have been Larry. He likes to fool with things, so he probably took the bell thinking he could make it louder or something."

"Speaking of Larry, is he still at school?"

"Jah."

Jake leaned on the counter and stared at Ella. She had a good heart and cared deeply for her family. He wished she liked

him better, though. The wall she'd built between them was thicker than dense fog,
and at this close range he could see the
fine lines on her forehead. She might be
prettier if she didn't frown so much. Jake
didn't know why, but he found himself
strangely attracted to her. He just wished
he could figure out some way to break
through that barrier she'd built. He also
wished he knew what she had against
him. He was tempted to ask but didn't
want to start an argument. They'd had
too many of those already.

"What can I do for you?" Ella asked. "Are
you after more baked goods?"

"Not this time." He rubbed the glass
countertop with the sleeve of his jacket
in an effort to dispel the fingerprints that
were there. "I. . .uh. . .wondered if you
needed my help with anything."

"Huh-uh. We're fine."

"I thought you might need some wood
chopped or something."

"I'm planning to do that after I close the
bakeshop for the day."

"Why don't you let me do it for you? I'm
sure you've got better things to do than try
to chop wood."

"*Try* to chop wood?" Her forehead wrinkled deeply. "Are you saying that I'm not capable of chopping wood?"

"I'm not sayin' that at all. I just meant. . ."

She pushed past him, slipped into her jacket, and rushed out the door.

Jake quickly followed. *I'm here to help out,* he reminded himself. *And it's not because I have an interest in a sharp-tongued woman who clearly doesn't want me around. It's because I care about her family and want to do the right thing, so despite Ella's protests, I'll continue to offer my help.*

～❧ ❧～

Ella sloshed her way through the snow out to the woodpile behind the barn. She picked up a hunk of wood and was about to reach for the ax when Jake stepped in front of her. She gulped. With him standing only inches away, it was hard to think. . . hard to breathe. She was about to ask him to move back when he spoke first.

"I have a few hours free this afternoon, and I'd really like to give you a hand. Isn't there something you'd like me to do?" Jake's tone was soft, his face sincere.

Ella hesitated. Since Papa's death, she'd come to realize that as much as she wanted to be independent, she couldn't do everything in her own strength. Then last night, she'd read Galatians 6:2: *"Bear ye one another's burdens, and so fulfil the law of Christ."* It was a gentle reminder that she needed to let others help out during their time of need. She guessed that even meant Jake.

Jake touched Ella's arm. "Did you hear my question?"

She nodded and lifted her lips in a slow smile. "How much experience have you had at baking?"

His eyebrows lifted. "Huh?"

"When I'm done chopping wood I'll be doing some more baking. Since you're so anxious to help out, I thought maybe. . ."

Jake held up his hand. "I can do a lot of chores, but there's one thing I can't do, and that's bake." He crinkled his nose and winked at her. "Unless, of course, you like things burned."

Ella's cheeks grew warm. Was Jake flirting with her? Oh, surely not; he was just trying to be funny. She shivered and picked up the axe, but Jake grabbed hold of her arm before she could take a swing.

"Why don't you head back inside where it's warm? I'll have this wood chopped in no time at all."

Jake's self-assured attitude only refueled Ella's anger. Didn't he ever give up? Did he enjoy making her mad?

He moved closer, so close she could feel the tension between them. "I'm not leaving here until I chop some wood, so you may as well hand me that ax."

"From what I remember, you're kind of accident-prone. How do I know you won't cut yourself?"

"If I do, then you'll have to doctor me up." He wiggled his eyebrows playfully. "You'd better get inside now and make sure you have some bandages ready for me."

She grunted and started for the bakeshop. Jake Beechy was impossible! She didn't know what Loraine had ever seen in him—for that matter, what Jolene saw in him now.

Ella cringed. She hoped Jolene didn't end up marrying Jake. The thought of him being her cousin-in-law didn't set well with her.

She stopped walking, turned, and cupped her hands over her mouth. "Make sure you don't leave any of that wood unchopped! Things done by halves are never done right."

"You think you know everything, Ella!"

Her jaw clenched against the cold, and she fired back, "Jah, well, you think everyone should do as you say!"

"You're kind of cute when you're riled like that! Your nose twitches, and your cheeks turn red!" His voice carried in the crisp, cold air.

Ella glared at him, sensing that he was making fun of her. How did Jake always manage to make her feel so stupid? "The only reason my nose is red is because it's so cold out here!" She leaned down, grabbed a wad of snow, and formed it into a ball. Then she pulled her arm way back and chucked the snowball at Jake.

"Hey!" He brushed the snow off the sleeve of his jacket, bent down, and grabbed some snow of his own.

Ella knew what was coming, so she

hurried for the bakeshop as fast as she could. She'd just stepped onto the porch, when—*splat!*—a chunk of icy snow hit the back of her neck. She was tempted to retaliate, but it was cold out here, and she had baking to do. She'd get even with Jake some other time.

Ella stepped into the bakeshop and headed straight for the stove to thaw out.

Maybe what I need is something to warm my insides. After she'd poured herself a cup of coffee, she glanced out the window and watched as Jake swung the axe. He made it look so easy. She'd never have admitted it to him, but she hated chopping wood and knew it would have taken her twice as long as it would Jake.

Ella noticed Jake glancing toward the bakeshop, so she moved quickly away from the window. No point in letting him think she'd been watching. He might get the wrong idea.

She took a seat at the table near the stove and continued to fume. Why hadn't Jake ever seen her as a capable woman? Why did he think he was so much better at doing things than her? Why couldn't Jake. . .

Ella halted her thoughts and pushed away from the table. She had to quit thinking about Jake and get some baking done.

~✺ ✺~

Sometime later, Jake entered the bakeshop. His face was red and glistened with sweat. "Whew! It's gettin' colder out there by the minute." He rubbed his hands briskly together. "Sure feels good to be inside where it's warm."

"Danki for cutting the wood," Ella said.

"No problem. What else would you like me to do?"

Go home. She forced a smile. "I don't need anything else done right now."

"Sure you do. There's always chores that need to be done. Would you like me to muck out the stalls in the barn?" Jake pointed to the sink. "Or I could wash those dishes you've got piled up from your baking."

She shook her head. "I can do them." *That's one thing I'm sure I can do better than you.*

"If you won't let me help with anything else, then at least let me give you some money."

"Money for what?"

"To help with a few bills, which I'm sure you must have." Jake pulled some money from his pocket and placed it on the table. "When I was at Jolene's the other day, she mentioned that things have been kind of slow for you here in the bakery. She said you're worried about not having enough money to get through the winter."

Ella avoided his steady gaze as an eerie silence moved in around them. It irritated her that Jolene had told Jake about things that were none of his business. She pushed the money toward him. "I've told you before; we're getting by fine on our own!"

"Then I'll buy some bread."

"What?"

"I said, 'I'll buy some bread.'"

"Fine. How many loaves do you need?"

"Ten."

Her eyebrows shot up. "What in the world are you going to do with ten loaves of bread?"

"I'll find a use for 'em."

"What are you planning to do. . .feed bread to your horses?"

"Maybe." He pointed to the wad of bills. "How much do I owe you?"

"Why do you think you need to help us, Jake?"

"My mamm always says, 'If you give a little, you get back much more.'"

"Just what is it you expect to get back?"

"I don't expect anything." Jake pushed the money toward her. "I'm going to give you this no matter what you say, so you may as well take it agreeably."

"And I say you're not!" she challenged. "Why don't you forget about helping us and stay home with your horses?"

"I can't do that. It'd be like trying to walk around with only one shoe."

"Then I guess you'd better get used to walking that way."

He jammed his hands into his jacket pockets, looking dejected. Ella couldn't be sure if he was actually hurt by her comment or just putting on an act.

A lump formed in Ella's throat as she stared at the money. They really did need it. Tears pricked the backs of her eyes, and she feared they'd soon be rolling down her cheeks. Jake had reduced her to tears again, yet deep down inside, she appreciated his help.

Ella rose from her chair and glanced out

the window. "It's snowing harder now, so I'll get your ten loaves of bread, and then you can be on your way. You wouldn't want to get caught in a snowstorm." She hurried to the other room before Jake could see the tears that had started dribbling down her cheeks. She hoped he wouldn't come over here again anytime soon.

CHAPTER 32

Ella dropped into a chair at the kitchen table and fanned her face with the corner of a cotton dish towel. "Whew, it's so hot in here!"

Mama, who sat across from Ella, dropping lettuce leaves into a bowl, nodded. "I'm wondering if we should hire someone to put a second oven in your bakeshop so you don't have to use this one when you have a lot of baking to do. All the baking you've done this morning has heated up the house like nobody's business. Come summer, it'll only be worse."

Ella nodded. "I try to do most of my baking in the morning, but it doesn't seem to make much difference. A hot oven makes for a hot house, that's for sure." She sighed. "Don't see how we can afford to buy a second oven for the bakeshop right now, much less hire someone to put it in. What I'm making from the bakery is barely enough to put food on the table."

Mama dropped a few more pieces of lettuce into the bowl and yawned. "Sure wish there was more I could do to help out, but I'm so tired much of the time." She groaned. "I still can't believe the results of my blood test showed that I have diabetes."

"The dokder said it might take awhile to get your blood sugar regulated, and you've only been on the diet he gave you a few weeks. I'm sure between changing your diet and taking the medication he prescribed, you'll feel better soon."

Tears gathered in the corners of Mama's eyes. "When your daed and I were first married, I had the energy and strength of two women my age. I feel so worthless now."

Ella swallowed hard. She hated to see Mama looking so sad. She left her seat and bent to give Mama a hug. "You're not worthless. You might not be able to do as much as you once did, but you do what you can, and that's what counts. So please don't worry about it."

"'I can do all things through Christ which strengtheneth me,'" Mama quoted from the book of Philippians. "Without His help I couldn't do anything. We just need to keep joy in our souls and praise on our lips as we trust God to provide for our needs." She patted Ella's arm. "We'll be okay; you'll see."

Mama's words made Ella aware that she still tried to do too much in her own strength. She motioned to the packages of cakes and cookies on the counter. "I'll be glad when spring's here and the tourists come to the area. If I do a little advertising, hopefully some of them will come out here to our bakeshop."

"*Your* bakeshop, Ella." Mama's light tone contrasted with the serious expression on her face. "It's *your* bakery that's supporting us right now."

"I've never thought of it as being mine. You and Charlene help out, and even the younger ones do whatever they can."

"That's true. We all chip in whenever it's necessary, and we'll continue to do our best."

"I know you will." Ella glanced out the window and sighed. *"Ich bin bereit fer frie-hyaahr."*

Mama laughed. "Winter's barely started and you're ready for spring?"

"Jah. In the spring I'm planning to take some of my baked goods to the farmer's market in Elkhart, and when the Shipshe-wana flea market opens in May, I might sell some things there, too."

"That's a good idea," Mama said, "but you can't be in three places at once. With the exception of Charlene, and maybe Larry, the kinner can't run a stand by them-selves at either one of the markets."

"Maybe by then we'll be making enough money so I can hire someone to work the stands. Guess we'll have to wait and see how it goes."

"Give me that piece of puzzle!" Amelia shouted from the living room.

"No! You took the one I was gonna choose!" Helen hollered.

Mama's eyebrows furrowed. "Sounds like two of my girls are arguing again. Seems like all Amelia and Helen have done since they got out of bed is argue and fuss." She rubbed her forehead with the back of her hand. "I'll be glad when Monday comes and they're back in school."

"It's not your turn! If you don't let go of that, I'll tell Mama!" Helen's shrill voice carried into the kitchen.

"All that chitter chatter is hurting my ears," Mama said, dropping the lettuce and placing both hands against her ears.

Ella pushed her chair aside. She didn't care how loud the children hollered when they were outside, but not in the house. There was no excuse for them to be arguing that way and upsetting Mama. "I'll take care of their childish prattle," she said as she hurried from the room.

⚜

Lonnie drew in a deep breath and smiled as he watched the cows in the stall closest to him crunch away on the sweet-smelling hay he'd given them earlier that morning. For the last hour, he'd been out in the barn, sanding the legs of the small end table he'd made to give Mom for Christmas. He rather liked being out here. It gave him a sense of peace to be alone with the animals. It was a good time to think. Unfortunately, all he'd been able to think about so far today was Jolene, and that bothered him. Whenever he was with her, his insides felt warm and comforted, but he didn't know if he could trust those feelings. Jolene had an inner beauty about her that went much deeper than her pretty face and sparkling blue eyes. He was sure Jolene's beauty started in her heart and shone through her eyes and smile. If being too sweet could be considered a flaw, then maybe Jolene wasn't as perfect as she seemed. There had to be something about her that Lonnie didn't like, but for the life of him, he couldn't think of what it was. He'd have to be careful not to let himself get any closer to her than he already had. He couldn't allow himself to fall in love again.

Forcing his thoughts aside, Lonnie stood and moved the stool he'd been sitting on closer to the stove. If it weren't for the warmth from the fire, his hands would have numbed quickly in the biting cold.

Someone touched Lonnie's shoulder, and he jerked around. He was relieved to see Wayne standing there and not Pop wanting him to do some chore that involved smelly pigs.

Wayne smiled and withdrew a notebook and pen from his jacket pocket. He wrote something on it and handed it to Lonnie. Lonnie was glad Wayne had written his thoughts, as he still wasn't able to read lips very well.

I have a few things I need to pick up in Shipshe and wondered if you'd like to go along. Thought maybe we could stop someplace for coffee and doughnuts.

"That sounds nice, but I'm in the middle of something right now." Lonnie motioned to the legs he'd been sanding.

Did you make that? Wayne wrote.

Lonnie nodded. "It's a surprise for Mom. I'm planning to give it to her for Christmas."

Wayne's lips puckered like he had whistled. Lonnie missed not being able to hear the melody of a whistle.

Wayne picked up the tablet again and wrote something else: *I'm impressed. I had no idea you had a talent for woodworking.*

"I've fooled around with it off and on ever since I was a boy but never figured anything I made was very good."

Well, this sure is. Wayne ran his fingers over one of the table legs. *You've done a fine job with it.*

Lonnie's face heated. He wasn't used to receiving such compliments, especially not for his woodworking skills.

Would you be interested in coming to work for me? Wayne wrote.

"In your taxidermy shop?"

No, in my new woodworking shop. I'm only helping my daed part-time with taxidermy right now because there's not really enough work for both of us. But I've been able to sell several things that I've made in my woodshop to some of the furniture stores in the area. I think that might turn into a profitable business for me.

Lonnie wasn't convinced that the table he'd made was really that good, but feeling a sense of nervous excitement, he said that he'd be willing to try working for Wayne.

Wayne smiled and wrote, *Let's head*

for Shipshe, and we can talk about this some more.

❧ ❧

The landscape was barely visible under the blanket of white that had fallen the night before, and Jake was on his way home after shoeing an unruly horse. To make matters worse, he'd had to fight slippery roads and blustery snow, both coming and going.

Good thing my truck has four-wheel drive, Jake thought as he peered through the front windshield. He wondered how things would be if he sold his truck and joined the church. He'd have to drive his horse and buggy everywhere except for when he went places that would require him to hire an English driver. *Guess it would take some getting used to for me to let someone else haul me around, but if I were to get my own business going here, I wouldn't have to shoe horses anymore.*

Jake thought about some of the fellows he'd grown up with and how many of them were married and raising families. He wondered if it had been hard for any of them who'd owned vehicles to give them up when they joined the church. He knew it hadn't been an issue for Wayne, because he'd never owned a car. Even if he had, Wayne loved Loraine so much that he'd probably have given up most anything in order to marry her.

Jake wondered if he'd ever feel that much love for a woman. Even when he'd thought he was in love with Loraine, he'd run off to Montana and done his own thing. Soon after he'd moved to Montana, he'd become interested in his boss's daughter, Roxanne, but that hadn't lasted long and had never been really serious. Maybe he was incapable of the kind of love Wayne had for Loraine. Maybe he really was self-ish and self-centered, like Dad had accused him of being on several occasions. *Guess I need to pray more and ask God to take away any selfish desires that aren't pleas-ing to Him.*

Jake's musings halted when he turned up his folks' driveway. He parked his truck behind the barn so Dad didn't have to see it every time he looked out the window.

As Jake started walking toward the house, a bird flew from a nearby tree, send-ing a shower of snowflakes onto his head. He brushed it off and hurried on.

As soon as Jake stepped onto the back porch, he heard his folks' voices coming from the kitchen window, which was open a crack.

"Er hot scheins sei verschtand verlore," Dad said.

Who seems to have lost his reason? Jake wondered. He stood there a few minutes, listening; then, when he realized it was him they were talking about, he decided to wait a few minutes before going in so he could hear more of what they were saying.

"I blame you for nagging Jake to join the church and for trying to make him do things your way. Truth is, I think it's your fault Jake left home in the first place."

"Stop badgering me. We've been through all this before."

"But if you hadn't pressured Jake so much and worked him so hard when he was a buwe, I'm sure he'd have stayed in Indiana and would have joined the church by now."

There was a long pause, and then Mom started up again. "I'm just heartsick that Jake will be going back to Montana soon. I've gotten used to him being here, and I'll miss him so much."

Jake leaned against the wall and drew in a couple of deep breaths. First he'd had to deal with slippery driving conditions; then a contrary horse that didn't want to be shoed; and now this? The day couldn't get much worse!

"You baby Jake too much; that's what I've gotta say."

"I do not baby him. I just—"

Jake opened the door and stepped into the kitchen. Mom and Dad looked up. Dead silence fell on the room.

Jake turned to Mom and said, "Where'd you get the idea that I'd be leaving for Montana soon?"

Mom blinked a couple of times. "I. . . uh. . .ran into Eunice at the grocery store the other day. She said you told her that you'd be leaving soon."

Jake shook his head. "I never said any such thing. All I told Eunice when I met up with her at Jolene's the other day was that I needed to make up my mind soon about whether to return to Montana or not."

"Have you made up your mind?" Dad asked, leveling Jake with a piercing look.

Jake dug his nails into the palms of his hands. He hated being put on the spot.

"Have you made up your mind or not?"

"You don't have to shout," Mom said. "Is it any wonder Jake doesn't want to live near his family?"

Dad grunted. "That's not the reason, and you know it. Our son thinks he's too good for us. He's never been happy doing what he does best. Wants to own a bunch of wild horses like he's been tryin' to train out west."

Irritation welled in Jake's soul. It took all his willpower not to dash out the door and take off down the road in his truck. "I wasn't *trying* to train horses, Dad. That was my job. I'm not bragging, but I think I did it rather well." He glanced out the window at the barn. "Besides, the kind of horses I want to train aren't wild—they need to learn how to pull a buggy. And I don't just want to train horses," he added. "I'm also hoping to raise a certain breed of horses that I can sell for profit. That's what I've been working and saving my money for."

Dad folded his arms. "Makin' lots of money. That's all you're interested in, isn't it, Jake?"

"No, it's not! I want to raise and train horses because that's what I enjoy doing.

And while I might be good at shoeing horses, I've never enjoyed it all that much."

"Maybe you could train horses to pull our buggies here," Mom said. "That would bring in even more money than you're making now filling in for your daed in his business."

"I'll give it some thought," Jake said.

"What is there to think about?" Dad hollered. "Do you have to think about it 'cause you don't know if you're staying here or not?"

"I wish you would lower your voice, Joe." Mom's chin trembled. "This isn't the way God intended for family members to speak to each other."

Dad frowned. "Jah, well, if he'd listen to what I have to say and quit walkin' through life with one foot in the world, there'd be no dispute here or any raised voices."

Jake tapped his foot as his patience waned further. He'd been on the verge of telling his folks that he'd decided not to return to Montana, but now he was having second thoughts. With the snowy weather making it hard to travel, he figured the best thing to do was to wait until spring to make his decision. In the meantime, he needed to put as much space between himself and Dad as possible, so he whirled around and started for the door.

"Where are you going?" Mom called. "It's almost time for lunch."

"I'm not hungry. I'm going outside to the barn so I can have some time alone to think." Jake jerked open the door and let it close behind him a little harder than usual. If things didn't improve around here by spring, he would definitely return to Montana.

CHAPTER 33

Jolene had just entered the bath and body store in Shipshewana to do some Christmas shopping, when she spotted Katie at the cash register. She waited until Katie finished paying for her purchases, and then she stepped up to her and said, "I'm surprised to see you in town this afternoon. I figured you'd be at the stamp shop waiting on desperate customers buying last-minute Christmas presents."

"I was there earlier, but I had a dental appointment this afternoon and decided to come here afterward to do some Christmas shopping of my own." Katie grinned.

"I want to get something nice for Freeman."

Jolene smiled. "It won't be long before spring is upon us. Are you getting excited about your wedding in April?"

"Oh, jah, I can hardly wait."

A pang of jealousy stabbed Jolene's heart. She didn't even have a boyfriend, and even if she had one, there were no guarantees that she'd ever get a marriage proposal.

A vision of Lonnie popped into Jolene's head. She'd never admit it, but she was beginning to have strong feelings for him. Of course, it didn't matter how she felt, because he'd told her that he would never look for love again.

To complicate matters, Jolene suspected that Lonnie might be interested in Ella, for he talked about her a lot. But given his reservations about marriage, it was unlikely that he'd ever act upon those feelings.

"Are you all right?" Katie asked, nudging Jolene's arm. "Your eyes are misting up like you're on the verge of tears."

Jolene gave Katie a hug. "I'm just happy for you and Freeman."

Tears welled in Katie's eyes. "I never thought I could be this happy. After all the depression and anxiety I went through after Timothy died, I never thought I'd live a normal life again." Her eyes brightened, and a smile stretched across her face. "God is so good. Every day, I praise and thank Him for helping me to overcome my panic attacks."

"We all have much to be thankful for," Jolene agreed.

～❧ ❧～

You look like you're enjoying your work, Wayne wrote on the tablet he then handed to Lonnie.

"Next to tuning wind chimes, I've never had a job I enjoy so much." Lonnie signed as he spoke, since Wayne had sat in on a few lessons while Jolene was teaching her family and Jake. Lonnie figured it might help his new boss learn quicker if he signed whenever he spoke.

I'm glad to hear you like the work. Don't forget what I told you earlier. I want you to feel free to use my tools to work on your own projects during your lunch hour and breaks, Wayne wrote.

"I'll remember that." Lonnie had plans to

not only make his mother and sisters something for Christmas, but Jolene as well. He wanted it to be a thank-you gift for her teaching him to sign and read lips. Although he still wasn't comfortable with lip reading, he hoped he'd eventually get better at it and could use that skill in public rather than relying on the tablet and pen he kept in his pocket.

Lonnie worked quietly for the next few hours. When it was time for lunch, he ate quickly and started working on a bird feeder for Jolene. As he cut the pieces of wood, he thought about how kind and patient she'd been with him. Even when he'd been irritable and negative, she'd remained optimistic and helpful, always encouraging him to keep trying and not to give up. There was something about Jolene's gentle, sweet spirit that drew him to her. There'd been times when he'd been tempted to ask her out, but fear of her rejection had always held him back. Besides, what did he have to offer a woman? He couldn't make any kind of commitment. The thought of becoming a husband and maybe a father scared him to death.

Lonnie wanted to believe that God would

provide for his needs and help him through any situation, but being deaf limited him in so many ways. Sometimes the fear he felt was almost paralyzing. Other times, especially when he was with Jolene, he felt as if he could accomplish most anything. But did he trust his feelings enough that he could open his heart to her?

Pulling his thoughts aside, Lonnie picked up the hammer and a nail. He needed to get busy on the bird feeder or he'd never get it done.

"Yeow!" The hammer missed the nail and hit his thumb instead.

He grimaced and stuck his thumb between his teeth. *Guess that's what I get for thinking more about Jolene than what I'm doing.*

When the throbbing subsided, Lonnie went back to work. A short time later, Freeman showed up with his dog.

Penny leaped into Lonnie's lap, and he dropped his hammer. "Ouch!" It landed on his toe.

Freeman picked the dog up and said something, but Lonnie couldn't make out the words. Oh, how he wished he could hear.

Wayne came to his rescue, handing Freeman a tablet and pen.

Sorry my excitable mutt jumped on you, Freeman wrote. *She got nervous on the way over because she's scared of the wind. Sometimes she gets so scared that her whole body vibrates.*

"It's okay. No harm was done." Lonnie went back to work on the bird feeder, and Freeman moved over to Wayne's desk. A few minutes later, the dog jumped into Lonnie's lap again. This time she knocked the birdhouse to the floor, and a piece of the roof chipped off.

Lonnie groaned. At this rate, he'd never get Jolene's gift done in time for Christmas.

∼⁂∼

For the last week Jake had been planning to do some Christmas shopping, but between the horses he had to shoe and the horses he'd begun training recently, he hadn't made it to town. He was glad he'd taken Mom's suggestion and run an ad in the paper, because he'd already gotten some business from folks who needed their buggy horses trained. He'd also bought a few horses that he planned to train and then sell to folks who were in need of a good buggy horse. He enjoyed the training process a lot more than shoeing, but until Dad was working full-time again, Jake knew he'd have to keep shoeing horses.

Jake had just finished shoeing two of their bishop's buggy horses and had a few hours free until it was time to head for home, so he was on his way to Shipshewana to buy a few gifts. He wanted to get Mom a new set of dishes, as she'd mentioned the other day that her old ones had several chips. Buying presents for his younger siblings should be easy enough, since they were usually happy with most any toy. What to get Dad was the question. Whatever Jake decided on, he was sure Dad wouldn't like it. He never liked much of anything Jake said or did. Jake knew it wouldn't be right to leave Dad out, however, so he figured he'd better come up with something.

Jake parked his truck in front of the Red Barn and went inside to look around the various shops. He bought a couple of toys for his younger siblings then decided to head over to the furniture store outside of

Shipshewana. Maybe he'd buy Dad a new reclining chair. The one he had now was falling apart, and Dad did like to put his feet up at night and recline while he read the newspaper. Jake hoped if he bought something Dad actually needed, it might improve his attitude toward him. It might make him realize that Jake could do a few things right.

Jake was about to get into his truck when Eunice Byler walked by. She smiled sweetly and said, "It's nice to see you, Jake. What brings you to Shipshe on such a cold, snowy day?"

"I might ask you the same question," he said.

"I've been delivering some of my candles and soaps to a few of the stores in the area. The ones I brought in before to sell on consignment have all sold." Her smile widened. "I think it must be because everyone's buying them for Christmas presents."

"Guess that makes sense." Jake started to walk away but changed his mind. He'd been wanting to confront Eunice about telling Mom that he planned to leave Indiana, and since there was no one around to hear their conversation, this was the perfect opportunity.

"I've been meaning to ask you something," Jake said.

"What's that?"

"I'm wondering why you told my mamm that I planned to leave Indiana soon."

"I never said that."

"Mom said you did. Said you told her that the last time you spoke with her."

Eunice's cheeks flushed a bright pink. "I. . .uh. . .did talk to her, but I didn't really say you'd be leaving soon. I just mentioned that I figured you might be leaving soon since your daed's legs have healed and he's back at work. Besides," she quickly added, "you did say you might be going back to Montana, remember?"

"That's true, but I only said 'might.' I think you jumped to conclusions. And about my daed—the doctor said he should wait until he's fully recovered to start shoeing horses again." Truth was, with the way Dad limped around, Jake wasn't sure he'd ever be able to shoe horses again. Jake didn't want to keep shoeing horses permanently. It would mean he'd have less time for training horses. Besides, Dad needed something to do. If he kept busy, he wouldn't have so much time to think of things he didn't like about Jake.

"I'm sorry to hear your daed's still not able to work. I didn't realize. . ." Eunice stopped talking, leaned closer to Jake, and touched his arm. "I hope what I said about you leaving didn't create a problem between you and your mamm."

Jake shrugged. "It's no big deal. I just told her I'd be sticking around—through the winter at least."

"Does that mean you might not go back to Montana?"

"It all depends."

"On what?"

Jake grimaced. Eunice was sure the nosy one. He'd never met a woman so full of questions—or so irritating. Except for Ella, that is. Nobody, other than Dad, could get under his skin the way Ella did. He still couldn't figure out what she had against him, and that bothered him nearly as much as his strained relationship with Dad. He'd tried to be nice and help Ella's family, but she didn't seem to appreciate it. If he could only do something to convince her that he wasn't as bad as she thought. *Maybe I should buy her a Christmas present. Maybe then she'd realize—*

"Did you hear what I said?" Eunice gave the sleeve of Jake's jacket a tug.

Jake's mind snapped back to the present. "Wh–what was that?"

"I was wondering if you're going to the Christmas program at the schoolhouse next week."

"Guess I'll have to, since some of my brothers and sisters have parts in it."

Eunice smiled. "I'll be there, too, because my brother Richard will be playing the part of Joseph." She shifted her purse to her other arm. "I'd better get into the store now and see how many bars of soap they need. It was nice seeing you, Jake."

"Same here," Jake said as he climbed into his truck.

~❧ ❧~

As Andrew stood beside his horse and buggy watching Eunice and Jake, disappointment flooded his soul. He'd thought Eunice was interested in him, but he guessed he'd been mistaken. From the way Eunice kept touching Jake's arm and leaning so close to him, Andrew was sure she must be interested in Jake. *He'll prob-*

ably end up breaking her heart the way he did Loraine's. Maybe I should warn her. Andrew shook his head. *No, she might not appreciate that, and I don't want her to know that I'm jealous. Guess the best thing for me to do is to wait and see what happens. If Eunice and Jake are seeing each other, there's probably nothing I can do about it.*

Andrew had been planning to buy Eunice something for Christmas, but after seeing her and Jake together, he decided against it. He didn't want her to think he was being pushy or trying to buy her love. No, the best thing for him to do was to stay clear of Eunice for a while and keep his focus on more important things. The only trouble was, he couldn't think of anything or anyone more important than Eunice.

Andrew's shoulders slumped as he crossed his arms over his chest. He felt totally defeated.

CHAPTER 34

I can't believe Christmas is only two days away," Jolene said to Andrew as she made his lunch on a Saturday morning toward the end of December.

"I know. I hope Mom's over the flu by then. None of us will enjoy the holiday if she's sick." He signed the words as he spoke.

Jolene was pleased that Andrew had caught on so quickly to signing. He was the only one in the family who had, although Mom and Dad were still trying. She would continue to teach them until they could sign well enough to communicate easily with her. Even Eunice was able to sign fairly well now. Jolene wondered what Andrew would think when he found out.

Andrew glanced out the kitchen window and groaned. "It's snowing again, and I'm sure the roads will be slippery. Sure wish I didn't have to go to work today."

Jolene nodded, feeling empathy for him. "Since it's Saturday, I won't have to teach, but I do have some work to do around here." She sighed. "I'll be glad when spring comes and we don't have to worry so much about the roads. At least not the kind of worry that winter weather causes."

"You know what Mom always says: 'In the winter our blood runs more slowly and we can let go of last year's worries.'" Andrew grinned at Jolene and signed, *"So I'm with you. Let's look forward to spring."*

"I certainly am. In the meantime, though, I need to get your lunch finished so you can be off to work."

"Is there anything I can do to help?"

"Guess you can get out whatever you want to drink."

"Sure, I can do that." Andrew went to the refrigerator and took out a bottle of apple juice, which he placed on the counter

beside his lunch pail. "Can I ask you something, Jolene?"

"Of course."

"If someone's beginning to have strong
feelings for someone, but they think that
person has strong feelings for someone
else, should they say anything?" Andrew
hesitated and pursed his lips. "I mean
should the person who has strong feelings
for someone tell them and risk rejection,
or would it be better if they kept it to themselves?"

Jolene tipped her head and stared at Andrew. "Would this 'someone' who has strong
feelings for someone happen to be you?"

His face reddened, and he gave her a
sheepish grin as he nodded.

"Is the other someone Eunice Byler?"

"Jah."

"Are you in love with her?"

"I haven't gone out with Eunice enough
to know if what I'm feeling for her is love,
but I do have strong feelings for her." Andrew frowned. "But I'm worried that she
might have feelings for Jake."

"What makes you think that?"

"I've seen them together a few times.
The other day I saw them with their heads

real close, and Eunice was touching Jake's arm."

Jolene bit back a chuckle. The hound dog look on Andrew's face was humorous enough, but the thought that Jake might be interested in Eunice was ridiculous.

"Jake will be going back to Montana in the spring," Jolene said. "So I don't think he's much of a threat."

"How do you know he's going back?"

"Eunice told me, when she came for a. . ." Jolene stopped talking. She'd almost blurted out Eunice's secret.

"What were you going to say? You really don't think there's anything going on with them?"

"I. . .uh. . .think the only person Eunice is interested in is you."

Andrew shrugged. "Guess I'll have to wait and see how it goes."

She smiled. "I guess you will."

꙳ ꙳

Eunice watched the swirl of snow out the front window of her buggy and knew she'd better concentrate on the road. She didn't want to end up in the ditch like so many other buggies had during frigid weather like this.

I hope Andrew's working today, she thought. She'd been disappointed that she hadn't been able to speak to him at the school Christmas program last week. He'd left before she'd had the chance. She glanced at the small package on the seat beside her. She hoped he'd like the leather wallet she'd bought for him as a Christmas present. She also hoped he wouldn't think she was too forward by giving him a gift, but he had come to her place for supper a few times, and he'd brought her home from more than one young people's gathering. Still, that didn't mean he cared for her as much as she cared for him. Maybe it was only a strong attraction she felt for Andrew, but when she was with him, she found herself wanting to be a better person. . .someone he could trust. . . someone he might even come to love.

Eunice's buggy jerked to one side, halting her thoughts. She gripped the reins as the horse picked up speed, but despite her best efforts, her buggy slid off the road. "Easy, Dolly. Easy, girl," she clucked. "We'd better take it easy or we'll end up stuck in some ditch."

Eunice was relieved when she was able

to guide the horse and buggy back onto the road. She knew she'd better stop thinking about Andrew and pay attention to the road.

A short time later, Eunice pulled her horse and buggy up to the hitching rail outside the harness shop in Topeka. Her excitement mounted, but when she entered the shop, her palms grew sweaty as nervous tension took over. Drawing in a deep breath to help steady her nerves, she moved toward the back of the shop. She found Andrew in front of his workbench, punching holes in a bulky leather strap. Not wishing to disturb his concentration, she stood off to one side.

When he finished the strap and reached for another one, he looked up. That's when he noticed her.

"Wie geht's, Eunice? What brings you out on such a cold, snowy morning?"

She moistened her lips with the tip of her tongue. "I've been delivering some soap and candle orders, and I stopped by to. . ."

"Maybe you should have asked your daed to make the deliveries. The roads are really nasty this morning, and a horse can be hard to handle on snow and ice."

"You sound like Jake. I heard him mention to my daed that. . ."

Andrew's face reddened. *"Duh mich net mit ihm vergleiche!"*

Eunice slapped one hand against her hip. "Don't get so testy, Andrew. I was not comparing you to Jake. I only meant that you and Jake. . ."

"I'd rather not talk about Jake."

"How come?"

"Because I think my cousin Ella's right about Jake. He can't be trusted." Andrew pulled another hunk of leather toward him.

Eunice had begun to realize, here of late, that she never listened carefully enough to what was being said, but she was sure Andrew had just said that Jake couldn't be trusted. What that had to do with Jake telling her dad that horses could be hard to control in the snow, she couldn't imagine.

"I didn't come over here to talk about Jake or start an argument with you, Andrew." Eunice hoped her voice sounded calmer than she felt right now.

"What did you come for?"

"To deliver your Christmas present," she signed.

Andrew set the hunk of leather aside and stared at her with a blank expression. He must not have understood what she'd signed. She'd probably messed it up, but good.

His blank expression faded, and his face broke into a wide smile. "When'd you learn how to sign?"

"Did—did you understand what I said to you?"

"Sure did. You said you came to deliver my Christmas present."

Eunice felt the tension in her shoulders and neck dissipate. "That's what I said, all right."

Andrew's mouth hung slightly open as he continued to stare at her. "But how? I mean, you said you were too busy to take signing lessons."

"I have been busy, but I used it as an excuse not to take lessons with you and your family."

"How come?"

Eunice's face heated as she dropped her gaze to the floor. "Because I thought it would be hard to learn, and I. . .I didn't want to make a fool of myself in front of you."

"You thought if you couldn't learn signing I'd think you were foolish?"

She lifted her gaze and nodded. "I was never very bright in school, and there are so many things I can't do well. I've felt like a failure most of my life, and I didn't want you to be disappointed in me, too."

"If you were trying to learn to sign, I sure wouldn't have been disappointed." Andrew moved away from his workbench and took a step toward Eunice. "How did you learn, anyway?"

Eunice explained how she'd been secretly taking lessons from Jolene at the schoolhouse on the days Jolene wasn't teaching Lonnie or Ella. She ended by saying, "I wanted it to be a surprise."

"It's a surprise, all right. A very pleasant surprise."

She smiled. "I don't know how to sign a lot yet, but I plan to keep learning from Jolene and practicing at home. Hopefully I'll get better with time, but it may take me longer than most because I'm not very good at catching on to new things. As I said, I've always felt like a failure, and—"

Andrew held up his hand. "I've never considered you to be a failure, and you're not dumb, either. You created a good business for yourself, and that had to have taken some doing. Not only that, but you're a real good cook." He moved a bit closer. "I've enjoyed myself whenever you've had me over for supper."

"Really?"

"Said so, didn't I?"

She smiled and handed him the gift she had tucked under one arm. "I hope you like what I got you."

Andrew gave his left earlobe a quick tug and made a funny little grunting sound. "Uh. . .how come you bought me something for Christmas?"

"I bought you a gift because you're my friend, and I—"

"Did you buy Jake something for Christmas, too?"

"What? No! Besides what I got for my family, you're the only one I've bought a gift for."

He scratched the side of his head. "But I thought you and Jake. . ."

"What did you think about me and Jake?"

"I thought you liked him and that the two of you might be going out."

"What in the world gave you that idea?"

"I've seen you talking to him a few times, and the other day in Shipshe, I saw the two of you standing real close." Andrew leaned on his workbench, as though he needed it for support. "For a minute there, I was afraid Jake was gonna kiss you."

Eunice almost laughed out loud as she shook her head. "The only man I care about is you, Andrew Yoder."

"Really?"

"Really."

Andrew stepped close to her side, so that his left arm was brushing her right arm.

She trembled from the wave of warmth she felt whenever he was near.

He glanced around, as though worried they might be seen, but there was no one else in the room. Then slowly, he lowered his head until his mouth was almost against her ear. "I've come to care for you, Eunice, and I hope you'll consider what I'm about to say."

"Wh–what's that?" she asked breathlessly.

"I'd like you to be my steady girlfriend and go out only with me, but there's one little problem."

"What problem?"

Andrew raked his fingers through the back of his hair.

Confusion, mingled with fear, converged on Eunice. "Andrew, what's the matter? What problem is there between us?"

He cleared his throat a couple of times. "It's a problem with your mouth."

Instinctively, she reached up and touched her mouth. "You—you don't like my mouth?"

Andrew took a step back. "Actually, it's not your mouth I have the problem with, it's what comes out of your mouth, in the form of gossip."

She moaned. "Oh, that."

"The Bible says in Proverbs 11:13 that a talebearer reveals secrets. And in Proverbs 10:19 we're told that 'in the multitude of words there wanteth not sin: but he that refraineth his lips is wise.'"

"Jah, Andrew, I know that. I read those same passages in the Biwel the other night, and it made me realize that I have a weakness. But God spoke to my heart." Tears welled in Eunice's eyes. "And with His help I'll try to do better because I know that gossiping is wrong."

He nodded. "It can hurt others when we talk about them."

"You're right, and I don't do it to be mean. Sometimes I'm just not listening close enough to what's being said and I get mixed up about things." She grimaced. "Of course, I guess the best thing is for me not to repeat what I've heard."

Andrew nodded and looked like he was going to reach for her hand, but just then, the door of the harness shop opened and an English man stepped in with a saddle.

"I'd better go," Eunice said. "I'll see you at church tomorrow, Andrew."

"I'll look forward to that." He lifted the gift she'd given him. "Danki for this. I'll bring you a gift on Christmas morning."

Feeling as though she were floating on a cloud, Eunice stepped out the door. When she was a safe distance from the shop, she laughed and spun around in the cascade of heavy snowflakes falling from the sky. They clumped her lashes together and melted on her nose and lips. She licked them and giggled. Her starched head covering absorbed the heavy wetness of the snow, but she didn't care. Andrew cared for her and wanted her to be his steady girlfriend, and he didn't think she was stupid.

Eunice lifted her gaze to the sky. *Please help me, Lord. Help me to remember to bridle my tongue.*

❧❧

As Lonnie trudged up the road toward Jolene's house, he shivered. The long walk through the snow had dampened his back with sweat, and a chill had set in. His horse had thrown a shoe last night, so he'd decided it would be best not to make him pull the buggy until Jake could put on new shoes. Besides, a walk in the brisk air wouldn't hurt him any. It would give him time to think about some of the things that had been weighing heavily on his mind.

In an effort to keep his thoughts off the cold, Lonnie quickened his steps and focused on the scenery and peacefulness of this silent winter day. He recalled that days like this were often silent, even to those who could hear. Every branch and twig was covered under a thick blanket of white. Ice crystals clung to the fence posts surrounding some of the farms he passed. He was tempted to stop and pull one off the way he had as a boy, but he figured he needed to keep going.

Lonnie glanced across the road, where two German shepherd pups frolicked in the snow. Winter was a beautiful time of the year. He just wished it wasn't so cold.

By the time Lonnie reached Jolene's house, he was sweating profusely and had begun to shiver. He was both excited and apprehensive about giving her the gift he'd made. He didn't know exactly when it had happened, but sometime during these last few months, he'd come to care deeply for Jolene. That scared him—a lot. He wasn't sure if she cared for him, and even if she did, he knew they had no future together. Maybe he'd made a mistake in making her a gift. Maybe he should turn around and head for home.

I'm here now, so guess I may as well give her the gift, Lonnie decided. Besides, it would feel good to get out of the cold for a few minutes. With a sense of determination he didn't really feel, he tucked the package for her under one arm and rapped on the door.

A few seconds later, Jolene's mother, Leah, answered his knock. "Guder mariye," he signed as he spoke the words. "Is Jolene at home?"

"She's in the kitchen," Leah signed in reply. Lonnie felt good about being able to communicate with her this way.

He brushed the snow off his jacket and followed as Leah led the way to the kitchen. He was relieved when she left the room and padded down the hall. It would be easier if he spoke to Jolene alone.

He found Jolene sitting at the table, reading her Bible. When he touched her shoulder, she looked up and offered him a friendly smile. "Good morning. You look really wet," she said, signing and speaking at the same time. "Is it snowing again?"

"Not at the moment. I walked over, so I've been sweating."

She motioned to the stove. "You should stand over there and get warm."

He set the gift on the table and moved across the room, enjoying the heat radiating from the stove. *"The gift is for you,"* he signed.

Her eyes lit up. *"Do I have to wait until Christmas to open it?"* she asked, signing the question.

He shook his head. "It's not really a

Christmas present. It's just something I made to say thanks for teaching me total communication."

"I've been glad to do it, so no thanks is—"

"What was that?" Lonnie hadn't understood all the words she'd said.

"I appreciate the gesture." Jolene picked up the gift and tore the wrapping from it. When she removed the bird feeder, she smiled. *"This is nice. I'll enjoy using it to feed the birds the rest of this winter."*

Lonnie was on the verge of saying something else when Jake stepped into the room. He grinned at Jolene and handed her a gift.

"What's this for?" she asked, tipping her head.

"It's a Christmas present, and it's my way of saying thanks for teaching me to sign. You can open it now if you like."

Jolene tore the wrapping aside and withdrew a box full of scented candles in various sizes. There was also a beautiful leather journal inside.

Jolene sniffed the candles and smiled at Jake. "Thank you. That was very thoughtful of you."

"I bought the candles from Eunice. Figured you might like the journal to write down your thoughts about teaching."

"I appreciate them both."

Lonnie cringed. He'd been able to read their lips, and even if he hadn't, it didn't take a genius to see how much Jolene liked Jake's gift. The homemade bird feeder Lonnie had given her didn't look nearly as good as Jake's store-bought gift. He was sure she liked Jake's gift better.

"I should be going," Lonnie said, and he moved quickly toward the door.

Jolene touched his arm and he turned around. *"I offered Jake a cup of coffee. Would you like one, too?"*

"I'd better go." Lonnie hurried out the door. Keeping the way he felt about Jolene to himself was a difficult task. Seeing the way she'd looked at Jake was unbearable.

~❧ ❧~

Exhausted after arising early to get her baking done, Ella took a seat by the fireplace in the living room and draped one of Mama's old quilts around her. Hopefully she'd have a few minutes of quiet to herself before it was time to open the bakeshop.

She pulled the quilt tighter around her shoulders and moved her chair closer to the fire. Flames leaped from the glowing embers, sending a wave of warmth into the room.

Ella leaned her head against the back of the chair and closed her eyes. Christmas was only a few days away, and there was still so much to do.

Tears burned the backs of Ella's eyes as she reflected on last Christmas. *Oh, Papa, I still miss you so much. This will be our first Christmas without you.*

She mentally shook herself. *I can't let the pain of losing Papa ruin our Christmas. I need to put on a happy face for the rest of the family.*

Ella rose from her chair and headed for the kitchen, where she removed the tea kettle from the stove. She'd just poured herself a cup of tea, when she heard the whinny of a horse. She glanced out the window and saw a horse and buggy parked in the yard. Figuring it must be an early customer, she hurried to the back door. As soon as she opened it, a swirl of cold air entered the house. She was surprised to see Jake plodding through the snow toward the bakeshop.

"I'm not open yet!" she hollered.

Jake turned and tromped up to the house. "Thought I'd see if you were there before I came here," he said, stepping onto the porch.

"You just visited my bakeshop two days ago, so please, don't tell me you need more bread," Ella said.

Jake shook his head. "Came to bring you this." He withdrew an envelope from his pocket and held it out to her.

"What is it?"

"Something I thought you might need during the holidays. Call it an early Christmas present." He handed her the envelope. "Go ahead, open it."

Feeling a bit awkward because she had no gift for him, Ella opened the envelope and gasped. There was five hundred dollars inside! Irritation welled in her soul. "What's all this money for, Jake?"

"I thought you could use it to buy your family some gifts."

She dropped the money into the envelope and handed it back to him. "I don't need your money. I've already bought gifts for my family."

"I just thought. . ." Jake stopped talking and dropped his gaze to the porch.

Ella could see the hurt look on his face. She squeezed her eyes shut, knowing she should take back her unkind words but was somehow unable to do so. She was tired of Jake coming over here all the time, buying baked goods she was sure he didn't need and volunteering to do chores she didn't want him to do. Now he wanted to give her money again! Why did dealing with Jake have to be such a challenge? This had to stop!

She opened her mouth to spew angry words, but before she could say anything, Jake dropped the envelope to the little table near the door, turned, and sloshed his way through the snow to his buggy.

Ella's legs trembled as she stepped into the house. Then she dashed into the living room, flopped onto the sofa, and gave in to her threatening tears.

CHAPTER 35

Would you please pass the potatoes?" Jolene's mother signed. She then pointed to the bowl of potatoes sitting in front of Jolene.

Jolene smiled and handed the potatoes to Andrew, who sat beside her, and then he passed them to Mom. It was good to see Mom doing more signing. She was getting so much better at it, too.

Dad looked over at Jolene and signed, *"It's real good to have you back with us."*

Andrew nodded. *"We've missed not having you here for Christmas the last couple of years."*

"I've missed being here, and I'm glad to be home," Jolene said as she signed.

"Do you enjoy teaching Sylvia and Irvin?" one of Jolene's married sisters, Barbara, who was visiting from Wisconsin, asked.

"I sure do."

"I heard you got some nice gifts from your two older students." Barbara grinned and nudged Jolene's arm. "It appears that you might have two men interested in you."

Jolene shook her head. "Lonnie and Jake are just my friends." *Although I wish Lonnie could be more than that,* she mentally added.

Jolene's other married sister, Anna Rose, needled Jolene in the ribs. "Friends who like to give you Christmas presents. I wouldn't be surprised if you don't end up marrying one of them."

"That's not going to happen," Jolene said with a shake of her head.

"How do you know?" Dad asked.

"Because I'm quite sure that Jake will be leaving for Montana in the spring."

Mom pursed her lips. "That's too bad. I'm sure Jake's folks will be very disappointed when he goes."

"I'm sure they will." Jolene forked a piece of ham onto her plate. "Even if Jake should decide to stay in Indiana, I'd still have no interest in him—at least not in a romantic sort of way."

"What about Lonnie?" Anna Rose asked. "From what you've said about him in your letters, I think he'd make a good husband."

"Lonnie told me once that he has no plans to marry," Jolene said around a mouthful of mashed potatoes.

"How come?"

"He was deeply hurt when his girlfriend broke up with him. Besides, he thinks his deafness would hamper him from being a good husband and father." Jolene blotted her lips with a napkin. "I can relate to that kind of thinking because I'm not sure I'd make a good mother, either."

"That's lecherich," Andrew said. "A lot of deaf people get married."

Figuring they needed a new topic of conversation, Jolene quickly changed the subject. "Are you planning to go over to see Eunice today?" she asked Andrew.

Andrew's face turned crimson. "Uh-huh. Thought I might head over there after we've finished our dinner."

"Is Eunice your *aldi*?" Anna Rose asked.

Andrew ate a piece of ham then washed it down with a drink of water. "I believe she *is* my girlfriend."

"Are you sure getting involved with Eunice is a good idea?" Mom asked with a look of concern. "She has been known to spread quite a bit of gossip."

"Eunice is trying to change," Andrew said. "She has a lot of good qualities others don't see, and she told me the other day that she knows it's wrong to gossip, and I believe she's mending her ways."

"If Andrew's interested in Eunice, then I think we should give her a chance," Jolene put in.

Mom reached over and patted Andrew's hand. "We'll support your decision to court whomever you want."

"I appreciate that." He looked over at Jolene and smiled. "You did good at keeping Eunice's secret. She surprised me when she came by the harness shop the other day and signed a few words."

Jolene grinned back at him. "I'm pleased with her progress."

They continued to visit as they ate their

meal, and when everyone was finished, all heads bowed for a second silent prayer.

Heavenly Father, Jolene prayed, *Thank You for the opportunity for us all to be together this Christmas. Thank You for my teaching job and for my students. Please guide and direct each of us in the days ahead.*

"I have presents for all of you," Jake said to his family after they'd eaten their Christmas dinner. "I'll get the ones that are in my room, but I'll need help with the one I have for Dad that's hidden in the barn."

Dad's eyebrows shot up. "You hid something there without me knowing it?"

"Uh-huh, that was the purpose—to keep you from knowing about it. It's behind a stack of hay in one of the empty stalls." Jake smiled, feeling in a cheerful mood. "I'll get the gifts that are in my room first, though." He hurried out of the dining room and returned a few minutes later with a sack full of presents.

Dad sat stony-faced as Jake handed out the gifts, but everyone else seemed happy enough.

"This is great!" Kyle said after he'd opened the fishing pole Jake had given him. "Maybe you and me can do some fishin' when spring comes around."

Deciding it might be best not to discuss his plans for the spring, Jake thumped his brother's arm. "We'll have to see how it goes."

Next, Jake gave his teenage sister, Marilyn, a gift. Her face fairly glowed when she opened a box full of rubber stamps. "Danki, Jake."

He smiled. "I thought you might enjoy them since I know you like to keep all the postcards and letters you received from friends in your scrapbook."

"What'd ya get for me, Jake?" his younger brother Vern asked with an expectant look.

Jake handed the boy a box. "See if you like this."

Vern tore the wrapping aside and lifted the lid on the box. When he reached inside and pulled out a baseball bat and a glove, his eyes lit up. "Danki, Jake! This is just what I've been wantin'!"

Jake looked over at Elmer then. "Your gift's out on the porch."

Elmer jumped up and raced out the door. A few minutes later he returned, pushing a shiny new bike into the room. "Danki, Jake. I really needed a new bike!"

Dad, who'd sat quietly as the children opened their gifts, grunted and frowned at Jake. "Looks to me like you spent a lot of money on those presents."

"From the way my sister and brothers are grinning, I'd say it was money well spent." Jake placed a large box on the table in front of his mother. "Now it's your turn, Mom. I hope you like what's inside."

Mom fumbled with the box, and when she saw finally got it open, a wide smile stretched across her face. "A new set of dishes is exactly what I need. Danki, Jake."

"You're welcome." Jake looked over at Kyle and Elmer. "You two look like you're pretty strong today. How'd you like to help me bring in Dad's gift?"

The boys nodded agreeably and raced to get their jackets, as did Jake. "We'll be back soon," Jake called over his shoulder as they hurried to the door. "Meet us in the living room!"

When Jake and his brothers returned to the house with a large box, he found the rest of his family seated on chairs in the living room.

Dad, who'd taken a seat in his old easy chair, looked up at Jake and said, "What in the world's in that big box?"

"It's your Christmas present." Jake took out his pocket knife and cut the sides of the box open, revealing a beautiful new recliner, upholstered in blue. He stood off to one side, awaiting Dad's response.

"Now why'd you waste your money on something I don't even need when we've got bills that have to be paid?" Dad mumbled.

Jake opened his mouth to reply, but Dad cut him off when he thumped the arm of his old chair and said, "There's nothin' wrong with this old chair. I sure don't need a new one."

"Now, Joe," Mom was quick to say, "Jake must have wanted you to have a new chair, so I think—"

"I don't care what you think," Dad bellowed. "I'm gettin' tired of you always takin' Jake's side!" Before Mom could say anything in her own defense, Dad turned to Jake with a scowl. "As far as I'm concerned, you buying this expensive chair is just your way of showing off."

Jake's mouth dropped open like a broken window hinge. "How is me buying you a nice Christmas present showing off?"

"You're trying to remind us of how much money you made workin' in Montana." Dad snorted. "If you want to throw your money around why don't you buy something sensible like a horse and buggy?"

"I have a horse and buggy," Jake retorted.

"Jah, well, when you left Indiana the first time I laid claim to that horse and buggy. I've just been lettin' you borrow it since you came home."

White-hot anger surged in Jake's soul. He wished he'd never bought Dad the new chair! He shouldn't have bought him anything at all! He wondered why he'd bothered to come home and help out. Dad didn't appreciate it; that was for sure.

"You gonna try out that chair, Dad?" Kyle asked.

Dad shook his head and grunted. "Nope."

"So what do you want me to do?" Jake asked, his irritation mounting. "Am I supposed to take the chair back to the furniture store?"

"The chair's here's now," Mom was quick to say. "If your stubborn daed won't sit in it then I sure will." She flopped into the chair and reclined it back as far as it would go. "Now this is a very comfortable chair, and it looks much nicer than our old one does."

"I like it, too," Kyle spoke up.

"Nobody asked you, boy!" Dad's eyes narrowed as he glared at Kyle. "So just keep your opinions to yourself."

Mom looked at Dad and shook her head. "You don't have to be so harsh. Jake bought you a nice gift for Christmas, and you should appreciate it."

Dad rose from his chair with an undignified grunt and limped across the room.

"Where are you going?" Mom called to his retreating form.

"Out to the barn, where I won't have to look at that expensive chair!"

When the door slammed shut behind Dad, Jake sank to the sofa. He felt like a heel. "I'm sorry for ruining everyone's Christmas," he mumbled.

Mom shook her head. "It's not your fault, Jake. You were only trying to make everyone happy by buying those gifts. Your daed. . .well, he's just so frustrated right now that he can't accept anything from you."

"Frustrated because I won't do everything he says, you mean?"

She shrugged.

"Dad will cool down soon; you'll see," Kyle said, touching Jake's arm. "I'll bet in a few days he'll be sittin' in that new chair with a big ol' smile on his face."

Jake wasn't so sure about that, but he didn't voice his thoughts. Instead, he turned in his chair and stared into the glowing fireplace embers.

After a few minutes, he closed his eyes and tried to relax, but suddenly, Ella came to mind. He thought about the encounter he'd had with her the other day. She hadn't been any happier about the money he'd given her than Dad had been with his new chair. Jake had to wonder if she would keep the money he'd left there or if she'd end up throwing it in his face.

He grimaced and opened his eyes. *Guess I probably ruined Ella's Christmas, too.*

❧ ❧

It had been difficult for Ella to look happy when she'd gotten up Christmas morning, but for the benefit of her family, she knew she had to. While she was sure that her younger siblings still missed Papa, they were full of excitement. Everyone had seemed pleased with the small gifts she'd given them, and although Mama's face looked strained, she'd put up a brave front.

As they sat at the table, eating their Christmas dinner, all the earlier chatting had ceased, and everyone seemed intent on finishing their meal.

"What's for dessert?" Larry asked after he'd cleaned his plate.

"I made apple and pumpkin pies," Ella said. "They're in the kitchen."

Larry licked his lips. "Umm. Think I'll have some of both."

"None for me," Mama said with a shake of her head. "My blood sugar was higher than it should have been when I tested it this morning, and I don't want to send it any higher by eating a piece of sugary pie."

"I made one sugar-free pie, just for you." Ella reached over and patted her mother's hand.

"That was considerate of you, but I think I'll wait awhile to have dessert." Mama sighed. "I hope you get more bakery business soon, because with the cost of my diabetes medicine, I'm worried that we won't have enough money to pay for that as well as all the other things we need."

Ella forced a smile. "We'll get by somehow, Mama. We just need to hang on until spring, and then I'm sure things will pick up."

"I hope so."

Ella pushed her chair away from the table and stood. "Guess I'll go get those pies now."

"Want me to help?" Charlene called as Ella started across the room.

"Thanks anyway, but I can manage."

When Ella stepped into the kitchen, lit only by the propane light above the table, she headed over to the counter where she'd set the pies. She was about to pick up one of the pumpkin pies when she spotted an envelope on one end of the counter.

She grimaced. The money Jake had

given her the other day was inside that envelope. In her haste to get everything done before Christmas, she'd forgotten that she'd laid the envelope there after he'd left it on the porch. She planned to take it back to him one day this week.

Ella removed the money from the envelope and stared at it a few seconds. *We really could use this right now. What's more important: preserving my pride or seeing that my family's needs are met?* With Mama in need of regular medication, the answer came through to Ella rather quickly. She would take the money into Mama and tell her it was a gift from Jake. Then, when she saw the look of gratitude and relief on Mama's face, she'd remember to be thankful.

CHAPTER 36

When spring arrived, the snow left in a rush, and the air was soon scented with budding flowers and trees. Ella's bakery business had picked up a bit, and for that she was thankful. Mama had been managing her diabetes better, too, which meant she was able to help out more. Charlene, though still busy helping Mama with household chores, had more time to spend in the bakeshop with Ella.

When Ella stepped outside one Monday morning in the middle of March, the shrill cry of a crow drew her attention upward. Soon the birds would be building nests, and babies would be born not long after that.

Ella smiled. Katie and Freeman would be getting married in a few weeks, and Loraine was due to have her baby soon.

She shook the dust mop she held and sighed. *I wonder if I'll ever have the privilege of becoming a mother. Probably not, since I don't have a boyfriend. No, there's not much prospect of marriage for me.*

She glanced up the driveway, where Larry, Amelia, and Helen were heading to school. *Guess I'll have to be content helping Mama raise my little brother and sisters.*

She squeezed her eyes tightly shut. *I hope Mama never marries again. I don't think I could bear it if some other man moved in here and tried to take Papa's place.*

"Are you sleeping or just holding that dust mop in your hand?"

At the sound of Charlene's voice, Ella whirled around. "I was just thinking, that's all."

"Thinking about some fellow, I'll bet."

"Of course not." Ella gave the dust mop a couple of good shakes. "There is no fellow in my life."

"What about Jake?"

"What about him?"

"He comes around here often enough. I figured the two of you might be going steady by now."

Ella swatted her sister's arm. "You're such a kidder."

Charlene shook her head. "I'm not kidding. I've seen the way Jake stares at you when he thinks you're not looking."

"More than likely Jake's glaring, not staring at me. As I'm sure you've noticed, Jake and I don't see eye to eye on much of anything." Ella turned toward the door. "We need to finish cleaning up the kitchen before it's time to go out to the bakeshop. Are you coming?"

"Work. . .work. . .work. That's all we ever do," Charlene mumbled as they stepped into the house. "Why don't we close the bakeshop for a few hours this afternoon and go over to Katie's stamp shop? We could buy a few stamps and make some cards or do some scrapbooking this evening."

"We don't have extra money to buy stamps right now. Even if we did, I don't have time to make cards." Ella motioned to the bakeshop. "In case you've forgotten, we have a lot of baking that needs to be done today."

Charlene groaned and leaned against the kitchen counter.

Feeling a little guilty for making her sister work so hard, Ella said, "If you'd like to visit the stamp shop this afternoon, go right ahead, but you'll have to go alone."

Charlene's brows puckered, and she shook her head. "If you're not going to the stamp shop, then neither am I."

~❧ ❧~

Jake stuck his pitchfork into a pile of manure and quickly mounted the cart in front of the spreader. Giving his horse the signal to go, he guided the rig down the lane toward the field. He'd promised Dad he'd help him get the field ready for planting corn, and they needed to get it done quickly because the shadowy sky overhead signaled that rain might be forthcoming.

Unexpectedly, Jake's thoughts went to Ella. He hadn't seen her since their last church service nearly two weeks ago. He'd decided to quit going over to her place to offer his help so often, since he knew it wasn't appreciated. Despite the desire he had to help Ella's family, he was trying hard to stay away, knowing he couldn't let himself get involved with her.

"Not that she'd ever let me be involved," Jake mumbled. He smacked the side of his head. "Why would I want to be involved with someone who clearly can't stand me, and why do I think about Ella so much? All we ever do is argue and get on each other's nerves."

Jake remembered when he and Ella were children that he'd seen a different side of her—a softer, pleasanter side. She'd been cute and spunky back then, and still was, really. Ella hadn't been so defensive and edgy when she was a girl, and even though he'd never told anyone, for a while he'd had a bit of a crush on her. He'd even carried her books a few times as they'd walked to school. Ella had been full of smiles and acted like she was his friend.

I wonder what happened to change her attitude toward me. Was it because I took off for Montana to work on the horse ranch and left her cousin in the lurch? Should I bring that up and see what her reaction is, or would it be better to leave it alone?

Jake grew more confused about his feelings for Ella all the time. Something about her fascinated him. Maybe it was her spunky spirit, or it could be her pretty, reddish blond hair and pale blue eyes.

He shook his head. *No, I just think I'm attracted to her because she's a challenge. She's like a wild, untamed horse that needs to be broken.* Not that he wanted to break Ella's spirit. He just wished he could get her to lower her defenses.

Determinedly, Jake pushed Ella to the back of his mind. He needed to think about something else.

His thoughts went to Kyle, who had asked Jake if the two of them could go fishing after school. Knowing he needed to give Kyle more of his attention, Jake had agreed. As soon as Kyle got home from school, if it wasn't raining, they'd head out.

❧❧

"Sure can't wait to show Larry the fish we caught in his pond," Kyle said as he and Jake walked across the field behind the Yoders' place that afternoon.

"You should have invited Larry to fish with us; then you wouldn't have had to compete with me." Jake thumped his brother lightly on the head. "I did catch the biggest fish, after all."

Kyle snorted. "That's only 'cause you got lucky when that big old fish snagged your line."

Jake chuckled. "What can I say? He must have liked my bait."

When Jake and Kyle entered the Yoders' yard, he spotted Ella taking clothes down from the line. Before he had the chance to say anything, Kyle bounded up to her and announced, "Guess what? My bruder caught the biggest fish I've ever seen, and he took it outa your pond!"

Ella quirked an eyebrow. "Is that so?"

Kyle bobbed his head and grinned. "Show it to her, Jake. Show Ella that big old fish you caught!"

Jake reached into the plastic sack he'd brought along and withdrew the fish. "What do you think?"

Ella gasped, and her cheeks flushed a deep crimson. "Th—that fish was never meant to be caught!"

Jake's forehead wrinkled as he stared at the fish. "What do you mean?"

"It's a plecostomus. My daed put it there last spring to keep the pond clean."

"What's a pleco—whatever you called it?" Kyle asked.

"It eats algae and can grow up to two feet long." Ella motioned to the fish. "It's also known as a suckermouth catfish."

Jake groaned. He felt like a dunce. "I thought I'd caught a plain old catfish. If I'd had any idea it was a suckermouth, I'd have thrown it right back."

"You should have asked before you decided to fish in our pond."

"Guess maybe I should have, but I've seen other people fish there, so I figured you wouldn't care."

She dropped the towel she held into the clothes basket and slapped her hand against her hip. "Well, you figured wrong!"

Kyle, who stood at Jake's side with a worried expression, gave Jake's shirt-sleeve a tug. "I think we oughta go, don't you?"

Jake didn't want to go. He wanted to make Ella see that she was making too much out of him fishing without her permission. And she ought to realize that he hadn't caught the suckermouth on purpose.

Kyle gave Jake's shirtsleeve another tug. "Are we goin' or not?"

"In a minute." Jake moved closer to Ella. "How much did you pay for the plecosto-mus? I'll pay you whatever it's worth."

"I have no idea what Papa paid for the fish. Even if I did, I don't want your money."

"How come?" Kyle asked before Jake could respond.

"Because your bruder has given us enough already." Ella bent down, lifted the clothes basket into her arms, and stomped off toward the house.

"Guess you're in big trouble with Ella, huh, Jake?" Kyle asked.

Jake nodded. "Jah, but then that's nothin' new."

⚜

By the time Ella entered the house, she'd worked herself up so much that she could barely breathe. Jake had a lot of nerve fishing in their pond without asking! As much time as he'd spent fishing over the years, he ought to know the difference between a regular catfish and a sucker-mouth!

"What's that long face all about?" Mama asked when Ella entered the kitchen and placed the basket of clothes on the table.

Ella told Mama how Jake had caught the

plecostomus and mentioned how angry she'd been when he'd told her about it.

"It doesn't sound to me as if Jake caught the fish on purpose, and I don't think you should have made such an issue of it." Mama shook her head. "I'm not sure how much good that fish did for the pond anyway. The last time I looked, there was quite a bit of algae in it."

Ella frowned. "Well, it was a waste of a perfectly good fish. I don't think it's edible, so Jake's getting just what he deserves. . . a worthless suckerfish!"

Mama blew out her breath and rolled her eyes, looking thoroughly disgusted. "I don't know what's happened to my carefree girl, but ever since your daed died, you've been negative and edgy." She shook her finger at Ella, the way she'd done when Ella was a girl. "Jake's been nothing but helpful to us. I think you ought to apologize for getting so upset about the fish."

"Me, apologize to him? Oh, Mama, you don't know how many irritating things Jake's said to me since he came back from Montana. He's never said he was sorry, either. Not even once."

"Jake might not be aware that he's said or done things that have irritated you."

"I'm sure he's aware of it, all right. I think he does certain things just to irritate me."

"Whether that's true or not, the Bible tells us in Matthew 7:12 that we are to do to others as we would have done to us." Mama motioned to the Bible she'd left on the table after they'd had their devotions that morning. "Matthew 6:14 reminds us that if we don't forgive others, our Father will not forgive us."

Ella nodded slowly. "I know that Mama, but with Jake. . ."

Mama held up her hand. "In God's eyes, Jake's no different than anyone else. It's God's will that you forgive him."

Ella's face heated with shame. She knew Mama was right. She also knew she was being petty and overly sensitive about the plecostomus. "I'll apologize to Jake the next time I see him," she said.

≈ ≈

Jake dropped his brother off at home, and then he got his horse and buggy and headed over to Crist's taxidermy shop with the fish. He figured since he'd caught the dumb thing and couldn't eat it, he may as well have it stuffed.

When Jake stepped into the taxidermy shop, he was surprised to see Wayne working there instead of Crist.

"Where's your daed, and how come you're here and not in your woodshop?" Jake asked as he stepped up to Wayne.

"Pop took Mom to see the chiropractor. Her back kinked up last night when she was getting ready for bed." Wayne motioned to the deer hide on the workbench in front of him. "So I told Pop I'd work here while he's gone, and I put Lonnie in charge of my shop."

"Oh, I see." Jake removed the plecostomus from the plastic bag and told Wayne how he'd accidentally caught it, including the part about how mad Ella had become when he'd told her about it.

"You know Ella," Wayne said as he rubbed the side of his nose. "She's always gotten upset easily. It's just in her nature."

"Tell me about it. But I think she gets more upset with me than anyone else." Jake pointed to the fish. "So can I leave this with you to have it stuffed? Thought it'd make a nice little trophy to hang on the wall."

Wayne shrugged. "Suit yourself."

Jake leaned against one end of the workbench, and after they'd visited about a few others things, he picked up a stuffed squirrel sitting on the shelf behind him and tossed it into the air like it was a baseball.

Wayne snickered and shook his head. "Are you ever gonna grow up and quit fooling around?"

"Beats me."

"You'll never find a woman if you keep acting like a *bensel*."

Jake frowned. "I'm not a silly child, and I'm not lookin' for a woman, so I should be able to act any way I want."

Wayne lifted his gaze to the ceiling. "I think we'd better change the subject."

"Good idea." Jake placed the squirrel back on the shelf. "What's new with you these days?"

"Not a whole lot. Loraine and I are just waiting patiently for the boppli to make its appearance." Wayne pulled his fingers through the ends of his beard. "Speaking of babies, Tripod, that pet ewe of mine with only three legs, gave birth to twin lambs this morning. Would you like to go out to the barn and take a look?"

Jake nodded, but before they could make a move to leave the shop, Loraine rushed into the room with a worried expression. "I've been in labor for the last few hours." She touched her bulging stomach. "I think it's time to go to the New Eden Care Center, because I'll soon have this boppli."

CHAPTER 37

When Lonnie pedaled his bike up the drive-way leading to the schoolhouse, he noticed some of the scholars were taking advantage of the nice weather to play an after-school baseball game. What took him by surprise was seeing Jolene standing near second base. Had she forgotten about their lesson, or had she just gotten caught up in the game?

Lonnie had kept an emotional distance from Jolene ever since he'd given her the bird feeder for Christmas. He'd been on the verge of asking her out that day, but after Jake had shown up with his gift for

Jolene and Lonnie had seen her response to it, he'd chickened out and changed his mind. It was probably better that way, since he really had nothing to offer her.

Lonnie moved closer to the baseball field and watched as Kyle Beechy stepped up to home plate, wearing a determined look on his face.

Fifteen-year-old Daniel Stoltzfus was the pitcher, and he threw the ball right over the plate.

Kyle swung the bat hard but missed. He gritted his teeth and took his stance again.

Daniel took aim and threw the ball once more. This time Kyle hit the ball with such force that it sailed over the pitcher's head and landed clear out in center field. Several boys scrambled for the ball, but by the time James Smucker had picked it up, Kyle was halfway around the bases. Unless someone acted fast, he was sure to make a home run.

James quickly threw the ball toward second base. Jolene, however, wasn't looking his way and didn't see the ball coming.

Lonnie cupped his hands around his mouth and hollered, "Look out, Jolene!"

Of course, she couldn't hear him, and

he was too far away for her to read his lips.

The ball smacked Jolene's knee with such force that she crumpled to the ground.

Lonnie raced onto the field and dropped down beside her. *"Hold still. Your leg might be broken,"* he signed.

"I'm sure it's not broken; I think it's just bruised." Jolene grasped Lonnie's arm and slowly rose to her feet.

Everyone clambered around. Lonnie felt frustrated because they all seemed to be talking at once, and he couldn't make out what anyone was saying.

Finally, Jolene held up her hand to quiet them. Then with a brave smile she said, "I'm fine. Lonnie will help me into the schoolhouse. Go on with your game."

As Lonnie walked beside Jolene, letting her lean on his arm, he thought this was just another example of why he could never consider asking her to marry him. It would be difficult enough for a deaf person to be married to someone who could hear, but if two deaf people got married, it was just asking for trouble. How could either of them be good parents? What if they had children and one of them called for help? Beyond that, what if Jolene betrayed him the way Carolyn had done? So many unanswered questions all led to one thing: He'd stupidly allowed himself to fall in love with Jolene.

⊰≈⊱

When they entered the schoolhouse, Jolene gasped at the stark emotion she saw in Lonnie's eyes. Her heart pounded with sudden hope. Maybe he cared about her as much she cared for him. If he did, he'd sure been keeping it to himself. Ever since Christmas, he'd only come around when he needed a lesson, and he never said much to her of a personal nature. The day he'd given her the bird feeder as a Christmas present, she'd hoped he might ask her out. Instead, soon after Jake had shown up, Lonnie had rushed out the door.

Maybe it's a good thing I'm not going out with anyone, she told herself. *Men are hard to figure out, and I've got enough to deal with just teaching school.*

"If your leg's hurting too much, maybe we should forget about my lesson today," Lonnie signed, pulling Jolene's thoughts back to the present.

She shook her head. *"I'll be fine. I don't*

think I should try to tackle the stairs, though. If you don't mind, we'll have our lesson down here in Fern's classroom."

"I don't mind." Lonnie pulled out the chair at Fern's desk, and Jolene took a seat. *"Should I go upstairs and get the hand mirror?"*

"Yes, please."

"How about some ice to put on your knee?"

"That'd be good. There's an ice pack in my lunch box."

Lonnie hesitated a few seconds; then when she waved him on, he hurried from the room. He returned a few minutes later with the mirror and Jolene's lunch box. When he handed it to her, the gentle, caring expression on his face was almost her undoing.

She fought the urge to tell him how much she'd come to care for him, but that would be too bold. Unless he made the first move, she would keep the feelings she felt for him locked away in her heart.

⚜ ⚜

When Jake stepped into the taxidermy shop, Crist turned from the job he was working on and offered him a friendly smile.

"Afternoon, Jake. If you came to check on your fish, I'm afraid it's not ready yet."

"No, I didn't think it would be done this soon. Came to see Wayne and find out whether Loraine had her boppli."

Crist nodded enthusiastically. "She had a baby boy two days ago. She and the little guy are doin' real well." He glanced out the window. "Wayne's probably working in his shop, but Loraine, Ada, Priscilla, and the boppli are up at the house if you'd like to stop in and say hello."

"Maybe some other time. I just stopped by to find out if she'd given birth, and I wanted to know if everything went okay. I'm sure my mamm will expect a full report when I get home."

Crist chuckled. "Most women are like that, all right. I know my Ada sure is. Nothing much goes on in this community without her knowing it."

"Speaking of Ada," Jake said, "when I was here the other day Wayne said she was having trouble with her back. Is she feeling better?"

"Jah, the chiropractor fixed her right up."

"That's good. Well, guess I'd best be on my way. I have one more stop to make before I head for home." Jake turned toward the door. "Tell Wayne I said congratulations on becoming a daed."

"I will."

※ ※

Ella had just put the CLOSED sign in her bakeshop window when the door swung open, nearly knocking her off her feet. Her heart pounded when she saw that it was Jake.

"I'm just closing. But if you really need something, I can stay open a few more minutes and get it for you."

"I don't need anything this time." Jake shifted his weight from one foot to the other then leaned against the display counter as he stared inside.

"Are you sure you don't want something? Chocolate chip cookies are on sale this week."

"Sounds good, but I'd better not." Jake patted his stomach. "Can't afford to get fat if I'm gonna have the energy to keep training horses." He cleared his throat a couple of times. "Actually, the reason I stopped by is to say—"

"I'm sorry," Ella blurted out.

Jake tipped his head. "What was that?"

"I said, 'I'm sorry.'"

A funny little grin spread over Jake's face. "That's exactly what I was going to say." He stepped closer to Ella. So close that she could feel his warm breath on her face. "What is it that you're sorry for?"

The gentleness in Jake's voice surprised Ella. She swallowed a couple of times and wiped her damp hands on the sides of her apron. "I'm. . .uh. . .sorry for the way I acted when you told me you'd caught our plecostomus."

His grin grew wider. "You were pretty mad about that."

She clenched her fingers against her sides. Was he trying to goad her into another argument? "What are *you* sorry for, Jake?"

"I'm not sorry for catching the fish because it wasn't my fault that the critter took hold of my bait." He took another step toward Ella. "But I am sorry that I didn't take the fish off my line and put him back in the pond."

She shrugged. "What's done is done. Let's just forget about it, shall we?"

"I can't really forget about it because I took that old sucker catfish over to the taxidermy shop to have it stuffed. When it's done, I thought I'd bring it over here so you can hang it on your wall." Jake looked quite pleased with himself. Did he really think he'd done a good thing?

"What are you trying to do, Jake, rub salt in my wounds?"

"'Course not. I just thought. . ."

"Oh, I know, you expect me to put in on my wall so that every time I look at it I'll remember how you killed our fish!"

Jake's eyebrows furrowed. "Are you saying you don't want the fish?"

"That's exactly what I'm saying!"

He took two steps closer. . .so close, they were almost touching noses. "Fine then, I'll take the fish and hang it on *my* bedroom wall!"

"That's a good idea; you do that, Jake!"

"I will!"

Jake continued to stare at Ella; then, in a surprise gesture, he reached out and tipped her chin up with his thumb.

Ella was surprised by the wild flutter of her pulse when he touched her. She stood motionless, caught up in the moment. Her heart thumped so hard she could barely breathe.

Slowly, Jake lowered his head and captured her lips in a kiss so tender and sweet that it stole her breath away. As the kiss continued, Ella wrapped her arms around Jake's neck.

Suddenly Ella pulled away, heat flooding her face.

"S—sorry about that," Jake stammered. "I—I'd better go." He stared at her a moment longer, as though trying to memorize her face, then turned and rushed out the door.

Ella flopped onto the stool behind the counter and closed her eyes. *Dear Lord, please make me strong. Help me not to lose my heart to Jake all over again.*

CHAPTER 38

Ella tied her horse to a post on the back porch, prepared to give it a bath. She was planning to visit Loraine today, because she hadn't seen the baby yet. But her silly horse had decided to roll in the mud in the corral.

For some reason, the horse acted more fidgety than usual, and it made her think about Jake and how easily he handled horses. She found herself wishing that Jake was here right now. Two days had passed since their unexpected kiss, and Ella still hadn't shaken off the feelings it had brought on. For the life of her, she couldn't figure out why she'd allowed Jake to kiss her. Or for that matter, what had possessed him to do it. It wasn't like they were a courting couple. Since they mostly argued when they were together, it made no sense that he'd want to kiss her.

Ella let her mind wander back to the past. . .back to when she'd had a school-girl crush on Jake and had waited anxiously at the end of their driveway for him to show up and walk her to school every day. She knew now that what she'd felt for Jake back then wasn't love, but she sure had liked him a lot. Ella had often wondered how things might have gone if Jake had taken her for a ride in his buggy when he'd turned sixteen. Would they have started going out? Would she have become his steady girl? Even if they had started dating, Jake might have left for Montana. It could have been her instead of Loraine left pining for Jake and hoping for a letter.

I'm not that little girl with a crush on Jake anymore, Ella told herself. *I'm a grown woman who should know better than to let herself fall for Jake again.*

A horsefly buzzed nearby, and Ella's

horse whinnied and jerked its head. "Hold still, Pet," Ella mumbled. "You know you're only making things worse!"

Pet continued to thrash her head and snap at the fly, while Ella tried to steady the animal with one hand and hold onto the hose with the other hand.

Whoosh!—Pet jerked again, flicking the hose with her tail. That, in turn, caused the water to squirt Ella right in the face.

"Thanks a lot," Ella mumbled. "You're the one who needs a bath, not me." She grasped the hose and sprayed some water on Pet's legs.

The fly buzzed again, and Pet tossed her head and stamped her front hooves. Ella shot a spray of water at the fly but hit the horse's head instead. Pet reared up, knocking the hose out of Ella's hand and breaking the rope that had secured her to the post. The hose flipped this way and that, shooting water in all directions. By the time Ella was able to grasp it, her clothes were soaking wet. She looked around and spotted the horse's hind end as it disappeared into the barn.

"I don't need this today," Ella grumbled. She was about to turn off the hose, when a horse and buggy pulled into the yard. It stopped in front of the hitching rail, and Jake got out. "Are we having a bit of trouble?" he asked when he joined her. "You look like a cat caught in a rainstorm."

Ella wrinkled her nose. "Very funny."

Jake chuckled. "If you're trying to give yourself a shower with the hose, then maybe you'd better go inside and get a bar of soap."

"For your information, I was trying to give my horse a bath, but she got upset when a horsefly kept buzzing her. Then she broke free from the porch post where she was tied, and the hose got knocked out of my hand and shot water all over me."

"What made you tie the horse to the post on the porch?"

"Well, I. . ."

"Probably would have been better if you'd tied her to the corral fence or the hitching rail."

"I wanted to be close to the hose, so I thought—"

"Horses are very powerful animals, Ella. You never know what they're going to do."

"I realize that, but—"

"You've got to let the horse know who's

boss right away, or it'll take advantage of you."

"Are you saying I know nothing about my horse?"

"No, I'm just saying that you need to be in control."

Ella's temper flared, and she opened her mouth to defend herself but stopped when she felt a nudge at her heart. Angry words didn't solve a thing. Like Mama had mentioned the other day, the Bible taught that she should treat others the way she would want them to treat her.

"I'd like to continue this discussion," Ella said, "but I need to get inside and change into some dry clothes so I can go see Loraine and Wayne's new boppli."

"Would you like me to get your horse and hitch it to the buggy while you change clothes?" Jake offered.

Ella almost said she could do it herself but changed her mind. "Jah, sure, I'd appreciate that." She started up the stairs but turned back around. "Pet's in the barn."

"I kinda figured that, since I didn't see her out here." Jake sprinted for the barn, and Ella entered the house.

When she stepped outside a short time

later, carrying the gift she'd bought for Loraine's baby, she saw Jake standing beside her horse, shaking his head.

"What's wrong? How come Pet's not hitched to my buggy?" Ella asked.

He pointed to the horse's right front foot. "She's missing a shoe."

Ella grimaced. "That's just great! Guess I won't be going over to see Loraine's boppli after all, because Charlene and Mama had some errands to run in town, and they took our other driving horse."

"I'd shoe the horse for you right now," Jake said, "but I don't have any of my tools with me."

"That's okay. I can go over to Loraine's some other time." She flopped onto the porch step with a weary sigh.

Jake put Pet in the corral then joined Ella on the porch. "Why don't I drive you over to Loraine's and we can both see the baby? After that, I'll stop by my place, pick up my tools, and shoe your horse when I bring you home."

Ella hesitated but finally nodded.

They headed for Jake's buggy, and when Jake reached for Ella's hand to help her up, she felt an unexpected tingle. *It must be my imagination.*

As they turned onto the road, tension wound around them. Ella figured she needed to say something to help herself relax, so she pointed across the road and said, "Looks like there are plenty of trees being tapped for maple syrup this spring."

"Yep. Sure looks that way."

Ella searched for something else to talk about. Anything to keep from thinking about the kiss that she and Jake had shared the last time they were together. "Do you enjoy working with horses and training them to pull buggies more than you do shoeing them?"

"I definitely prefer to train 'em." Jake looked over at her and smiled. "Once I get my own business going, I probably won't do any shoeing."

His own business? Did that mean Jake was planning to stay in Indiana? Did Ella dare to ask?

"Of course, training horses isn't all fun and games," Jake continued. "Some horses can be real stubborn, and some are just plain high strung. I once had a horse that kept throwing his head back, so I had to come up with a way to make him stop."

"What'd you do?"

"I took a plastic bag and filled it with warm water. Then I got a split piece of leather, and whenever the horse threw his head back, I smacked the leather strap in the air so it made a loud *crack*. At the same time, I broke the bag of water between the horse's ears."

Ella's interest was piqued. "What did that accomplish?"

"The noise and the warm water made the horse think he must have been hurt and was bleeding. Believe it or not, it settled him right down."

"Hmm. . .that's interesting. Are there some specific things that might make a horse spook or act up?"

"Yep. When a horse is going down the road pulling a buggy it can get spooked by several things. Mailboxes; flower beds; people walking; cows or horses running in an open field. Oh, and a horse can get pretty upset when a loud semitruck roars past." Jake's nose crinkled. "Some horses like to rear up and take off, and I have to be ready for that. Of course, some horses are so temperamental that they can never be trained to pull a buggy."

"Where do you buy the horses you train?" Ella questioned.

"From horse dealers, who get them from the race track. When I get the horses, they're already harness trained but not trained to pull a buggy. So that's my job. I always start by getting them to pull a cart, and then we progress to the buggy."

"I know how important it is to have a dependable horse," Ella said. "We have enough buggy accidents caused by other vehicles on the road. We don't need unruly horses causing more accidents."

"That's for sure. Buggies aren't cheap, and when one's destroyed because of an accident, the Amish man who owns the rig is out a lot of money." Jake let go of the reins, lifted one hand, and turned it palm up. "Since an Amish man doesn't have insurance to replace the buggy, the way most Englishers have with their cars, it's not always easy to get a new rig right away."

"That's true."

They rode in silence awhile; then to Ella's surprise, Jake draped his arm over the back of the seat, so his hand touched her shoulder. "Would you like to go out to supper with me one night next week?"

Ella's spine tingled and she sat up straight. "I. . .uh. . .don't think that's a good idea, Jake."

"Why not?"

"Because we'd probably end up arguing the whole evening."

"That's what we do, Ella." Jake's eyes sparkled with laughter, and Ella found herself smiling in response.

"I'm not sure why we argue so much," she said in a near whisper.

"Maybe it's because we're so much alike."

She shook her head. "I don't think so. We're about as different as the sun and the moon."

"So are you saying that you won't go out with me because I'm not like you?"

"That's not what I meant." Ella thought about the kiss they'd shared the other day. She had a feeling Jake had been as shocked by it as she'd been. She also thought about the promise she'd made to herself, not to let herself get involved with Jake.

What happened between us was noth-

ing more than a fleeting attraction, she decided. *Jake and I have nothing in common, and I'm sure that I'd never be able to trust him again.*

Jake bumped Ella's arm. "Answer me, Ella. Is the reason you won't go out to supper with me because I'm not like you?"

"No, not really. It's just that I don't think we should start something we can't finish." Ella steeled her heart against Jake's lopsided grin and looked away.

Jake reached over and tucked a wayward strand of hair under Ella's head covering, and then he let his fingers glide down the length of her face. His gentle touch was almost her undoing.

❧ ❧

Jake moistened his lips and fought the urge to kiss Ella. Ever since he'd tasted her lips the other day, he'd wanted to kiss her again. *What's wrong with me?* he wondered. *Why would I want to kiss someone who clearly doesn't like me? It just has to be because I see Ella as a spirited challenge—like one of my unruly horses.*

Jake forced himself to keep his eyes on the road. It was ridiculous to think such thoughts.

When they pulled into the driveway leading to Wayne and Loraine's place, Jake halted his horse and buggy.

"What are we stopping here for?" Ella questioned.

"I. . .uh. . .had an urge to. . ." Jake never finished his sentence. Instead, he pulled Ella into his arms. When his lips touched hers, it seemed as if the whole world had receded into nothingness. The kiss was exhilarating and had been worth the wait.

Ella was the first to pull away again, and he couldn't help but notice that her fair complexion had become mottled with red.

"I probably should apologize for that," he murmured, "but I'm not going to. You know why?"

"Wh–why?"

"Because I enjoyed it, and I think you did, too."

Ella looked down at her hands clasped in her lap.

As Jake continued to stare at her, the truth slammed into him with such force that he almost fell out of the buggy. He was in love with Ella!

Clearing his throat, he was prepared to declare his love and take his chances on her reaction, but before he could get a word out, Ella spoke first.

"I. . .uh. . .hope you didn't get the wrong impression when I let you kiss me."

"What do you mean?"

"I'm not sure what's been happening between us lately, but I think we both realize that we can never be more than friends."

Disappointment flooded Jake's soul. It made no sense, given the way she'd responded to his kiss. For some reason, Ella seemed to be holding back. He'd been hoping for more than friendship, but if that was all Ella wanted, then he'd have to accept her decision no matter how much it hurt. Her friendship was better than nothing—and it'd be better than them arguing all the time.

CHAPTER 39

For someone's who's going to a wedding, you sure look glum today," Charlene said to Ella as they met each other in the hall outside their bedrooms.

"I'm not glum, just tired." Ella yawned. "I worked hard yesterday getting Katie's cake done, and after I delivered the cake, I spent the rest of the day helping Katie and several others set things up for the wedding meal." She smiled at Charlene and gave her shoulder a gentle squeeze. "I appreciate your taking over in the bakeshop for me so I could help Katie."

"No problem; I was glad to do it."

Ella sniffed the air as she descended the stairs behind her sister. "Smells like Mama has the coffee going already."

"Jah, she's been feeling better lately and seems to be getting a lot more done." Charlene halted when she got to the bottom of the stairs and turned to face Ella. "Are you looking forward to being one of Katie's witnesses today?"

"I am, and I'm sure Jolene is, too."

"Who'd you say Freeman asked to be his witnesses?"

"Andrew and Lonnie."

"Do you wish he'd asked Jake so you could be with him all day?"

Ella's mouth went dry. Why did Charlene have to bring up Jake? She'd been trying so hard not to think about him.

Charlene poked Ella's arm. "Well, do you wish you could be with Jake today?"

"Of course not."

"Are you sure? I mean, every time Jake comes around, I see a look of longing on your face."

Ella shook her head. "You're wrong. The only look you see on my face when Jake's around is a look of frustration." Even as Ella spoke the words, she couldn't deny her own feelings to herself. The fascination she'd had for Jake as a child had resurfaced soon after he'd started coming around offering to help out. She'd never have admitted it to Charlene, but she'd begun to see a side of Jake she hadn't seen before. He could be kind, helpful, and interesting to talk to. Every time Jake came over, Ella found herself wishing Jake would see her as more than someone who needed his help. Maybe he did. He'd kissed her, not once, but twice. And he'd invited her to have supper with him. Was Jake just toying with her affections, or did he have feelings for her? The question that haunted Ella the most was whether Jake could be trusted not to hurt her again.

"Guess we'd better get into the kitchen and help with breakfast," Charlene said, bumping Ella's arm. "It wouldn't be good for one of the bride's attendants to be late for the wedding."

Still half asleep from getting to bed too late the night before, Jake stumbled across the room and stubbed his toe on the end of the bedpost. A burst of pain shot up his leg, and he groaned. Limping over to the dresser, he jerked the bottom drawer open to retrieve a pair of clean socks. He'd slept longer than he'd planned to and needed to get dressed and down to breakfast soon, or he'd be late for Freeman and Katie's wedding.

Jake reached inside the drawer for a pair of dark-colored socks but only found one. The rest were all white. "There's gotta be another black sock in here somewhere. They can't all be in the wash," he muttered. He fumbled around for the matching sock but found none. In exasperation, he pulled the drawer out and set it on the floor. After a bit more fumbling, he finally located another black sock near the back of the drawer. When he lifted the drawer to put it back in place he caught a glimpse of something wedged between the bottom drawer and the wood that separated it from the drawer above. It looked like a piece of paper.

Jake reached inside and pulled it out. The paper had been folded in half, and one end was torn clean off. He unfolded it and squinted at the words written there.

I can't believe you lied to me, Jake. You promised when you turned sixteen

and got your own buggy that I'd be the first one you took for a ride. I'll never trust you again!

Jake stared at the note for several minutes. The rest of the page—probably where the person who'd written the note had signed their name—was gone.

Jake scratched the side of his head. *I wonder who wrote this note and how it got in my drawer.*

He sat there a few minutes, letting his mind take him back to the past. The first girl he'd taken out after he'd turned sixteen was Loraine, so the note couldn't have been from her. *Who'd I make such a promise to?* he asked himself. *Who wrote me this note, and how come I don't remember anyone giving me the note?*

Tap! Tap! Tap! Someone knocked on Jake's door. "Who is it?" he hollered.

"It's me, Kyle. Mom said to tell you that breakfast is almost ready, so you'd better get a move on, 'cause it'll be time to leave for the wedding soon."

"Okay. Tell her I'm coming."

Jake put the drawer back in place and stuck the note inside his coat pocket, which he'd laid out the night before to wear to the wedding. He'd think more about this later.

~ ~

When Jolene and her family pulled into the Bontragers' yard to attend Katie and Freeman's wedding, she was surprised to see Lonnie, dressed in a dark-colored frock coat and matching trousers, pacing in front of the buggy shed, where the wedding would take place. She'd known him long enough to tell when he was nervous, and the fact that he was pacing was a good indication that he must be quite anxious this morning.

As soon as Dad stopped the buggy, Jolene climbed down and hurried over to Lonnie. *"How come you're pacing?"* she signed.

He grimaced. *"I'm nervous about being one of Freeman's witnesses."*

"There's no need to be nervous. You won't have to do a lot—just sit with Freeman during the wedding service and also the meal afterward."

Lonnie nodded, although he didn't look convinced. He'd come a long way these last few months, but it was obvious he still had some doubts.

"**I mean it. Everything will be okay.**"

"**I'm not so sure about that. There will be a lot of people here today. I'm still having trouble reading lips.**"

"**Don't worry; we'll have Jake and Andrew to interpret for us through signing.**"

"I think it would have been better if Freeman had picked Jake as one of his witnesses, instead of me," Lonnie signed.

"**What makes you say that?**"

"**Jake has more confidence than I do. If he'd been asked to be one of Freeman's attendants, the two of you could have been together today.**"

"**I'd rather be with you than Jake.**"

Lonnie tipped his head. *"What was that?"*

"I'd rather be with you than Jake," Jolene repeated, speaking as she signed.

"**You don't have to say that just to make me feel better. I've accepted the fact that you and Jake are going out.**"

Jolene's mouth dropped open. *"Where'd you get that idea?"*

"**I've seen you two together a lot, and**

you liked his Christmas gift more than—"

"Jake and I are not going out."

Lonnie didn't seem to grasp what she'd said, so she repeated it, signing as she spoke.

"You're not interested in Jake?"

"Only as a friend."

Was that a look of relief she saw on Lonnie's face? Could it possibly mean that he might have feelings for her? Had he been holding back all this time because he thought she and Jake were going out, or was his deafness the reason he'd been keeping his distance? Jolene wanted to say more, but she spotted Katie on the other side of the building, motioning for her to come. *"The bride is waiting for me, so I'd better go."*

"Guess I'd better find Freeman, too," Lonnie signed.

A sense of sadness crept over Jolene as she joined Katie and saw the happiness glowing on her face. Lonnie had given no definite indication that he saw her as anything more than a friend. And with Lonnie being set against marriage, the chance of him asking her out was slim.

She'd have to accept that fact and focus on being happy for Katie and Freeman today.

❦

As Jake sat on a backless wooden bench on the men's side of the buggy shed, he couldn't keep his eyes off Ella. She sat in a straight-back chair between Katie and Jolene, facing Freeman and his two witnesses, Andrew and Lonnie. Ella looked prettier than ever today. She wore a dark blue dress that brought out the color of her pale blue eyes, and a white cape with matching apron. On her head, she wore the black head covering that was typically worn to their church by young women before they were married.

Ella glanced over at Jake then quickly looked away, turning her attention to the message Bishop Hershberger was preaching from the book of Ruth. Toward the end of his message, he quoted from 1 Corinthians and Ephesians. Jake paid special attention when the bishop read Ephesians 5:31: "'For this cause shall a man leave his father and mother, and shall be joined unto his wife, and they two shall be one flesh.'"

Katie seemed to radiate a blissful glow as she and Freeman left their chairs and stood before the bishop to say their vows, but Jake could only concentrate on Ella. He wondered how she would look on her wedding day. He knew Ella would be a pretty bride, and he found himself wondering what kind of wife and mother she'd make.

A vision of Ella sitting in a rocking chair, holding a baby with reddish blond hair, popped into Jake's head. He knew Ella could bake, because he'd tasted many of her baked goods. He'd also seen how well she managed a home and had witnessed the love and gentleness she showed, not only to her mother, but to her younger siblings as well. He felt sure Ella would make a good wife and mother.

Ella looked his way again then quickly averted her gaze. *Sure wish I knew when Ella started disliking me so much. When we were kinner, I thought we were friends.*

As Jake continued to ponder this question, he realized that Ella had cooled off toward him around the time he'd started courting Loraine. He just wasn't sure why. Until recently, after she'd let him kiss her,

Ella had shown no interest in him at all. At least not in a positive way. It made no sense. . .unless. . .Jake's spine stiffened, and he nearly fell off his bench. Unless Ella had written that note.

As Katie and Freeman spoke their vows before the bishop, Jake made a decision. The first chance he had to speak with Ella alone, he'd come right out and ask if she'd written the note.

～※ ※～

As Ella sat on one side of Katie during the wedding meal, she had a hard time concentrating on anything other than Jake. He sat at a table directly across from her, looking more handsome than usual in a white shirt, dark trousers, and matching jacket. He kept looking at her, and she wondered what was going through his mind. Was he thinking about the day they'd gone to see Loraine's baby, and the kiss they'd shared in his buggy? Ella still couldn't believe she'd let her guard down like that—not once, but twice she'd been foolish enough to let him kiss her. The mixture of feelings she had for Jake made no sense at all. One minute she felt irritated by everything he said. The next minute she was melting in his arms like butter left out on a hot summer day.

Ella's mouth went dry as a sudden realization hit her full in the face. She was in love with Jake and wished she could be his wife!

That's crazy thinking, she told herself. *Jake doesn't love me. Besides, he's given me no reason to trust him. He probably only kissed me just to prove he could do it. He probably thinks he's such a good catch that any woman would throw herself at his feet.*

Ella reached for her glass of water and was about to take a drink, when Jake left his seat and headed toward the bride and groom's corner table.

"I have a couple of horses to shoe this afternoon, so I have to leave soon," he said, looking first at Katie and then Freeman. "Just wanted to say congratulations and wish you all the best."

"Danki, Jake." Freeman's smile stretched ear to ear, and Katie fairly beamed. Ella couldn't help feeling a bit envious. If only she and Jake could be that happy. If only it was their wedding day.

Jake glanced her way, but she quickly

looked away, and as he talked more with Katie and Freeman, she began a conversation with Jolene. "Did you ever see so much food?" she asked, signing as she spoke.

Jolene smiled and patted her stomach. "After today, I probably won't have to eat for the rest of the week."

"Me neither," Andrew spoke up. He nudged Lonnie and signed, *"How about you? Are you getting enough to eat today?"*

"I've already had more than my share," Lonnie said with a grin.

Ella was about to ask Jolene another question when someone tapped her on the shoulder. She turned and gulped. Jake stood behind her wearing a serious expression. "I wonder if I could speak to you for a minute," he whispered, bending close to her ear.

"Uh. . .sure. What did you want to say?"

"Not here." Jake motioned toward the door with his head. "Can you meet me outside?" His voice was so low, she could barely hear him.

Ella shook her head. "In case you hadn't noticed, I'm busy eating."

"I don't see anything on your plate right now." Before Ella could respond, Jake leaned over her shoulder and reached for her plate. In the process, he bumped her glass of water, knocking it over and soaking the front of Ella's dress.

Jake grabbed the glass and set it upright. "Oops, sorry about that. You'd better go outside and let the sun dry your dress."

Ella gritted her teeth, but before she could formulate a response, Jake disappeared outside.

Ella waited a few minutes then excused herself. When she stepped outside, she found Jake leaning on the corral fence, as though waiting for her.

"What's so important that you had to drag me away from the wedding meal?" she asked, stepping up to him.

He chuckled. "I didn't drag you anywhere. Looks to me as if you came out here of your own free will."

"Jah, well, that's because I needed to let my dress dry out." She frowned. "Do you enjoy humiliating me, Jake?"

"No, of course not. Why do you always assume the worst where I'm concerned?" He touched her arm, and she shivered.

"Are you cold?"

"No, I'm fine."

"I don't think so, Ella. I don't think you're ever really fine when you're with me."

"What's that supposed to mean?"

He reached into his pocket, pulled out a piece of paper that had been folded in half, and handed it to her. "Is this *your* handwriting?"

Ella opened it and gasped as she stared at the words. "Wh–where'd you get this?"

"Found it this morning. It was stuck in the back of my sock drawer."

"Oh, I see." Ella's voice quavered, and her hands shook so badly that she had to hold them tightly against her sides.

"I vaguely remember finding the note in our mailbox soon after I turned sixteen, but I'm not sure how it got in my sock drawer." Jake leveled Ella with a look that could have stopped a wild horse in its tracks. "Did you write that note?"

Tears welled in her eyes, and she blinked several times to keep them from spilling over. "You do enjoy humiliating me, don't you, Jake?"

He shook his head. "'Course not. I just want to know if—"

"I wrote the note, okay? In case you've forgotten, you used to walk me to school every day, and you even carried my books. Then one day you promised that I'd be the first person you took for a ride when you got your own horse and buggy. You lied to me, Jake." Ella's voice rose higher, but she didn't care. Jake had forced her to admit she'd written the note, and she wasn't going to stop until she'd told him everything she'd been keeping bottled up inside her these last ten years. "There was a day when I would have fallen at your feet just to be near you, but did you care about that? No! You just made promises you never planned to keep!"

"Ella, I'm sorry. I never meant to hurt you." Jake took a step toward her and reached out his hand.

She jumped back, afraid that if he touched her she'd dissolve in a puddle of tears. "To you, I was probably just a little girl with a big crush, but you shouldn't have made me a promise that you didn't plan to keep."

Jake's face turned red. "I wasn't intentionally trying to break a promise. I—"

Ella's hand shook as she pointed her

finger at Jake. "It wasn't bad enough that you lied to me; you had to go and break my cousin's heart by lying to her, too."

"If you're referring to the fact that I went to Montana, I did plan to come back and marry Loraine, but things happened, and I—" Jake broke off his words and took a deep breath. "I know what I did was wrong, but I've apologized to Loraine. She's forgiven me, so why can't you?"

Ella knew she was being childish, holding a grudge for something that had happened ten years ago. Even so, it was hard to believe that Jake wouldn't lie to her again. If she only knew for sure that Jake would be staying in Indiana. If she just knew how Jake felt about her now.

"I think my dress is dry enough, and I need to get back in there," she said. "Besides, you've got a horse to shoe."

"That's true, but I'd rather talk to you."

"No, Jake, there's really nothing else for us to talk about." Ella turned and fled.

CHAPTER 40

Ella dropped the silverware they'd used at breakfast into the sink's soapy water and glanced out the kitchen window. It was the third week of April, and the grass had turned a deep emerald green. She smiled when she spotted several white butterflies hovering over the field near their barn. New life: That's what spring always brought. New life and a new hope.

Ella's thoughts went to her cousins. Katie and Freeman were happily married and settling into a routine in the home they shared with Fern. Loraine and Wayne were enjoying little Jonas, the precious baby boy

Loraine had given birth to several weeks ago. Ella had gone over there a couple of times since she and Jake had first paid the baby a visit. It was always a joy to hold little Jonas, and it made the longing she felt to be a mother even stronger.

"Jake," Ella murmured. He'd seemed so interested in the baby and had even asked if he could hold him. Ella wondered what kind of father Jake would make—if he ever married and had children, that is. He'd probably fool around and tease quite a bit, the way he'd done when he was a boy and still did now, for that matter. But he'd probably make his children behave, the way she'd seen him do with his siblings. A healthy balance of love and discipline is what all children needed.

Ella's face heated as she thought about the discussion she'd had with Jake at Katie and Freeman's wedding. She'd had trouble thinking of much else. Jake had come over a few times to buy baked goods since the wedding, but there'd been no mention of the discussion they'd had. He had, however, mentioned that he planned to stay in Indiana and buy some land so he could start his own business. Ella wondered if Jake's decision to stay had anything to do with her. She wouldn't ask, but did she dare hope?

No, I can't be the reason Jake's decided to stay. He doesn't even know I'm interested in him. Ella's face grew hotter. *Maybe he does know how I feel, since I allowed him to kiss me. Not once, but twice, no less! I wish I knew how Jake felt about me. I wish I knew if. . .*

She sloshed the sponge in the warm water as more confusing thoughts swirled in her head. The day she and Jake had gone over to Loraine's, he'd asked her to have supper with him, but she'd turned him down. Had that been the right thing to do, or should she have said yes? He might have taken her answer to mean that she wasn't interested in him.

If I'd have said yes, he'd have known I was interested, Ella reasoned. *Can I trust my feelings for Jake, or should I keep a safe distance from him?*

A prayer came to mind, and she closed her eyes. *What am I supposed to do, Lord? Tell me what to do, and I'll do it.*

～✖✖～

Jake had spent the last two weeks trying to figure out what to do about Ella. He'd read Proverbs 17:25: "A foolish son is a grief to his father, and bitterness to her that bare him." It had caused him to realize that one of the reasons he'd left home in the first place was to get away from Dad and his constant accusations. But that had been a foolish thing to do, because he'd managed to hurt his folks, Loraine, and Ella, too. Even though he and Dad didn't see eye to eye on many things, Jake's place was at home. He'd never be truly happy if he stayed in Montana and remained English. Oh, he'd be returning to Montana, and soon, but it was only to pick up his things and buy a few horses.

He didn't want to go, however, until he'd spoken to Ella first. Now that he knew why she didn't trust him, he hoped to put her mind at ease. He also hoped that once she realized he was going to stay in Indiana and join the Amish church, she'd be more receptive to the idea of going out with him. Maybe, if she went out with him a few times, she'd realize that they weren't so bad together and could actually have a good time. Maybe she would forgive him for not keeping his promise to her when she was a girl. Maybe, if she'd let him, Jake could start over and do things right.

I wonder if I should talk to someone about Ella, Jake thought as he headed out to the barn to check on the new horse he'd bought. *It should be someone who knows her well and might have some influence with her.*

He was almost to the barn when an idea popped into his head. He could speak to Jolene about Ella when he had his next signing lesson. Better yet, he could stop by the schoolhouse that afternoon.

～❦～

"How come your scholars look so sad?" Jolene asked Fern as the children filed out of the school.

"Allen Stutzman's daed was here a few minutes ago and gave us the news that Allen's been diagnosed with leukemia." Fern's face revealed her sorrow as she slowly shook her head. "Things don't look good for Allen. Ella's brother Larry took it the hardest, and I'm worried about him because it hasn't been that long since he lost his daed. I'm afraid if he loses his best friend, too, he might sink into depression."

Jolene's heart went out to Larry, but she felt especially sad for Allen and his family. She hoped the boy's folks would be able to get him the kind of treatment he needed, and she prayed that he would live.

"One of the scholars told me that, on the way out, Larry said something about not wanting to go home," Fern reported.

"I'm sure he was just talking. From what I know of my cousin, he always goes straight home from school so he can have a treat from Ella's bakery."

"I hope he went straight home today, because he's going to need a bit of consoling." Fern stepped out the door. "See you tomorrow, Jolene."

Jolene watched as Fern climbed onto her bicycle and pedaled down the driveway. She was almost to the end when a horse and buggy rolled in. Jolene was surprised when she recognized the driver as Jake, because he wasn't supposed to have a lesson until Monday evening at her home.

⚞ ⚟

When Jake strolled up to the schoolhouse, he greeted Jolene with a smile, but she didn't smile in return.

"What's wrong? You look like you've lost your best friend."

Jolene motioned for Jake to take a seat on the porch step, and she did the same. Then she told him about Allen Stutzman and about Larry's reaction to his friend's illness.

"That's a shame." Jake rubbed his chin. "I was planning to stop by Ella's bakeshop today. While I'm there, I'll ask how Larry's doing. In the meantime, there's something I'd like to talk to you about."

"What's that?"

"Umm. . .it's about Ella." Jake ran his hand across his sweaty forehead. It wasn't going to be easy to admit how he felt about Jolene's cousin, but if she had any influence on Ella, it might be worth the embarrassment.

"What about Ella?"

"I'm. . .uh. . .well, I think I'm in love with her." There, it was out. Jake sat back and waited for Jolene's response.

She stared at him for several seconds, and then her face broke into a wide smile. "I suspected as much."

His eyebrows lifted. "You knew?"

She nodded. "Does Ella feel the same way about you?"

"I'm not sure, but I think she used to."

"What do you mean?"

Jake explained about the promise he'd made to Ella when she was a girl and said he'd never thought much about it before. He went on to explain that he now realized that Ella'd had a crush on him back then. He blew out his breath in one long sigh. "Some time ago, I asked her to go out to supper with me, but she said no."

"That doesn't mean she doesn't like you. She could have been too busy."

"I wish that were true, but the real reason Ella won't go out with me is because she doesn't trust me, and besides, she says we argue all the time." Jake touched Jolene's arm. "Would you be willing to put in a good word for me with Ella?"

"I suppose I could do that," Jolene said, "but I think it would be better if you did some things that might help win Ella's heart."

"Got any suggestions?"

"You might buy her a gift; say some nice things about her when she's around; stop over to see her more often; maybe volunteer to do some chores around their place."

"I've already done plenty of chores, and that hasn't helped me win her favor. I've also bought lots of baked goods and given her some money at Christmas." Jake grimaced. "I've stopped over there more often than I probably should, and I think I've worn out my welcome. The only thing I haven't done is to say some nice things about Ella to her face."

"I don't suppose you've told her that you're in love with her?"

"No. I was afraid she wouldn't believe me, and I'm even more afraid of her rejection."

"You won't know until you try." Jolene gave Jake's arm a gentle squeeze. "My advice is to go see Ella and say something nice, then wait and see what her reaction is."

"Okay! I'll do that right now." Jake grinned as hope rose in his chest. "And while I'm there, I'll have a talk with Larry and see if I can cheer him up a bit." He raced across the yard to his buggy, more anxious than ever to see Ella.

CHAPTER 41

Ella glanced out her bakeshop window. Amelia and Helen had come home from school over an hour ago and said that Larry had walked home by himself, a different way. Ella was getting worried and felt tempted to go look for him but didn't want to leave the shop unattended. Charlene had taken Mama to a doctor's appointment, and Amelia and Helen couldn't watch Sue Ann and also wait on any customers who might come into the bakeshop.

Why would Larry walk home by himself? Ella fumed. *He knows he's supposed to walk with the girls.* She sighed. *Guess if he's not home by the time Mama and Charlene get here, I'll have to look for him.*

Ella ushered her three young sisters into the back room of her bakeshop and gave them some cut-up apples and milk to snack on. When she heard her shop door open, she headed that way to see who'd come in. She was both pleased and surprised to see that it was Jake.

He offered her a dimpled, kind of shy-looking grin. "Afternoon, Ella."

"Hello, Jake," Ella said, feeling suddenly shy herself in his presence. She wondered if whenever he looked at her, he thought about the kisses they'd shared. "What can I do for you today?"

He cleared his throat a couple of times. "I. . .uh. . .wanted to tell you how much I enjoyed those sweet rolls you sold my mamm the other day. They were sure good."

"I'm glad you liked them." Ella swallowed hard. Jake was looking at her in a peculiar way that made her toes curl inside her sneakers.

"With your baking skills, you'll make a good wife for some lucky fellow someday."

A wave of heat flooded Ella's face. "I doubt that I'll ever get married."

"What makes you say that?"

Ella leaned on the counter for added support. The intense look on Jake's face made her squirm. "For one thing, I need to help my mamm raise my bruder and schweschdere. Then there's the fact that I don't have a—"

"Speaking of your brother—I stopped at the schoolhouse before I came here, and Jolene mentioned how upset Larry had been when he'd heard about Allen Stutzman."

"What about Allen?"

"He has leukemia. Figured you knew."

She shook her head. "I knew he hadn't been feeling well, but I had no idea he'd been diagnosed with leukemia."

"Guess all the scholars took it pretty hard, Larry most of all. Jolene said she overheard him telling one of the scholars that he didn't want to go home."

Alarm rose in Ella's soul. "Larry's over an hour late. You don't suppose. . ."

"He's probably off by himself some- where, thinking about his friend and trying to come to grips with it."

"Larry took Papa's death pretty hard. If he loses Allen, I don't know what he'll do." She glanced at the battery-operated clock on the far wall. "I'd like to go look for him, but Mama and Charlene are still at the doctor's, and I don't want to leave my younger sisters unattended."

Before Jake could respond, an idea popped into Ella's head. "If you wouldn't mind staying with them for a short time, I'll hop on my bike and go search for Larry."

"I've got a better idea," Jake said. "I'll look for Larry, and you can stay here with your sisters."

"You wouldn't mind?"

"'Course not. What are friends for if not to help each other?"

Friends. At least Jake considered her a friend. She managed a weak smile. "I appreciate that, Jake."

He leaned across the counter and gave her shoulder a quick squeeze. "Not to worry; I'll find Larry and bring him home."

⊰✂⊱

Jolene's arms swung at her sides as she hurried toward the variety store in Topeka. She needed to buy a baby gift and get over to Loraine's before it was time to start supper. Jolene had visited Loraine and her baby a few times, but she still hadn't bought him a gift.

She'd no sooner entered the store when she saw something that made her blood run cold. A man wearing a ski mask that covered his eyes and nose stood near the counter, holding a gun in his hand. Sadie Smucker, the store owner, along with Eunice Byler and an English woman Jolene didn't recognize, stood next to the counter with their hands raised over their heads.

Jolene halted her footsteps, not sure what she should do. Gathering her wits about her, she decided that the only thing she could do was to run back outside and get some help. She was about to do that when Eunice turned and looked at her. So did the gunman.

He pivoted the gun toward Jolene. "Come over here!"

With her heart pounding and her legs shaking so badly she could barely walk, Jolene made her way across the room. When she reached the counter, the gunman grabbed her arm and pulled her roughly to his side. She winced but made no move to protest for fear that he might shoot her or one of the other women.

The man said something to Sadie then, but his head was turned away from Jolene and she couldn't make out what he'd said. Then he said something to Eunice and the other woman. They nodded, cast a quick glance at Jolene, and followed Sadie out the door.

Jolene looked up at the gunman and said, "Please, let me go."

"Not a chance! You're my ticket to freedom."

CHAPTER 42

Lonnie had just tied his horse to the hitching rail near the grocery store in Topeka when he spotted Jolene going into one of the stores down the street. He was tempted to follow but wasn't sure what he'd say to her if he did. He wanted to believe things could work out for them, despite their inability to hear, but he was still full of doubts and fears. He needed to trust God to help him not be afraid, but ever since his accident, he'd struggled with a lack of faith.

Lonnie was about to head for the grocery store when he saw Sadie Smucker, the owner of the store where Jolene had gone, rush out the front door with Eunice Byler and a middle-aged English woman. They stood in a huddle for a few minutes, and then Sadie scurried next door to the pharmacy.

Lonnie glanced at the store again, wondering what was going on. Why had the others come out but not Jolene? Maybe one of Sadie's clerks was inside waiting on Jolene, but if that was the case, then why were the English woman and Eunice wearing panicked expressions while clinging to each other? And why had Sadie appeared to be in such a hurry to go to the drugstore?

Lonnie hurried down the sidewalk and stepped up to Eunice. "I saw Jolene go in there a few minutes ago," he said, pointing to the store. "Is she still there?"

Eunice nodded, her eyes wide with fear. Her mouth moved quickly as she spoke, making it difficult for Lonnie to read her lips.

"I can only understand what you're saying if you speak slowly enough so I can read your lips. Would you please repeat what you said?"

Eunice spoke again, slowing her speech,

and she signed a few of the words. "There's a man with a gun in the store. He's holding Jolene hostage. He told Sadie to phone the police and to say that he'd be waiting for them when they got here."

Lonnie's heart gave a lurch. "Doesn't the man know that when the police get here he'll be arrested?"

The English woman spoke this time. "He told Sadie that he wanted money. When she said that she only had a few hundred dollars in the store, he said he needed a lot more." She paused and moistened her lips. "I believe he's holding the Amish woman, hoping he can make a deal with the police."

Lonnie's stomach twisted. Jolene was alone with a crazed man who held a gun. If the man didn't get what he wanted, he might kill her. The thought that he might lose the woman he loved chilled Lonnie to the bone.

As he stared at the store, emotion tightened in his chest. The sense of longing to share his life with Jolene suddenly filled him with purpose. He'd do anything to protect her, even lay down his own life if necessary.

Lonnie drew in a deep breath, sent up a quick prayer, and dashed down the street.

~≈ ≈~

Jake had driven up and down the road between Ella's place and the schoolhouse several times without finding a single sign of Larry. He figured the boy had probably taken a shortcut through the woods, but it would only be a shortcut if he'd come straight home. *Or maybe,* Jake thought as he came to a dirt road leading to one of the neighboring ponds, *Larry hiked in there to do some thinking.*

Jake guided his horse and buggy up the dirt road and followed it until he came to the pond. He breathed a sigh of relief when he spotted Larry sitting on a log near the water.

Not wishing to startle the boy, Jake tied his horse to a tree and headed for the pond, whistling loudly as he walked.

Larry turned and looked, but as soon as he saw Jake, he jumped up and started for the other side of the pond. Jake hurried after him. "Hold up, Larry! I need to talk to you!"

"What about?" Larry called over his shoulder as he kept walking.

"Just want to share a couple of things with you."

"What kind of things?"

"Let's have a seat, and I'll tell you."

Larry took a few more steps then halted and turned to face Jake. "Is it about Ella? Are you wantin' me to put in a good word for you with her?"

"Huh?"

"'Cause if you are wantin' me to put in a good word, you can forget it. I heard Ella tell Mama that she don't trust you; and neither do I." Larry's chin quivered. "I think you came here to try and make me go home."

Jake caught up to Larry and put both hands on the boy's shoulder. "You're late getting home from school, and Ella's worried about you."

"I ain't goin' home."

"Why not?"

"Just ain't, that's all."

"Is it because you're upset about Allen being so sick?"

Tears welled in Larry's eyes. "How'd you hear about that?"

"Jolene told me. She said you were pretty upset when you left school today."

Larry blinked a couple of times. "You'd be upset, too, if your best friend was gonna die."

Jake shook his head. "You don't know that Allen's going to die. You need to pray and trust God where Allen's concerned. I'm sure his folks will see that he gets the best possible care."

"Maybe so, but that don't mean Allen won't die."

"There are no guarantees in life," Jake said. "The only guarantee we have is that God loved us so much that He sent His Son to die for us." He waited a few minutes, to let Larry think about what he'd said. "There are many people with leukemia who've been helped. Allen has a good chance of surviving if he gets proper treatment."

"You really think so?"

"Sure do." Jake squeezed Larry's shoulders. "Your family needs you. Since your daed died, you're the man in the family. Don't you think your place is at home with your mamm and schweschdere?"

Larry stared at the pond, his shoulders shaking. With tears streaming down his cheeks, he finally nodded. "I really do care about Mama and my sisters."

"Then let's go." Jake led the way to his horse and buggy, but they'd only gone a short ways when the toe of his boot clipped a rock, and he stumbled. The ground spiraled up toward him, and then everything went black.

CHAPTER 43

Ella had just stepped onto the porch of her bakeshop to shake some flour from her apron, when Larry came running up the driveway. Relief flooded her soul.

Red-faced and sweating profusely, Larry dashed across the grass and leaped onto the porch. "Jake f–fell and hit his h–head on a rock! I th–think he might be dead!" Larry's eyes were wide with fear, and his chin trembled so bad that he stuttered.

Ella sucked in her breath. "What happened? Where's Jake?"

Larry quickly told Ella how Jake had talked him into going home. He sniffed a couple of times, struggling to hold back his tears. "If Jake hadn't come lookin' for me, he wouldn't have stumbled. If he dies, it'll be my fault."

Ella didn't have time to argue; she needed to get to Jake and see how badly he'd been hurt. She took hold of Larry's shoulders and bent down so she could look him in the eye. "Where's Jake now?"

"He's lyin' on the path leadin' to the Lehmans' pond. I can take you there right now."

Larry turned toward the driveway, but Ella stepped in front of him. "I need you to stay here and keep an eye on the girls."

"Can't Mama do that?"

"She's not here. Charlene took her to the doctor's this afternoon and they aren't back yet."

"But I can't stay here. I need to see how Jake's doin'." Tears rolled down Larry's cheeks. "Need to know if he's dead or not."

Ella swallowed around the lump in her throat. Jake couldn't be dead. She needed him to know how much she cared, needed him to know that she wanted to be more than his friend and that she'd forgiven him.

With a firm hand, Ella turned Larry toward the bakeshop. "Go inside now and watch your sisters. I'll be back as soon as I can."

Larry nodded and hurried inside. Ella raced to the barn and grabbed her bike. *Dear God,* she prayed as she pedaled quickly down the driveway, *please don't let Jake die.*

※ ※

Jolene's face broke out in a cold sweat as she sat in a chair, watching the gunman pace from the window to the counter and back. As the minutes ticked by, he seemed to become more agitated. Surely Sadie had phoned the sheriff by now. Would he and his deputies be here soon? Would they barge into the store and maybe shoot the gunman, or would they stay outside and try to talk him into giving himself up?

Jolene closed her eyes. *Dear Lord,* she prayed, *please give me the wisdom to know what I should do or say.*

When she opened her eyes, she was surprised to see the front door open, and even more surprised when Lonnie dashed into the store.

When the gunman rushed forward, pointing the gun at Lonnie, Jolene covered her mouth to stifle a scream. Gathering her wits about her, she leaped off the chair and hollered, "Don't shoot! He's my friend!"

Jolene had no idea whether the man had given a reply, for his back was to her. He did, however, lower the gun a bit and motion Lonnie to move away from the door.

As Lonnie's gaze connected with Jolene's, she saw the look of concern on his face. Had he come in here to save her, or was he just an unsuspecting customer like she had been?

The gunman said something to Lonnie, and then he quickly locked the door. Jolene was surprised he hadn't done that sooner. Maybe this was his first criminal act and he hadn't known what to do. Maybe the man behind the ski mask was as frightened as she was right now. Was it possible that she could talk him into giving himself up? It was worth a try, and it was better than doing nothing.

She moved forward and positioned herself so the man could see her face. "I don't know why you're keeping us here, but what you're doing is wrong, and I—"

"Shut up and sit down!" Although Jolene couldn't hear the intensity of the man's voice, she knew from the way his lips had formed the words that he'd yelled at her.

He kept pacing, waving the gun, and saying something Jolene couldn't make out. Every once in a while he stopped and looked at his watch, and then he started pacing again.

"We've got to do something," Lonnie signed to Jolene.

"I know, but what?"

"I'm not sure, but I need to get you out of here." He glanced toward the back of the store. *"Ask if you can use the restroom."*

"I don't need to use the restroom."

"Ask anyway. If he says you can use it, maybe you can sneak out the back door."

Jolene nodded. That made good sense. She didn't know why she hadn't thought of it herself.

She left her chair and approached the man cautiously. "I need to use the restroom."

"Sit down!"

"I really need to use it right away."

His lips compressed as he tilted his head. "You'd better not try anything funny."

Jolene's heart began to race. If she

were able to sneak out the back door, the man would soon realize she was missing. She was sure that would make him angrier than he already was, and if he got any angrier, he might hurt Lonnie.

"I guess I don't need the restroom that bad," she said. "I can wait."

"Suit yourself." He motioned to the chair beside Lonnie. "Now go sit with your friend and stop bothering me; I need to think."

Jolene complied.

"What happened? Did you ask about using the restroom?" Lonnie signed.

"I did ask, and he said I could, but I changed my mind."

Lonnie's forehead puckered. *"How come?"*

"Because I was worried that if I escaped, he might—"

The man stepped up to Lonnie and held the gun near his head. "What are you two doing, waving your hands around like that?"

"We're both deaf." Jolene signed as she spoke. "This is how we communicate."

"But you've been talking to me. How'd you know what I was saying if you can't hear?"

"We were reading your lips," Lonnie said before Jolene could respond.

"So you can only know what I'm saying if I'm looking right at you?"

Lonnie and Jolene both nodded.

He waved the gun over their heads. "Well, understand this: If someone doesn't show up soon with the money I asked for, neither one of you will make it outa here alive!"

CHAPTER 44

Jake! Can you hear me, Jake?"

Jake's eyelids fluttered, and he slowly opened his eyes. He saw Ella looking down at him with a worried expression. "Wh–what happened? Where'd you come from?"

"Larry came to get me. He said you'd fallen and hit your head on a rock." Ella dropped to her knees and cradled Jake's head in her lap. Then she gently probed his head with her fingertips. "I don't see any blood, but there's a lump on your forehead. I think you'd better see a doctor to be sure that you don't have a concussion."

"At least it's not you with a bump on your head this time."

Ella apparently didn't see the humor in what Jake had said, for she didn't even smile.

Jake reached up and touched his forehead. "Aw, it's just a little bump. I don't think there's any need for me to see a doctor." He made no move to sit up, however, enjoying the warmth of her hands as they cradled his head.

"Well, I think there is." Ella's expression turned to genuine concern.

Jake wondered if this might be a good time to tell her how he felt. Would she be receptive to what he had to say? He sat up and reached for Ella's hand. He was relieved when she didn't pull it away. "I. . . uh. . .know we've had our share of disagreements in the past. . . ."

"And still have," she said, a slight smile playing on her lips.

"Guess that's how it'll always be between us, but I hope we've come to the point where we can be friends again." He held his breath, waiting for her response. He didn't want to say too much until he knew how she felt about him. No point in making a fool of himself. Not that he hadn't done plenty of that in the past.

Ella nibbled on her bottom lip as he rubbed his thumb across her knuckles. "I'm not sure how it happened, but even though we don't agree on everything, I do think we can be friends—maybe even good friends."

"Friends don't always have to agree." He grinned. "They can agree to disagree."

"I guess you're right."

Jake rolled his tongue around in his mouth as he tried to figure out what to say next. He was on the verge of blurting out that Ella was more than a friend to him— that he'd fallen in love with her—but he decided this probably wasn't the best time or place to make such an admission. He needed to do a few things yet—things that would hopefully secure his future.

"I need to get home," Jake said, rising to his feet.

"What about seeing the doctor?"

"If I start feeling dizzy or have any other weird symptoms, I'll call the doctor," he promised.

"Jake, I really think. . ."

He leaned down and kissed her and

was pleased when she responded. When they pulled apart, he motioned to his horse and buggy, still tied to a tree. "I'll put your bike in the back of my rig and give you a lift home. Then I'll be on my way home, too."

"Do you promise to see the doctor if you start having any problems?"

"Said so, didn't I?"

"Guess I'll have to take you at your word." Ella smiled as he helped her into his buggy. "Larry will be relieved to know that you're not dead."

Jake's eyes widened. "He thought I was dead?"

Ella nodded. "He was very worried about you, and so was I."

"Really?"

She gave his arm a little squeeze. "Said so, didn't I?"

Jake chuckled and continued to do so as he climbed into the driver's side of the buggy.

"I'm glad you think what I said was so funny." Ella needled him in the ribs. "I really was worried about you."

"I'm glad you were." He clucked to the horse to get him moving, and then he reached over and clasped Ella's hand. "Does that mean you've forgiven me for not keeping my promise to take you out when I turned sixteen?"

"Jah." Tears welled in her eyes as she nodded.

"Should we go out to supper this evening and celebrate?"

"That offer's really tempting, but I think you ought to take it easy for the rest of the evening," Ella said, gently squeezing his fingers. "Your daed's doing better now, so maybe he can do your chores."

Jake winked. "Yes, Mother."

Tiny wrinkles formed across her forehead as she frowned. "I'm serious, Jake. You fell hard enough to knock yourself out, and you could have a concussion."

"You worry too much. I'll be fine, really."

When she leaned her head on his shoulder, a ripple of warmth shot through him. He thought he could spend the rest of his life sitting beside her like this.

"Were you able to talk to Larry about Allen?" Ella asked.

"Uh. . .yes. I think I gave him some hope when I said that Allen's folks would see that he got good care. I also told him that there's been many people with leukemia who've been helped."

"I hope and pray that Allen's one of those who makes it."

"Me, too."

They rode silently the rest of the way, but Jake didn't mind. He enjoyed this time alone with Ella, and words didn't seem necessary.

When Jake turned his buggy up Ella's driveway, she smiled at him and said, "I'll come over to your place to check on you in the morning."

Jake tipped her chin up so he could look into her eyes. "Would you mind giving me a couple of days?"

Her brows furrowed as confusion registered on her face.

"There's something I need to do before we talk again." Jake leaned over and kissed her cheek. "Why don't you come by next Monday?"

Her mouth formed an *O.* "Next week? But Jake, I—"

He held up his hand. "Please, Ella, for once, just do what I say, okay?"

She pursed her lips and lifted her shoulders. "Okay, but just this once."

~·⚡·~

Lonnie watched as the gunman looked out the window then suddenly pivoted and waved the gun in the air. He marched over to Lonnie and Jolene and said, "The sheriff's out there with a bunch of his deputies. They're calling for me to give myself up." He shook his head determinedly. "But that's not gonna happen."

Lonnie turned to Jolene and signed, *"I'm going to try talking to him."*

Fear shone clearly in Jolene's eyes as she nodded slowly.

Lonnie rose to his feet, praying for the right words. He could see that the gunman was getting more agitated all the time. If something didn't happen soon, he and Jolene could end up dead.

"Why are you doing this?" Lonnie asked the man.

"You really want to know?"

"Yes, I do."

"I've been out of work for nearly a year. If I don't get some money soon, I'll lose everything—my house, my car, and probably my family." He rubbed the side of his face, almost pulling the ski mask off in the process. "All me and my wife do anymore is argue. She said she's thinking about leaving me, and if things don't turn around for us soon, I'm sure she will."

"I think I understand a bit of how you must feel," Lonnie said. "I was out of work for a while after the accident that caused me to go deaf. I became bitter and feared that I'd never find a job. But I prayed and asked God to help me, and after a while, the right job came along." Lonnie smiled, although his hands were sweaty, and he figured his voice was probably shaky. "My new job is something I can do without being able to hear, and I'm happier now than I ever thought possible." As Lonnie continued to share with the man, he found that his own faith was being strengthened and a sense of peace had crept over him. For the first time since he'd lost his hearing, Lonnie realized that he wasn't a weak or incapable man. Despite his handicap, Lonnie could still be used by God if he was willing to listen and obey the Lord's gentle nudging.

In a surprise gesture, the gunman pulled off his ski mask. He was much younger than Lonnie had thought, and his face was pale and gaunt.

The man lowered his head into his hands and sobbed. "I can't pray and ask God for anything, because I'm a worthless, no-good bum."

Lonnie touched the man's arm. "What's your name?"

The man lifted his head. "Fred. Fred Hastings."

Lonnie prayed again, asking God to give him the right words. "I have good news for you, Fred."

"What's that?"

"God loved the world so much that He sent His Son to die for your sins. He doesn't care who you are or what you've done. He wants you to believe on His name. He wants you to confess your sins and ask Him to come into your heart. When you do that, He'll forgive you and cleanse your heart. You'll become a new creature in Christ."

Fred stared at him blankly. He might not be completely convinced, but at least he was listening.

"Here's something else to consider," Lonnie went on to say. "If the demands you gave the sheriff aren't met, which they probably won't be, you'll go to jail for a time. But if you kill us, you'll be faced with a murder charge."

Fred blinked a couple of times. "I hadn't thought about that. I was so desperate to get some money that I wasn't thinking at all."

"If you give yourself up right now, you'll probably go to jail if the state presses charges. But it'll go better for you if you don't carry this any further."

"You really think so?"

"Yes, and the Amish community will help you and your family. I can let some people know, and I'm sure they'll see that your family's cared for while you're in jail."

"The Amish would really do that?"

Lonnie nodded. "I think any Christian would want to help."

Fred stared at Lonnie then handed him the gun. "I'm giving myself up. You and your lady friend are free to go."

"All right, but we'll all go out together." Lonnie laid the gun on the counter, unlocked and opened the door, and then hollered to the sheriff, "Don't shoot! We're coming out!"

The minute they stepped out the door, the sheriff waved his hands and said something Lonnie couldn't understand. As they moved closer to the sheriff, Lonnie was able to read his lips and realized that he'd told the gunman to drop to the ground.

Fred did as he was told. A few seconds later, Lonnie grabbed Jolene's hand and hurried toward the sheriff.

After that, everything happened so fast. Fred was handcuffed, put in one of the patrol cars, and whisked away. Lonnie, Jolene, Sadie, Eunice, and the English woman spent some time explaining to the sheriff what had happened inside the store. Then Lonnie asked the sheriff if he could get the gunman's address so they could do something to help his family. The sheriff agreed, and by the time he'd finished taking their statements, Lonnie was exhausted. Noticing that Jolene had begun to tremble, he knew she must be exhausted, too.

Lonnie was about to suggest that he and Jolene go over to where he'd tied his horse and buggy, when Andrew dashed down the sidewalk, waving his hands.

"Someone came into the harness shop and said you were being held hostage in one of the stores," Andrew said, running up to Eunice.

"Ach, it was horrible," she said with tears

streaming down her face. "We're all lucky to be alive."

While Andrew consoled Eunice, Lonnie took Jolene's hand and led her away. When they reached his buggy, he pulled her into his arms and propped his chin on her head. He felt her sobs against his chest and gently patted her back. He loved this sweet woman more than life itself and knew he could never be truly happy unless they were together. He was no longer afraid to let her know how he felt. With God's guidance, he was no longer a helpless, fearful man.

❦ ❦

Jolene felt the vibration of Lonnie's heart beating under her ears. Had he been as frightened as she'd been while they were in the store? He certainly hadn't acted scared. The way he'd talked the gunman into giving himself up had amazed her. It made her love him all the more.

Jolene pulled slowly away from Lonnie and took a deep breath to ease the tightening in her throat. *"I know you think we can't be together,"* she signed, *"but don't you think you should let me decide what's best for me?"*

498   WANDA E. BRUNSTETTER

"What makes you think I think we can't be together?"

"You've said many times that—"

Lonnie lifted his hand and signed, *"I love you. You're my best friend."*

She made a circle with her right index finger. *"Always."*

His fingers curved under her chin, and his look went straight to her heart. At that moment, Jolene knew that Lonnie loved her as much as she loved him.

"I do believe we can be together, so when the time's right, do you think you might consider marrying me?" he signed.

She nodded affirmatively as she moved her right hand up and down, forming the word *yes.*

Lonnie helped her into his buggy, and when they were both seated, he lowered his head and kissed her tenderly on the mouth.

Jolene knew that she and Lonnie would face challenges, but if they kept their faith in God and sought His help every day, she was sure they could face anything together.

CHAPTER 45

Ella knew that Jake wanted her to wait until next Monday to see him, but by Friday, she couldn't wait any longer. She needed to know if he was all right; she needed to let him know how much she cared.

So she packaged up a loaf of friendship bread, climbed into her buggy, and guided her horse down the driveway. She'd left Charlene in charge of the bakeshop; Amelia, Helen, and Larry were still in school; and Mama and Sue Ann were both taking a nap, so this was a good time for her to go.

It was a beautiful spring afternoon, and Ella enjoyed the ride, absorbing the sweet smell of someone's newly mown grass, the beauty of budding trees and flowers in bloom. It was a perfect day to take a ride with Jake, and if he felt up to it, maybe they could.

Ella smiled as she thought about the way Jake had looked at her the other day—as though he only had eyes for her.

Is that the way he used to look at Loraine? Ella had cared so much for Jake, even back then, that she'd tried not to notice how he'd looked at Loraine.

Ella was sure that Jake was over Loraine and that he had no interest in Jolene. But one question remained: Was Jake ready to make a commitment to her?

A short time later, with a sense of anticipation, Ella pulled her horse and buggy up to the hitching rail by the Beechys' barn. After she'd climbed down and secured her horse, she reached into the buggy for the friendship bread and sprinted to the house.

Jake's mother answered soon after Ella knocked on the back door. "I came over to see how Jake's doing." Ella held out the bread. "And I brought this for him."

Lydia pursed her lips. "Didn't Jake tell you?"

"Tell me what?"

"He's not here."

"Where is he?"

"He left for Montana four days ago. Went by plane, despite his daed's protests."

Ella felt as if her heart had stopped beating. Despite what Jake had said about staying in Indiana, he'd left again.

"What a fool I was for trusting him," Ella mumbled.

Lydia tipped her head. "What was that?"

"Jake told me he was staying in Indiana, and I was foolish enough to believe him."

Lydia opened the door wider and motioned Ella inside. "I think we need to talk."

Ella reluctantly followed Lydia into the kitchen. She didn't see that they had much to talk about, unless Lydia planned to make excuses for her son's bad behavior.

"Are you sure Jake didn't tell you he was making a trip to Montana?" Lydia asked after they'd taken seats at the table.

Ella shook her head. "He never said a word."

"Maybe he wanted to surprise you."

"Oh, I'm surprised all right."

"Do you think Jake plans to stay in Montana? Is that why you're wearing such a long face?"

"Well, isn't he planning to stay there?"

"Nee. Jake has every intention of coming back here as soon as he—"

The back door flew open. Jake's dad stumbled into the room. His face was white, and his eyes were rimmed with tears.

"Joe, what's wrong?" Lydia hurried over to him.

He opened his mouth, but the only sound that came out was a strangled sob.

Lydia grabbed hold of his arm and gave it a shake. "Tell me what's wrong!"

"I was in the phone shed checkin' messages, and there—there was one from Jake's boss in Montana."

"What'd it say?"

Joe drew in a couple of shaky breaths and then dropped to his knees. "Jake's dead!"

CHAPTER 46

Ella stared at Jake's dad, trying to let his words register. As their meaning sunk in, a shaft of pain stabbed her heart. Jake was dead. But how? When? Where? A dozen questions filled Ella's head.

Lydia dropped to her knees beside her husband. "What happened? Tell me exactly what the message on our answering machine said."

Joe lifted his ravaged face and drew in a shuddering breath. "Jake borrowed his boss's truck to pick up some horses, but he never made it back to the ranch because he—he was in an accident." Joe sniffed deeply and swiped at the tears running down his cheeks. "Our son's body was burned beyond recognition."

Lydia gasped, and Ella grabbed the back of the nearest chair for support.

"This is all my fault," Joe lamented as he rose to his feet. He began to pace. "If I'd only been nicer to Jake, he'd never have left home in the first place."

Lydia ambled across the room as though in a daze and dropped into a chair at the table. Her whole body trembled as she clutched the folds in her dress. "Ach, my son, Jake!"

Ella sat beside Lydia and held the other woman's hands as she fought for control. She couldn't be sure whether the tears that splashed onto their hands were hers or Lydia's. She just knew they both loved Jake and would miss him terribly.

Ella could certainly relate to Joe's cries, for she, too, felt as if she were to blame for Jake's death. *If I hadn't been so mean to him after Papa died, he might have joined the church by now and never left Indiana. Why did Jake leave again?* she wondered. *Was he really planning to come back here, or had he changed his mind and decided that he liked Montana better?*

If there was only some way to undo the past. If Ella could just see Jake's face again and say that she loved him. If there'd ever been any doubt about that, it had been erased the day Jake had fallen and hit his head. Seeing him passed out on the ground had almost been Ella's undoing. Hearing that he was dead had broken her heart. Ella felt like she'd waited her whole life to find a man she could love, and just when she'd found him, he'd been snatched away.

Ella knew Jake's parents needed time alone to grieve for their son, and she needed to be alone as well. So as Joe reached for Lydia and they clung to one another, Ella slipped silently out the back door.

She stood on the porch, gazing at the Beechys' yard and losing herself in the memory of the way Jake had looked at her the last time she'd seen him. She knew now that Jake could be trusted, but he wouldn't be coming home.

When Jake's horse stuck his head over the corral fence and whinnied, she blinked hard and couldn't stop the flow of tears. Jake was dead. It was too late for them. Collapsing onto the porch step, she sobbed.

Ella heard the roar of an engine drawing closer, so she quickly dried her eyes with her apron, trying to pull herself together. An oversized truck was coming up the driveway, pulling an equally large horse trailer. Someone was probably bringing Joe some horses to shoe.

I don't think Joe's in any shape to speak with anyone right now. Maybe I should tell the customer what happened and ask him to come back some other time. Ella grimaced. *I hope I can explain things without breaking down.*

Ella stepped off the porch and started walking across the lawn. She'd only made it halfway there when the truck door opened. Jake stepped out. Her heart stopped midbeat. It couldn't be Jake. Jake was dead.

Ella blinked a couple of times, thinking she must be imagining things. But she wasn't, for Jake was strolling across the lawn with a huge grin on his face. As he drew closer, he opened his arms to Ella, and she ran into his embrace.

"Have you missed me as much as I've missed you?" Jake murmured, nuzzling the top of her head.

"Oh, Jake, we thought you were dead."

Jake pulled back and looked at her strangely. "As you can see, I'm very much alive. What gave you the idea I was dead?"

Ella quickly explained.

Jake's eyes widened, and he shook his head. "Oh, no! That wasn't me in my boss's truck. Andy, one of the fellows who works at the ranch, said he needed the truck, so I caught a ride with one of the other guys into town so I could pick up the truck and trailer I needed to rent in order to come back here." Jake paused and reached for Ella's hand. "That was three days ago. I've been on the road ever since."

Ella was so overcome with joy that all she could do was stare up at Jake and squeeze his hand.

Finally, as if coming out of a daze, she motioned to the house and said, "You've got to go inside and see your folks. They're in shock and grieving for you."

Jake bounded up the porch steps, pulling Ella along. When they stepped into the kitchen, Lydia looked at Jake as if she were seeing a ghost. Ella heard the poor woman's breath catch in quick, ragged gasps. "Jake! Is. . .is it really you?"

"Jah, Mom, it's me."

Jake's dad, who'd been standing in front of the sink, whirled around quickly, dropping a glass. "Jake! I. . .I can't believe it's you! We were told you'd been killed—that you'd been burned up in your boss's truck."

"It wasn't me, Dad." Jake moaned. "Andy must be the person who died. He borrowed our boss's rig, not me."

Lydia leaped out of her chair and threw her arms around Jake. "I'm sorry to hear about your friend, but I thank the Lord that you're alive!"

Joe joined Jake and his mother in a three-way hug. "Same goes for me, son. I can't tell you how glad I am."

Ella was so overcome with emotion that she could hardly speak, when Jake pulled her to his side and whispered, "Can I talk to you outside for a minute?"

"I guess so. If your folks don't mind."

Lydia grabbed a napkin from the center of the table and dabbed at her eyes. "Go right ahead."

Jake looked at his dad.

Joe gave Jake another hug. "It's fine with me, but I'd like to say something first."

"What's that?" Jake asked.

"I'm sorry for the way I've treated you. I've griped and complained and badgered you about joining the church." Joe reached for a napkin and blew his nose. "Will you forgive me, Jake? Can we start over? I'll see if I can make it better between us."

Jake nodded as tears coursed down his cheeks. "If you forgive me. I know I haven't been the ideal son."

"But you're *my* son, and that's what counts." Joe sniffed deeply. "I love you very much."

"I love you, too, Dad." Jake looked around. "Where are my little brothers and sisters?"

"They're not home right now," Lydia answered. "Fern and Jolene were taking their scholars on a field trip to celebrate the last day of school."

"So they don't think I'm dead?"

Joe shook his head. "They know nothing about the message."

"Hopefully, by now, my boss knows it wasn't me in his truck, but I'll need to give him a call, just the same." Jake glanced down at Ella and smiled. "As soon as I'm done talking to my aldi, that is."

Ella basked in the warmth of Jake's smile. It felt wonderful to hear him call her his girlfriend.

When they stepped onto the porch, Jake motioned to the truck and horse trailer parked in the driveway. "See that rig?"

Ella nodded.

"I've got some horses in there, and that's going to be the beginning of our future together."

"What are you saying, Jake?"

He slipped his arm around her waist and pulled her to his side. "I'm saying that I love you, and as soon as I join the church, I want you to become my wife."

She opened her mouth to respond, but he spoke again. "And I want you to know that even if you say you won't marry me, I'll love you until the day I die."

"Oh, Jake, don't even speak of it."

"You don't want me to speak of marrying you?"

"No, not that. I don't want to hear anything about you dying."

"The Bible says that it's appointed that everyone must die." He bent his head and nuzzled her ear. "Will you marry me and grow old with me until death takes one of us away?"

Ella's vision clouded as tears squeezed between her lashes. She cleared her throat so she could speak clearly. "Jah, Jake, I'll marry you—until death do we part."

Jake took Ella in his arms and kissed her tenderly. All the challenges she'd faced in the last several months faded. She could think only about her future as Mrs. Jake Beechy.

EPILOGUE

Five years later

As Jolene watched her husband and two little girls ride the carousel at Hershey Park, her heart swelled with love. Lonnie smiled at her, and she basked in its glow. Today, she and Lonnie had come here with their extended family, including Jolene's cousins Ella, Katie, and Loraine along with their husbands and children. Jolene's brother Andrew and his wife, Eunice, had been invited, too, but they'd stayed home because Eunice was due to have their second baby soon and wasn't feeling up to the trip.

Jolene thought about Fern. Last year, the schoolteacher had married Devon Bontrager, a widower. Fern, who'd been so sure she would never marry and have children, was now happily caring for Devon's six rambunctious boys.

Jolene chuckled as she looked at Ella and Jake's little boy, Joe. A chunk of cotton candy hung off his chin. He swiped it away with the back of his hand and grinned up at his mother. Wayne and Loraine stood watching their three children, two boys and a girl, as they scrambled onto a ride. Then there were Katie and Freeman, happily watching their two little towheaded boys holding stuffed tigers in their arms.

When Lonnie and the girls got off their ride, Lonnie signed, *"Hasn't this been a fun day?"*

Jolene nodded. *"Making a trip to Hershey Park was worth the wait."*

"Marrying you, now that was worth the wait." He reached for her hand and gave her fingers a gentle squeeze.

She smiled and closed her eyes as she sent up a prayer. *Heavenly Father, I'm thankful that the van accident, which nearly destroyed our lives, has somehow brought us all closer to each other—and to You. You used the tragic accident for Your good, and each of us cousins has learned that, despite the challenges we've had to face, trusting in You is the only way.*

RECIPE FOR ELLA'S FRIENDSHIP BREAD

1 cup starter (see recipe below)
2/3 cup vegetable oil
2 cups unbleached white flour
1 cup sugar
3 eggs
1½ teaspoons baking powder
1 teaspoon cinnamon
½ teaspoon vanilla
½ teaspoon salt
½ teaspoon baking soda
1 cup raisins, chocolate chips, chopped
   nuts, dates, and/or apples

Combine all ingredients in a nonmetal bowl and mix well. Place batter into two well-greased, lightly floured 9½ × 5½ × 3½ baking pans. Bake at 350 degrees for 45 to 50 minutes or until an inserted toothpick comes out clean. Place on a rack and cool for 10 minutes before removing from pans. Cool bread thoroughly on racks before cutting into slices and serving.

STARTER

    1 cup sugar
    1 cup milk
    1 cup unbleached white flour

Combine all ingredients in a large, nonmetal bowl. Stir with a nonmetal spoon. Cover the bowl lightly with plastic wrap. Do not refrigerate. Store at room temperature. Stir the mixture every day for 17 days. On day 18, do nothing. On days 19, 20, and 21, stir the mixture again. On day 22, stir and add the following ingredients:

    1 cup sugar
    1 cup milk
    1 cup unbleached white flour

Stir again. On days 23, 24, 25, and 26, stir the mixture. On day 27, add the following ingredients:

    1 cup sugar
    1 cup milk
    1 cup unbleached white flour

Stir well. You should now have about 4 cups of starter. Give 1 cup of the starter to each of two friends and keep the remaining 2 cups for yourself. Use one cup of the starter to make a loaf of friendship bread. Keep the other cup for your own starter.

To Keep the Starter Going

Do not refrigerate the starter, and do not use a metal bowl or spoon. On day 1 (the day you receive the starter), do nothing. On days 2, 3, and 4, stir the mixture. On day 5, stir in:

1 cup sugar
1 cup milk
1 cup unbleached white flour

Pour the mixture into a large, nonmetal mixing bowl; cover lightly with plastic wrap. This mixture will rise. On days 6, 7, 8, and 9, stir. On day 10, stir in the following ingredients:

1 cup sugar
1 cup milk
1 cup unbleached white flour

Give 1 cup of the starter to each of two friends to make their own bread, keep one cup for your own bread, and keep one cup as your own starter for future breads. Be sure to give the recipe for the starter, as well as the directions for making the bread, to each of your friends, too.

DISCUSSION QUESTIONS:

1. At first, some people in Jolene's family saw her deafness as a handicap. What are some ways we can help others who have physical limitations to see that they can live a useful life?

2. When Lonnie lost his hearing, he became bitter and angry at God. Why do people often blame God for the bad things that happen to them? If God can prevent bad things from happening, why doesn't He?

3. Everyone deals with death and other tragic losses in different ways. When Ella's father died, Ella dealt with her grief by staying busy and looking out for others' needs instead of her own. Is there ever a time when it's okay to hide our true feelings when going through

grief? Is it healthy to overlook one's own needs in order to minister to others?

4. When Jake returned home after his father was injured, he did his best to help out, even though he didn't enjoy shoeing horses. Why didn't Jake's father seem to appreciate the sacrifice Jake had made? Have you ever felt that a sacrifice you made was unappreciated? How did it make you feel?

5. When Jolene's family realized that they needed to learn how to communicate with Jolene, everyone in the family made an effort to learn how to sign. Has there ever been a time in your life when you've had to learn something new in order to help someone with a disability? Did it make you feel closer to that person?

6. A lot of misunderstandings occurred in this story. Misunderstandings are the biggest cause of dissension among family members and friends. What are

some ways we can deal with misunderstandings that occur between us and our friends or family?

7. Lonnie was afraid of making a commitment to Jolene because he thought their hearing loss would be a determent to marriage. Have you ever been afraid of doing something because you felt as if you were hindered by something? Did you shy away from it, or did you decide that with God's help you could overcome any obstacle?

8. Too often, children tease others with a disability. What are some ways we can teach our children to have more understanding toward someone who is physically or mentally challenged?

9. Were there any verses of scripture in this book that spoke to you personally? Did any of the verses help you see things in a different light? Without being preachy or pushy, how can we use scripture to help someone going through a difficult situation?

10. While reading *A Cousin's Challenge*, did you learn anything new about the Amish way of life? How can we incorporate some things that the Amish do into our own lives?

ABOUT THE AUTHOR

WANDA E. BRUNSTETTER enjoys writing about the Amish because they live a peaceful, simple life. Wanda's interest in the Amish and other Plain communities began when she married her husband, Richard, who grew up in a Mennonite church in Pennsylvania. Learning about her Anabaptist great-great-grandparents increased Wanda's interest in the Plain People. Wanda has made numerous trips to Lancaster County and has several friends and family members living near that area. She and her husband have also traveled to other parts of the country, meeting various Amish families and getting to know them personally. She hopes her readers will learn to love the wonderful Amish people as much as she does.

Wanda and her husband have been married over forty years. They have two grown children and six grandchildren. In her spare time, Wanda enjoys photography, ventriloquism, gardening, reading, stamping, and having fun with her family.

In addition to her novels, Wanda has written two Amish cookbooks, an Amish devotional, nine Amish children's books, several novellas, stories, articles, poems, and puppet scripts.

Visit Wanda's Web site at www.wanda brunstetter.com and feel free to e-mail her at wanda@wandabrunstetter.com.

White Christmas Pie

<u>NONFICTION</u>
The Simple Life
Wanda E. Brunstetter's Amish Friends
Cookbook
Wanda E. Brunstetter's Amish Friends
Cookbook, Vol. 2

<u>CHILDREN'S BOOKS</u>
Rachel Yoder . . . Always Trouble
Somewhere, 8-book series

The Wisdom of Solomon